DATE DUE

JAN 1 3	APR 13 '95	
JAN 2 3	SEP 1 1 '95	
FEB 4 1993	AUG 1 6 '97	
MAR 1 4 1993	AP 30 '01	
JUN 7 1993	JE 1 8 '02	
JUL 2 0 1993	AG 1 1 '03	
AUG 1 4 1993	SE 0 9 '03	
OCT 4 1993	DE 2 '04	
OCT 2 7 1993	NO 2 1 '05	
DEC 8 1993	MR 2 7 '10	
MAY 3 1 1994	AG 0 8 '10	
SEP 3 1994		

#5 in the
Dog Lover's Mystery
Series

M

CON

Conant, Susan

Bloodlines

Bloodlines

Bloodlines

Susan Conant

A PERFECT CRIME BOOK
DOUBLEDAY
NEW YORK   LONDON   TORONTO   SYDNEY   AUCKLAND

A PERFECT CRIME BOOK
PUBLISHED BY DOUBLEDAY
a division of Bantam Doubleday Dell
Publishing Group, Inc.

DOUBLEDAY is a trademark of Doubleday,
a division of Bantam Doubleday Dell
Publishing Group, Inc.

Book design by Tasha Hall

Library of Congress Cataloging-in-Publication Data
Conant, Susan J., 1946–
Bloodlines / by Susan Conant. — 1st ed.
            p.   cm.
"A Perfect Crime book."
            I. Title.
      PS3553.04857B57   1992
813′.54—dc20   92-21750
                                      CIP

ISBN 0-385-42484-1

Printed in the United States of America
January 1993

1   3   5   7   9   10   8   6   4   2

FIRST EDITION

To my beloved daughter, Jessica,
in memory of a cat of canine fidelity,
her irreplaceable Gray

Acknowledgments

I am blessed with the editor who defines the standard of the breed, multiple Best in Show and High in Trial, dog lover's dog lover, the legendary Kate Miciak.

For help in researching the background of this book, many thanks to Senior Investigator Bob Baker and Field Investigators Bob Reder and Frank Ribaudo of the Humane Society of the United States; Virginia Devaney, Voyageur Kennels, Cedar Crest, New Mexico, president of the Alaskan Malamute Protection League; Ann Kimball of the Elizabeth H. Brown Humane Society, Orleans, Vermont; and Mark Phillips of The Tattoo Shop, Portsmouth, New Hampshire. Many thanks to Barbara Beckedorff and Jean Berman for their astute comments, suggestions, and corrections. Thanks, too, to Joel Woolfson, D.V.M., who answered my questions about veterinary matters. Any errors are mine alone.

I am also grateful to my Alaskan malamutes, Frostfield Arctic Natasha, C.D., T.T., and Frostfield Firestar's Kobuk, whose joy restores my soul.

The only thing necessary for the triumph of evil is for good men to do nothing.

—EDMUND BURKE
Letter to William Smith
January 9, 1795

Bloodlines

1

I WAS WRITING A STORY about a tattoo artist in Newport, Rhode Island, who specializes in engraving dead-likeness portraits of dogs on the bodies of their owners. Her professional name —maybe even her real name—is Sally Brand, and she got started in dogs because she was tired of cover-ups.

Cover-ups? Seaman First Class Jack Doe comes home with "Jack and Jill Forever" freshly and painfully emblazoned on his forearm, only to discover that Jill's deserted him or that the one he really loves isn't Jill after all but the inconveniently polysyllabic Millicent. The tattoo's a misfit, right? What he needs is a cover-up. So Sally would update *Jill* to *Millicent,* which can't have been easy; or if the sailor had soured on love, she'd incorporate the entire original tattoo into the head of a black panther, which, Sally tells me, will camouflage anything; or, in the case of an unabashedly narcissistic Jack Doe, she'd cover up the *and Jill* with a pair of frolicking dolphins or an ebony-black-ink rococo anchor, thus leaving only the reliably apt "Jack Forever."

One night, though, when yet another sailor strolled into Sally Brand's storefront parlor and asked her to immortalize yet one more transitory human relationship on his upper back, Sally finally wised up and asked, "Hey, fella, you happen to own a dog?" So the guy pulled out his wallet and produced a photo of a Dalmatian with the unimaginative name of Spot. Sally'd done lots of Rottweilers and Dobermans before, but the images had been more or less generic. The head of Spot was her first real portrait. The rest is tattoo history. Human relationships are only skin deep. They're laborious, painful, and expensive to correct. But with dogs? With dogs, there are no misfits.

I first heard of Sally Brand at Crane's Beach, where I saw her work on the heavily muscled chest of a top handler named Larry Wilson, whose tattooed brace of Obedience Trial Champion black standard poodles not only looked just like the originals but even wagged their tails when he flexed his pectorals.

I was so crazy about the idea that I originally had only one question: Where? Rowdy is my right hand, after all, so that seemed like a good idea. But what about Kimi? Both of them? That felt better: two Alaskan malamutes, one on each upper arm, forever eyeing one another across my breasts. Then the guilt set in. What if Vinnie happened to peer down from above? Never having missed a thing on this earth, Vinnie could hardly be expected to overlook the sudden appearance of a sled dog on each of my biceps and the simultaneous nonappearance of a golden retriever bitch anywhere on my body. How could I explain it to her? *Sorry, Vinnie, but there just wasn't room for everyone?* I mean, how do you tell the best obedience dog you'll ever own that she got edged out by a pair of *malamutes,* for God's sake? So I could hardly leave Vinnie out.

Off. Not to mention Danny or Cookie or any of the others, even poor Rafe, who was terrified of everything, especially needles.

As I sat at the kitchen table writing up the notes of my interview with Sally Brand, I was still trying to decide *where* and also worrying about *who* and *how many*. Then the phone rang, thus probably saving me from becoming the first tattooed lady ever exhibited by the American Kennel Club.

Four or five times a year, I pick up the receiver to discover that someone's dialed my number by mistake. This call, though, was definitely for me: It was about a dog—not just any dog, either, but an Alaskan malamute.

"Holly?"

Holly Winter. Kute with a *k*, right? Welcome to purebred dogdom. And, no, the two litters whelped just before mine weren't Samoyeds or malamutes or anything else Christmasy. They were golden retrievers, but, yes, of course: December. Woof woof. Let me reassure you, though, and while I'm at it, let me remind myself: Although I'm a member in good standing of the Dog Writers' Association of America, this is not one of those tales—doubtless spelled *t-a-i-l-s*—told from the dog's point of view. I don't object to the dog's point of view, of course; I just don't know what it is. Although I've spent most of my life trying to imagine it, I still see it only through a glass, darkly, which is to say that, from what I can discern, it is remarkably like God's face. Anyway, I admitted to being myself.

My caller was Barbara Doyle. You know her? Well, if you show your dogs, you've seen Barbara. She has shepherds. (Foreigner? German shepherd dogs. Good ones, too.) She's a few years older than I am, I think—maybe in her midthirties?—and she's kind of frail and romantic looking. We train together at the Cambridge Dog Training Club.

"I happened to be at Puppy Luv this morning," she said

flatly. Like most experienced dog handlers, Barbara has complete control of her tone of voice: Even though she must have known what to expect from me, she did not sound ashamed, apologetic, defensive, or challenging. Puppy Luv is a Cambridge pet shop that sells my living birthright for a mess of green pottage, lots of green pottage, but pottage nonetheless.

My own control slipped. I may even have yelled. In fact, I'm sure I did, because Rowdy and Kimi, who'd been enjoying a morning doze on the kitchen floor, opened their gorgeous brown eyes and lifted their beautiful heads. Anyway, what I yelled was: "What were you *doing* there?" Barbara Doyle isn't a pet shop kind of person. In fact, she's a sire-won-the-national-specialty, dam-went-Best-of-Opposite-at-Westminster kind of person.

"Ran out of food," Barbara said, meaning, of course, *dog* food and not just any old kibble, either, but premium chow. "I know, I know," she added, anticipating the lecture that was already dripping from my lips like drool from the mouth of a Newfoundland. "I got the smallest bag they had. I never buy from that place. The point is, you do malamute rescue, don't you?"

"A little," I said. "Hardly any." I'd placed a few malamutes, sure, but most of my so-called rescue work had consisted of racking up giant phone bills while failing to find good homes for great dogs. Alaskan malamutes are big and strong, and, of course, they shed their coats, but that's not why they're hard to place. All rescue dogs, including all purebreds, are hard to place, all for the same reason: They aren't puppies.

"Well, there's a malamute at Puppy Luv," Barbara said. "I thought you might want to know."

"Damn." *Buy on impulse, neglect at leisure.* That's the real motto of every pet shop that sells dogs. "Damn it," I said. "Are you sure it's a malamute?"

The question wasn't quite as stupid as it probably sounds. Alaskan malamutes are much bigger and brawnier than Siberian huskies. A malamute's ears are set on the sides of the head, but a Siberian's ears are set high, and a Siberian's ears are fairly large in proportion to the size of the head, too, medium size, not smallish like a malamute's. A Siberian has a fox tail, like a brush, but a mal's tail is plumed and carried over the back. A Siberian has blue eyes or brown eyes or even one blue and one brown, but all malamutes have brown eyes. In brief, the two breeds are nothing alike, totally distinct, impossible to confuse, except—well, except that a great big brown-eyed Siberian husky looks quite a bit like a small malamute with a tail and ears that don't conform to the breed standard.

"According to the sign," Barbara said. "And it's a *big* puppy."

"Brown eyes?"

"Yeah. I took a good look. I just thought you might want to know."

"I do," I said mechanically. "Thanks."

Now that I knew, I'd have to do something. Or do nothing. Neither prospect felt good. Do you understand why? If so, and especially if you love dogs, stick around anyway, huh? It started that Friday morning in February when Barbara Doyle called to tell me about a malamute for sale in a pet shop. It ended less than a week later. If a dog had died during that time, I'd warn you right now. I promise. I wouldn't want to hear about it, either, you know. I wouldn't ask you to listen. Honest to *God* spelled backward.

2

"BARBARA COULD BE WRONG, you know," I told Rowdy and Kimi, who sat directly in front of me as I stroked their white throats. As I often remind them, they are certainly the two most beautiful and intelligent Alaskan malamutes in Cambridge, Massachusetts, and possibly in the entire world.

After I'd hung up the phone, I went into the bathroom to wash my face in cold water. Then I returned to the kitchen and reseated myself at the table, where I discovered that one of the two most beautiful and intelligent Alaskan malamutes in Cambridge, Massachusetts, and possibly in the entire world, had emptied the cup of milky tea I'd carelessly left in reach. Wet tan splotches dotted my pages of notes about Sally Brand. The dogs' black noses were wet, their muzzles white and dry, their expressions happy and innocent. When the sugar bowl is licked clean, the culprit is apt to be Rowdy. The shredded remains of a grease-soaked pizza carton mean that Kimi's raided the trash. She's usually the one who removes the ripening bananas and tomatoes from the kitchen windowsills, but Rowdy shares her spoils. I can even identify who's eaten what where: Kimi swallows the tomatoes whole, but Rowdy leaves a puddle of juice and seeds. Rowdy is fantastically adept at peeling bananas; a slimy brown and yellow mess bearing visible tooth marks means Kimi. An empty teacup, though, can be either one. When I warn prospective adopters that Alaskan malamutes are big, strong dogs that shed, I should probably add that they're opportunistic predators as well. On the other hand, they are highly intelligent listeners.

"So," I went on, "all I do is go take a look, and then I call Siberian Husky Rescue and break the news, and then, too bad, but it's their problem, not mine."

Have I lost you? Most pet shop dogs get flown in from the Midwest. The puppies are in crates, the papers aren't, and whoever picks up the pups at the airport matches up the puppies and papers. Got a fifty-five-pound pet shop "malamute" with pretty blue eyes? Well, now you know why. Don't let it worry you, though. Siberians are great dogs, too. Oh, but you wanted a *malamute*? What can I say? The obvious, I guess: You should have gone to a breeder.

The dogs gazed soulfully at me. Objectively speaking, they really are beautiful. If you're not used to our New England malamutes—Kotzebues—they'd look small to you, I guess, even though they're considered big around here. Rowdy's permanent diet usually keeps him reduced to eighty-five or ninety pounds, and Kimi weighs seventy-five, which happens to be ideal for a bitch. They're both dark wolf gray with white undercoats and white trim—white feet, legs, underbellies, and the undersides of their tails—but Kimi has some pale beige-tan, too. Their faces, though, are distinct: Rowdy has what's called an "open face." Yes, I know. It sounds like a Danish topless sandwich, but it means all white, in contrast to black facial markings like Kimi's. She has the works, a full mask: black cap, black bar down her nose, and black eye goggles. Her eyes are deep brown but slightly lighter than Rowdy's. His are so dark than you have to look closely in good light to see the line between the pupil and the iris. I might also mention in passing that Rowdy happens to have *the* ideal malamute head, rounded over the skull, with standard-epitomizing wedge-shaped ears set on the sides of his head precisely where they belong. Oh, and a nice blocky muzzle, too. Thick bones. Great front. And rear. And you really should see him move. Very typey dog. Breed champion, finished easily. Have I digressed?

Oh, yes. Puppy Luv. I'd never entered the place before. Ever since I'd started writing my monthly column for *Dog's Life,* I'd been warning my readers that pet shops that sell dogs support the puppy mill industry, and I'd urged my readers and everyone else not to buy so much as a single toy-size dog biscuit at a place like Puppy Luv. Obviously, then, I wouldn't have gone there to replenish my supply of food, collars, leads, Vari-Kennels, Redi-Liver, Souper-size Nylabones, Gumabone Plaque Attackers, Boodabones, Nylaflosses, chew-resistant Frisbees, undercoat rakes, wire slicker brushes, shampoos, coat conditioners, flea-control products, or any of the other bare necessities of life. In truth? I'd never entered the place because I'd been afraid to see a malamute puppy for sale there. Yes, I know. I should have been upset at the prospect of seeing any puppy of *any* breed sold to any dog-ignorant, dog-negligent, and maybe even dog-abusive credit card carrier who'd plunk down a Visa Gold. And I was distressed, too. But I cared more about my own breed than I did about the others. Not every human being *values* a great listener. Some people don't *want* a fascinating companion who takes an active, intelligent interest in the world. Many people don't *enjoy* a dog who's a mental and emotional equal. The average person does not actually *relish* being dragged along the street like a sledge on the permafrost. In brief, the Alaskan malamute is the wrong breed for most people, and one of the worst breeds for someone who should never own a dog at all.

So I knew I had to go to Puppy Luv, but I didn't quite trust myself. Was I afraid I'd shoot the salespeople, ransack the place, and steal the puppy? I'm not sure, but I definitely didn't trust myself. So I called someone I do trust, Steve Delaney, who is Rowdy and Kimi's excellent vet and my equally excellent lover, but, in this context, as one says here in Cambridge, a person who can be relied on to discourage a companion from shooting salespeople, ransacking pet shops, and shoplifting small malamutes.

"Steve, there's supposed be a malamute for sale at Puppy Luv," I said breathlessly, "and if I go there alone, at a minimum, I'll make a scene, and I need you to make sure the puppy's at least healthy."

Steve has a rumbly voice. "Good morning," he said slowly. "Last night was great for me, too."

"Yes," I said. It took me years to master this kind of seductive patter. Just imagine my pillow talk. "So meet me there when you finish for lunch, at what? Noon? Twelve-fifteen? It's in that sort of shabby little shopping mall near the—"

"I know where it is. Holly, you aren't going to buy—"

"Of course not. I've written about it a thousand times, okay? The puppies will be all right. It's the breeding stock that suffers." You know about that, don't you? Twenty-five hundred licensed puppy mills in this country, another twenty-five hundred unlicensed, only that can't be right, can it? Because there are four thousand just in Kansas, and Missouri is worse. I know all the stats. Ninety percent of puppy mills are filthy, close to a hundred percent of pet shop dogs come from puppy mills, pet shops sell about half a million dogs a year, and when you buy a puppy from a pet shop, all you do is perpetuate the suffering of the breeding animals. "I know!" I said. "I write about this!" I thought for a second and added feebly, "Or I try."

"Holly, you're going to have a real hard time seeing that puppy and walking out. Are you sure you want to do this?"

"That's the point! I *don't* want to do it. Steve, please come with me. I don't want to go all alone. I need you. Please come with me. The puppy could be sick. He might need help. *Please.*"

"Twelve-fifteen," he conceded. "On the sidewalk outside."

"Beautiful. And Steve? Uh, don't dress like a vet."

He laughed and asked what that was supposed to mean.

"You remember that sweater your mother gave you for Christmas?" I said. "Did you put it in the Saint Vincent de Paul?"

Just off Concord Avenue, a few blocks from my house, the Society of Saint Vincent de Paul maintains a large collection box in which prosperous Cantabrigians deposit wearable presents they don't like. When Steve opened his mother's Christmas package, saw the sweater, and said, "Huh. Saint Vincent de Paul," I suggested that he attach a stamped envelope addressed to his mother so that the true recipient could thank her for the gift, but he refused. Steve's main objection to the sweater was the crocodile. He said that his own mother should know that he didn't specialize in exotic pets and that whoever ended up wearing the sweater probably didn't, either, and wouldn't be any more grateful than he was.

3

Puppy Luv occupied one of ten or twelve storefronts in a uniform strip of low, plate-glass-fronted shops erected twenty or thirty years ago and evidently intended as the acorn from which a mighty shopping oak would sprout. The vacant lots on both sides and in back had even been plowed under and left fallow. The developer must have expected to add a branch of Filene's or Jordan's or a Star Market, some large enterprise to attract heavy spenders whose late-model cars would fill the blacktopped acre that yawned between the dull shops and the tedious street. As it was, this nameless would-be mall looked like a seedy desert motel with oversize rooms and unwashed windows left curtainless for the pleasure of exhibitionist guests and voyeurist passersby.

Well, there *was* ample parking. On that zero-degree, snowless, electric-blue-skied morning in February, I could have left the Bronco right in front of Puppy Luv, but just in case a pet shop employee happened to stroll by as I got out, I cruised past the pet shop, kept going, and parked in a remote corner of the cracked blacktop lot. I intended to visit Puppy Luv as someone other than who I am, and the Bronco might as well have had DOG PERSON painted in big professional red letters on its old blue doors. A new Euro-style wagon barrier fenced off Rowdy and Kimi's area, which also held two large metal-mesh crates and two old blankets originally made of wool but now richly interwoven with soft, pale malamute undercoat and long dark guard hairs. The new seat cushions and floor mats, Christmas presents from Steve, were the ones you may have noticed in the Orvis catalog—gray background with handsome black paw prints? The bumpers didn't proclaim that I heart Alaskan malamutes or urge "Caution: Show Dogs," but a bumper sticker on the front read "My dog is smarter than your dog or your brother," which is true except that they both are . . . and probably smarter than the average sister, too.

I could've stripped off the brag and removed the barrier, crates, blankets, cushions, and mats, of course, but I'd had barely enough time to transform myself from a malamute-owned dog writer—furry jeans and T-shirt—to a semblance of my image of the ideal pet shop client, which is to say, as people actually *do* say here in Cambridge, the Significant Other of the kind of husband who knows that the little lady needs something to love and senses that in spite of his MasterCard, Visa, and American Express Platinum, he isn't it. I'd washed and moussed my hair and blown it dry, rather skillfully, I might add, thanks to my experience in readying golden retrievers for the show ring and what my father flatteringly considers to be the uncanny resemblance of my own mop to their glowing coats. Marissa, my mother, disapproved of the AKC-banned practice of cosmetically eradicating pink spots on otherwise dark noses, and none of my show dogs has ever had pigmentation problems, anyway. Nonetheless, I own mascara, as well as foundation makeup, blush, and lipstick, all of which I'd applied rather heavily. I'd put on good knee boots and a suburban-looking green corduroy dress, and I hadn't removed the dry cleaner's suffocating plastic from my navy winter coat until I'd stepped out of my furry house.

Even so, when Steve found me in front of the optician's shop studying the display of tortoiseshell frames in the window, he managed to recognize me. In fact, I was the one who almost didn't recognize him. For one thing, he'd shaved and, for another, he'd obviously just had one of his twice or thrice yearly haircuts, if you can call it that. His hair, when he has any, is brown, and it's normally wavy, like the coat on the shoulders of a Chesapeake Bay retriever. Now he looked like a tall, upright Airedale with green-blue eyes and bad clipper burn.

I kissed him anyway and then removed a glove and felt his whiskery scalp. "Um, did Lorraine do that?" I asked. It was a stupid guess. Lorraine, the vet tech who really runs Steve's practice, is an excellent groomer.

Steve suppressed a grin, shook his raw head, and said, "Rhonda." His face shone with the amazed pride I'd last seen there three weeks earlier when India, his German shepherd, took Highest Scoring Dog in Open B. India is a wonderful obedience dog. Rhonda is no groomer at all. The German shepherd is not a clippable breed, but even if it were, Steve wouldn't have trusted India to Rhonda. At least before. "She did a great job, didn't she? I didn't want to ask her or Lorraine, but when I went to take a look and see how booked up I was, Rhonda was there, and I said, 'Damn, I don't have time for a haircut.' So she said she'd give it a try."

Steve was wearing the expensive Christmas-present V-necked cable-knit sweater over nondescript khaki pants. Despite weather almost too cold for my dogs, he'd left unbuttoned what is possibly the best men's topcoat in the city of Cambridge. I can't even imagine what it must've originally cost, but Steve picked it up at one of the world's most venerable used menswear establishments. You know Cambridge? If not, I should tell you that Keezer's is where gentleman's-C-student, son-of-alumni-admitted Harvard preppies short of cash sell their Brooks Brothers and J. Press apparel and where Max Keezer resells it to straight-A-student, admitted-on-merit, full-scholarship undergraduates, thus enabling the brainy nouveau-Cantabrigian proletariat literally to wear the cloak of the elite. Anyway, Keezer's is also open to the public and is how Steve happened to own a camel topcoat made of honest-to-God cashmere that felt as soft as a pussycat's throat and didn't advertise his profession by showing pet fur, either.

Puppy Luv was two doors down from the optician's shop, beyond a two-pairs-for-the-price-of-one women's shoe outlet and before a discount drugstore. A large permanent sign hanging in the window advertised AKC PUPPIES. Taped to the plate glass underneath was a big red heart with a message in white letters: LOVE IS A WARM PUPPY. Next Thursday would be Valentine's Day. Dotted around were small red hearts edged in white paper lace, each bearing a breed name: Scottish terrier, cocker spaniel, Italian greyhound, Pomeranian, Dalmatian, poodle, Boston terrier, Maltese, Norwegian elkhound, chow chow. And Alaskan malamute.

Steve stepped ahead of me, pushed on the door, held it, and ushered me in. Knowing what I knew about puppy mills, I expected . . . well, if you don't know what I knew, maybe you'll be offended, but I expected a canine Buchenwald Boutique, a woofy Auschwitz Annex—and if the comparison seems to make light of suffering, you know nothing whatsoever about puppy mills.

Puppy Luv, though, was anything but grim. Red crepe

paper streamers were looped from the ceiling, red hearts dangled here and there, and the place was bright, cheery, and spotless. A hint of the fragrance of small dog stood out against a pleasant background of cedar, Nilodor, and dog food.

Directly ahead of us was a check-out counter banked by bins of what the wholesale kennel supply catalogs always push as "the perfect impulse items": latex toy dragons, hedgehogs, ducks, fire hydrants, trumpets, pianos, and ears of corn in bright primary colors; rawhide chews ranging in length from three inches to a yard; plastic packets of beef jerky treats, freeze-dried liver, and dog cookies shaped like people. Ha-ha. Presiding over the cash register was a pretty woman with dark ringlets and the foreshortened face, wide cheekbones, and ever so slightly strabismic amber-green eyes of a Siamese cat. I am not making this up. Why should I? And if you don't trust my take on her, consider that she'd evidently noticed the resemblance herself and liked it enough to accentuate it: The pink-tinted plastic frames of her glasses narrowed and flared up at the outer corners. Also, under a white surgeon's coat she wore a pink angora sweater. Yes, angora. Real life, though, unlike fiction, never goes too far: According to the name tag pinned to the lapel of her white cotton coat, she was not called Kitty. There was nothing even remotely feline about her name, which, according to the tag, was Diane Sweet.

"Good morning," said Diane Sweet, briefly looking up from a pile of papers she was sorting. "Let me know if you need any help, okay?" Her unnaturally bright pink tongue darted rapidly in and out of her mouth. I wondered whether the intense rose color could be a sign of some mild zoonotic illness I'd never heard of: cat's tongue fever, Persian glossitis.

"Sure," Steve told her. "Thanks."

He led the way across the front of the store, past a rack

of greeting cards (basset hounds wearing sunglasses, goldens in silly hats), big displays of premium dog food (Eukanuba, Science Diet, Natural Life), and piles of plastic-protected dog beds in every size from ultratoy to maxigiant in colors to coordinate with every decor and ranging in shape from the basic circle to that popular anomaly, the dog-biscuit-shaped sheepskin nest. I mean, do you see children's double bunks in the form of a Big Mac? Well, maybe you do. Anyway, turquoise fiberglass cages lined the left-hand wall of the store. Directly ahead of us were two tiers of small cages, twelve above, twelve below. A waist-high clear plastic barrier parallel to the cage banks was evidently intended to deter customers from sticking their fingers into the cages or opening the wire mesh doors. Each cage bore a placard showing the puppy's breed. The labels were accurate. A neatly lettered and discreetly worded sign fastened to the wall above the cages read: "ASK ABOUT PUPPY LUV'S UNIQUE LUV ON TIME PLAN." Another sign advertised Puppy Luv's "SIX MONTH COMPLETE HEALTH GUARANTEE."

At the extreme right of the cage bank were four one-story cages meant for large-breed dogs. Each of these cages was about the size of the inside of a dishwasher and just as interesting, too. The Alaskan malamute resided twenty-four hours a day in the first dishwasher.

I wrapped my hands over the top of the plastic barrier and leaned toward the mal puppy, who sat alertly upright. She was in that unbelievably cute one-ear-up, one-ear-down stage that's supposed to be temporary but sometimes lasts forever. Walt Disney's Tramp? But a purebred, AKC-registered Tramp, of course. Just in case the ears didn't get to me —they did—the little malamute cocked her head and returned my gaze. I couldn't help bending forward toward her. She didn't prance or bounce—there wasn't room, anyway— and she didn't speak, beg, sit up, or do anything else cute.

She didn't have to. All she had to do was sit there with her head cocked and her eyes locked in mine. Her nose wasn't running. Her eyes were clear. She was almost irresistible.

"Her eyes are too light," I whispered to Steve. She had what are called "wolf eyes," golden-yellow-amber. According to the breed standard, dark eyes are preferred, the darker, the better, but, according to me, that wolf gold is a knockout color, especially when the dog's coat is a matching golden sable like this pup's. "That ear might not come up," I added, confident that it would. If it didn't? I knew at least fifty people who'd tape it for me. "Maybe her tail is too short?" I paused and sighed. "Maybe it isn't. God damn. Look at her. You can see the intelligence. And any stupid person—"

Steve spoke very quietly. "You see that? Look at those feet."

I did. The little malamute's feet looked fine to me— much too big for the rest of her, of course, but perfectly normal for a puppy of a big breed. "What's wrong with them?"

I tore my eyes from the puppy and looked up at Steve. His face was rigid and expressionless, his jaw tight, his eyes angry. I followed his gaze. In the upper of the two cages immediately to the left of the nameless malamute's, a tiny Boston terrier puppy lay asleep on his side, his legs outstretched as if to display the swollen pink pads and upward curving toes of his misshapen feet.

I spoke too loudly. "Jesus! What *is* that?"

High heels tapped lightly toward us.

"Later," Steve murmured.

"The Boston terrier is a lovely breed," Diane Sweet said truthfully. She lowered her voice and addressed Steve. "And that's a *very* good price." Her oddly red tongue darted out and in. It reminded me of the swollen pads of the little Boston's feet. "Valentine's special," Diane Sweet added brightly. She pursed her lips and tightened the muscles in her face so that her cheeks stood out. Maybe she was trying to smile. Then she quietly confided: "That's a five-hundred-dollar puppy you're seeing there."

I'd been concentrating so hard on the little dog's poor feet that I'd overlooked the paper Valentine heart fastened to his cage. His sale price was two hundred eighty-nine dollars. Diane Sweet was right, though, I reflected. He *was* worth five hundred: five hundred dollars in vet bills. Otherwise? As a specimen of the breed? Well, maybe you don't know the breed. The Boston terrier is a small dog, under twenty-five pounds, sometimes even under fifteen pounds, notable for the exceptional liveliness reflected in his intense but gentle eyes and a look of bold, unwavering intelligence—the famous "Boston terrier expression." A black and white coat is acceptable, but the ideal color is brindle with white markings— white blaze on the head, white muzzle, white down the chest, and white on the feet and up the legs. Have I lost you? *Brindle?* Black hairs in a light base color, for instance gray, tan, or brown. You've probably seen a brindle coat on a boxer? Or maybe on a Great Dane? Well, never mind. This puppy was predominantly white, a show fault; his body was black, not the ideal brindle; and irregular flesh-colored blotches freckled his black nose. Even with the three of us peering at him and talking, he remained asleep. So what was he worth as a show dog? Nothing. But as a companion? Simply as a dog? Any dog? Like all the others, he was beyond price.

"I was wondering about this one," I said, pointing to the malamute.

Diane Sweet once again did something odd with her mouth and cheeks, and then said in a congratulatory voice, "That's an excellent choice. This is a *very* special puppy." She made her way quickly and smoothly through a swinging door in the barrier, opened the cage, and gathered up the puppy, who wiggled and squirmed. Diane Sweet tilted her head toward the back of the store and said, "Come on this way, and I'll let you play with her. See that door?"

Just try missing a door marked CUDDLE SPACE. I remembered something I'd read once, something attributed to one of the head honchos of a chain of pet shops. "There are only two places you can buy love," the guy had said. "A brothel. And a Docktor Pet Center."

"Could you get that for me?" Diane Sweet asked Steve, who compliantly held open the door.

I followed Diane Sweet in. The Cuddle Space was a bright, cozy little white-painted room with red plastic-cushioned benches around the sides. Her eyes on me, not on Steve, Diane Sweet said, "Now you just play with her as long as you want. Do you know how to hold a puppy?"

Roger Tory Peterson, who devised the famous system of bird identification based on unique combinations of field marks—yes, the Peterson system—once went to an eye doctor who advised him to take up a hobby that would require him to focus on small objects seen from a distance. Something like, say, bird watching? I felt just like Peterson.

"I guess so," I said, lowering myself to the red bench.

"Well, there's nothing to it." Diane Sweet's tone was obviously intended to boost my weak sense of self-confidence. "Just hold out your arms. You'll get the hang of it in no time." And with that, she lowered the squirming little malamute into my lap and added, "Anyone who knows how to hug can hold a puppy."

The Alaskan malamute is a tough breed, and this was a tough, fearless little puppy who immediately scrambled up my chest, sniffed my neck, burrowed her head, and licked. I wrapped my arms around her and stroked her soft baby coat.

Against my own wishes, I lowered my head, rubbed my chin over the top of her head, closed my eyes, and breathed deeply.

Diane Sweet addressed Steve: "Aren't they the cutest thing you ever saw? This is the *perfect* picture of love." I can't even begin to imagine how Steve's face looked, and I was too busy with the wiggling puppy to take a peek. Diane Sweet went on. "You know, I just have to tell you: This is a nice friendly puppy, but she's never responded to anyone like *this* before."

Diane Sweet could have been telling the truth, of course. The puppy was nuzzling my neck and licking my hands. It's certainly true that dogs know who loves them, and, besides that, the pup must have smelled Rowdy and Kimi.

"She sure is cute," I said.

"Uh, how much is this dog?" Steve asked quietly.

"She's six hundred dollars. This is a show dog," Diane Sweet said shamelessly.

Well, look, it has happened. There are a few famous cases of pet shop puppies that went on to become and to produce AKC champions—a Maltese called Lover, the sire of the legendary "Aennchen dancers" who all went Best of Breed at Westminster—but those cases are famous because they're rare and improbable.

"And," Diane Sweet assured Steve, "you'll get the purchase price back the first time you breed her."

Steve cleared his throat.

"Think it over if you want," Diane Sweet said, "but I have to tell you that this puppy isn't going to be here long. It's Valentine's week, and this is a very special puppy. We'll get other malamutes, but I can't guarantee you one like this." Then her voice dropped almost to a whisper. "You know," she advised Steve, "it would really be a shame to separate them."

4

WHEN I GOT HOME, I forced myself to watch a videotape about
which I'll say nothing except that it showed a raid on a puppy
mill in the Midwest and that the dogs on the tape included
Siberian huskies, Dobermans, and Alaskan malamutes. This
tape is so gruesome that I'd put Rowdy and Kimi outdoors in
their fenced yard before I'd popped it into my new VCR. I
won't expose my dogs to filth. As for myself, I took the tape
as a booster shot, the sharp jab I needed to protect myself
from buying either the malamute puppy or the poor little
Boston terrier. Fact: Puppy mills breed their bitches the first
time they come in season and every six months thereafter
until the age of five or six, when the litter size decreases. And
then? If the bastards used needles instead of shotguns, I suppose it could be considered mercy killing.

While the tape was rewinding, I went to the door, whis-
tled, and called, "Rowdy! Kimi!" Then I backstepped to avoid
the dogs, who barreled up the steps, fled past me, and barged

into the kitchen, where they neatly planted themselves in front of the food closet and trained angelic eyes upon their favorite companion animal.

"You see that clock?" I asked politely. "Three hours to go." They eat at five. Actually, they eat from five o'clock until precisely twenty seconds after five. Tired of finicky eaters? Could I interest you in a nice rescue dog? "Find something else to think about, huh?"

Having offered that advice, I took it myself. My dogs weren't overweight, but when I spread my hands over their solid chests and rubbed hard, I could feel the healthy layers of muscle that hide their ribs from view even in the summer when they're shed out. I stroked their thick, clean, sweet-smelling coats, checked their ears and teeth—pristine—and glanced at their well-trimmed nails. Dogs don't absolutely need to be bathed and groomed like that. In fact, Rowdy is convinced that a warm bath is a life-threatening event, and, especially when I shampoo his tail and flanks, he yowls and shrieks so loudly and intensely that the sound waves whack against my head like breakers smashing into a seawall. Since acquiring Rowdy, I've certainly sustained a significant hearing loss and probably undergone a series of minor noise-induced concussions, too, but, as I've said, dogs don't actually require and often don't even enjoy show-ring perfection. But to remain healthy, they need basic cleanliness, not to mention food, shelter . . .

So I wasn't very successful in trying to think about something else, and, in any case, despite the limits on what anyone could do, I needed to do something. For advice about exactly what, I called Betty Burley, one of the most effective Malamute Rescue people around here. As I've confessed already, my own Malamute Rescue efforts had consisted largely of repeated failures to find good homes, not that I entirely blame myself. I mean, if you think about it, God

undoubtedly has exactly the same problem in placing rescued angels. The prospective adopters are all lined up,
they're full of enthusiasm, wild about the breed, and then all
of a sudden, they ask what seems like one last perfunctory
question, namely, "Say, they don't *shed,* do they?" And God,
eyeing those richly feathered white wings, clears Her throat,
ers, ums, and reluctantly spits out the truth. "But," the Deity
hastens to add, "only twice a year. And with a really powerful
vacuum cleaner and a good daily brushing, you'll hardly notice it!" The people, unconvinced, say thanks, hang up, and
dash to the nearest pet shop to pay six hundred dollars for a
toy-size lap demon. So, as I've said, why should I feel guilty or
inadequate? Everyone who does rescue has the same problem.

The exception is Betty Burley, who has been breeding,
showing, and rescuing malamutes for thirty or forty years.
Oh, and by the way, when I say that Betty does rescue, I don't
just mean that she takes back her own dogs. Every ethical
breeder does that. Let me add that although not everyone
around here is crazy about Betty Burley, she and I get along
fine. One reason I like her a lot is that she reminds me of
Kimi, and you're welcome to tell Betty I said that, too. She'll
probably be flattered. She should be. Kimi is highly intelligent, incredibly pretty, unmistakably feminine, outrageously
dominant, and genuinely tough. I first met Betty Burley at a
local kennel club's annual banquet, where we found ourselves
seated next to one another. After we'd exchanged only a few
words, I discovered that I'd draped my left arm around my
dinner plate and was keeping a vigilant eye on Betty in case
she made a Kimi-like lunge for my broiled Boston scrod. In
brief, despite the absence of a thick double coat, a full mask,
and, so far as I know, a long plumy tail, and despite Betty's
seventy-odd years, she is so much like Kimi that her presence
turns me food protective. All this is to say that Betty is good

at getting what she wants, namely, responsible homes for rescue dogs or, in the case of the kennel club banquet, the fish that I didn't finish. So Betty has more experience in rescue work and greater force of character than I do, and I needed help. I reached her at her kennel number and explained about Puppy Luv.

"That place!" Betty swore under her breath. "I'd like to strangle them."

"Failing that," I said, "is there anything we can do?"

Betty ignored the question. "That damned Puppy Luv. We've already got one of their dogs on our hands now." Coincidence? Let me repeat: Ethical breeders take back their dogs. The ones that end up with rescue are mainly strays and pet shop dogs. Betty continued. "As a matter of fact, I was going to call you today to see if you'd go and take a look." Betty gave the kind of sigh you hear from someone about to tell a familiar story. "This is some lady in Cambridge. Her husband died—it was his dog—and she says she's thinking about moving and doesn't have room and it's not fair to the dog and all that. Basically, she just doesn't want the dog. You live closer to her than I do. You think you could go take a look?"

"Sure," I said. "Where does she live?"

Betty gave me the woman's name, address, and phone number, and then a brief description of the malamute, a young unspayed female. The woman was named Enid Sievers, and she lived somewhere off Mass. Ave. in North Cambridge. The malamute was called Missy.

"There's no big rush," Betty said. "The lady's not threatening to take her to the vet or anything, and I really think she's trying to be responsible."

"I could go take a look today," I said. "I'll call. But I'd rather not have her here over the weekend unless it's an emergency. I'm really not set up for it, and I've got Rowdy entered on Sunday. I'll be gone all day, and my neighbors aren't going to love it if she and Kimi start anything."

If you don't show your dogs, you may not realize that shows, obedience trials, tracking tests, and other such events require advance entry and that the entry fees are usually not refundable. You're sometimes allowed to withdraw a bitch from a trial and get back your entry fee if you submit a veterinarian's certificate to prove that she came in season, but if you get the flu or just decide that the dog isn't ready, you lose your entry fee. But that's beside the point. I wanted to go, and I intended to spend tomorrow, Saturday, grooming Rowdy and doing a run-through as well as doing my own grocery shopping and errands. An unknown rescue dog wouldn't be much help. Want a few more excuses? On Sunday, when Rowdy and I went to the show, I wouldn't be able to leave Kimi and the rescue dog loose together in the house because Kimi harbors unsisterly feelings toward other malamute bitches; and if I crated both of them, their complaints would irk my neighbors, especially the male Scottie who belongs to Rita, my second-floor tenant and first-class friend. Also, Kimi, an indoor dog, lacked the superthick winter protection that malamutes develop only if they live outdoors. The rescue dog was probably an indoor dog, too. If the frigid weather continued through Sunday, it would be cruel to leave either of them outside. In brief, it wouldn't be convenient for me to take the dog until Monday.

"No problem," Betty assured me. "Like I said, there's no rush, and you don't need to keep her there. If it's a problem, I'll take her."

Although I honestly am not set up for a third dog, I felt guilty. "I'll drive her out to you," I volunteered. "I could probably do it Monday."

"Whenever," Betty said. "So did you get a look at the papers on this pet shop dog?"

If you're a breed loyalist, maybe you'll understand. If not, I'd better explain. Yes, but how? Look, suppose you're strolling through your local mall and happen to notice a baby shop that's selling an infant, and not just any old infant, either, but one that's unmistakably a member of your own family. Uncle Harry's nose, Grandpa's eyes, the whole bit. Wouldn't you be a little curious about how that baby got there? About who and where the parents were? And whether they were all right? Is that a little radical? If I've gone too far for you, take that raw sense of recognizing your own tiny relative for sale in a baby shop and tone down your feelings one small notch. Not all the way, just a notch. That's why Betty asked about the papers.

"No," I said. I hadn't even tried. "I just assumed she came from the Midwest or Pennsylvania or whatever."

Doesn't everybody know this? Maybe not. The big puppy mill states are Iowa, Kansas, Missouri, Arkansas, Oklahoma, Nebraska, and Pennsylvania.

"Probably Missouri," Betty said. "But not necessarily. Next time, see if you can get a look at the papers."

"I, uh, I wasn't . . . Betty, I really didn't know what to do. I mean, I still don't."

"First of all," she said firmly, "it's not the end of the world. Most of the people who buy from a pet shop just don't know where else to get a dog, okay? You've got to try and think that they aren't bad people. They just don't know any better."

Well, they damn well ought to, I thought.

Betty went on. "So what you want to do is go back there and be nice."

"I was nice this time," I said.

"What did you say?"

"They, uh, assumed I was interested in buying a puppy."

"Jesus," Betty said. "Why'd you . . . ? Look, just go

back there, say who you are, talk to them, and act nice. That's what the affenpinscher people say to do, and they know about it. They've got a much bigger problem than we do."

In case you didn't know, an affenpinscher looks something like a tiny terrier with the face of a really cute monkey. That combination of very small and very cute makes for a big problem: Puppies of large breeds rapidly enter a gawky preadolescence, but little bitty adorable balls of fluff have a long shelf life in a pet shop; a four-month-old Akita, malamute, collie, or chow is undoubtedly a *dog,* but a six-month-old affenpinscher, Maltese, bichon, or mini anything is obviously puppyish, which is what most buyers want. Consequently, it's the toy breed people who have the giant problem with pet shops.

"So I go back there and say I'm from Malamute Rescue?" I hated the idea.

"Yes," Betty said in a Kimi-like voice. "But act nice! Get them on our side. What you want them to do is put something with the papers. You have any of those booklets?"

The booklet, *The Alaskan Malamute: An Introduction,* is what we mail to people who inquire about the breed.

"Yes," I said.

"Okay, so put your name and address on it, or mine if you want, and go back there and try and talk them into leaving it with the papers. Or get them to pass along your name. That's the best you can do at this point."

"But what if—"

"Don't buy that dog!"

"I won't. But what if—"

"Look, how old is the puppy?"

"I'm not sure. Maybe seven weeks, I think. She's a baby."

Seven weeks is the minimum age at which a good

breeder will let a puppy go—most insist on eight weeks—but all good breeders warn buyers not to let the puppy have any contact with strange dogs until four months, when he's fully immunized. Pet shop conditions maximize a puppy's chances of getting sick: A large and changing population of incompletely immunized puppies from different but mostly dirty places, all living together indoors, isn't great, but it's especially dangerous with a ventilation system designed for people, not animals. Dogs require many more changes of air per hour than we do, much more fresh air than a pet shop provides, especially a shopping mall pet shop. Cat lover, too, are you? Kittens are the canary in the pet shop gold mine because they're the first animals to show upper respiratory diseases and ringworm. I didn't make up that canary business, either. It's a quote from an article in a magazine for pet shop operators: "Think of those kittens as the canary in your gold mine." Is that unbelievable? I mean, is that how you think about *your* cat? It's probably not even how you think about your *canary*, for God's sake.

"Seven weeks old," Betty said. "Honest to God. I would really like to strangle these people."

5

ENID SIEVERS LIVED IN ONE of those late-Victorian houses a few blocks off upper Mass. Ave. in North Cambridge on the Somerville line. It stood out from its neighbors by virtue—or sin —of being painted an unspeakably intense shade of raspberry. Because of that god-awful color, it was the kind of house that makes people gasp, titter, and return with friends who just have to see it and simply won't believe it when they do. But they do believe it, of course—its undiluted reality is undeniable—and ask one another whether that ultra-raspberry was the embarrassing result of some unimaginable misunderstanding with the house painter or whether, God forbid, it was chosen deliberately.

Thus the stunned queasiness on my face must have been the expression Enid Sievers saw whenever she opened her front door to anyone, and in case you've ever wandered by there and wondered the inevitable, the answer is, no, that raspberry was no accident, as I guessed the second Enid Sievers opened her door. Transpose that screaming raspberry into a violent electric green, and you'll see the color of the garment she wore, a silky pantsuit or polyester evening costume or possibly a pair of nineteen-thirties Hollywood-movie lounging pajamas minus the feather boa. Exactly what the outfit *was* didn't actually matter, I thought: Anyone willing to wear it at all would probably be willing to wear it anywhere.

The woman herself was in her late fifties, I guessed. She was very slim and had what my grandmother always refers to as "good posture," meaning that she held her shoulders back as if in perpetual defiance of imminent osteoporosis. Her most striking feature was exceptionally sparse black hair that had been cut, gelled, curled, fluffed, and sprayed to create the illusion of thick tresses, but a prominent part down the side revealed a good half inch of white scalp. Delicate, fragile, heavily moisturized skin stretched across the fine bones of her face. Thick glasses magnified the lines and pouches under her darting hazel eyes, which seemed to focus on a fascinating series of objects that didn't exist. I had the immediate impression that Enid Sievers believed something extraordinary: that alien beings had subjected her to grueling medical tests aboard their spaceship, or that Elvis regularly returned to earth to offer her spiritual counsel and tips on the lottery.

But her welcome was perfectly ordinary, even gracious. As soon as she introduced herself and made sure that I was, in fact, Holly Winter, she invited me in, saying proudly and confidently, "You didn't have any trouble finding the house, did you?"

"No," I said, half embarrassed. "Not at all. I spotted it right away." I was sorry I'd worn old jeans.

"No one ever has trouble finding us," Mrs. Sievers assured me as she led me through a little foyer and into a living room. "Edgar liked *cheerful* colors," she went on to explain. Her voice was high and wispy, as if amplified from a great distance, for example, Mars or Saturn. "Edgar always said that vision is a great blessing and that we should use it to the best of our ability and not just waste it."

She swept a bony green-swathed arm around to direct my attention to the room's furnishings, of which there were hundreds, maybe even thousands, and I'm not exaggerating. The windows were not so much curtained as red-velvet-barricaded against light, and above each window hung great swathes of the same red velvet augmented with heavy gold braid and thick tassels. Elaborately upholstered in a bewildering variety of red brocades and crimson patterns, dozens of Victorian love seats, fat couches, and old-fashioned over-stuffed armchairs battled for floor space against the armies of highly polished mahogany coffee tables, teak magazine racks, wrought iron plant stands, French provincial end tables, and standing lamps about which the less said, the better. Small area rugs with the bright, happy designs of Poland were scattered here and there on the richly textured bright maroon wall-to-wall carpet. The intricately carved green marble mantle of the fireplace supported an ormolu clock, two oversize modernistic jade green vases, a small collection of expensive-looking crystal owls, and a pair of china shepherdesses with candles sticking out of their heads.

Just as Enid Sievers invited me to have a seat, my legs seemed to go out from under me. When I'd caught my breath, I found myself in the soft depths of one of the love seats. Fringed pillows nudged at me like friendly lap dogs. The end table to my left held a large brass lamp, a foot-wide porcelain ashtray, a set of cork-and-plastic coasters, and two glass candy dishes piled with paper-wrapped caramels.

Enid Sievers took a seat on an equally pillow-laden

couch opposite me. Between us lay a pie-crust-edged coffee table crowded with glass objects and candy.

"Edgar was an optometrist," Enid Sievers explained brightly. She sat stiffly upright, her ankles crossed, her knees locked tightly together. "It taught him the value of *seeing*. He always said that we should use what God had given us."

"That seems like a good idea," I said stupidly or maybe even stuporously. The house was sickeningly hot and had a stale reek of perfumed soap and microwaved food additives. Where was the dog?

Enid Sievers leaned forward, picked up a candy dish, and graciously proffered it. "Would you like a caramel?"

"No, thanks," I said. "Uh, you, uh, called about your dog?"

"Missy is an Alaskan malamute." She sounded as if she were reciting something she'd memorized. "She is a registered purebred dog. Are you sure you won't have a caramel?" She pursed her lips and stared at me.

I cleared my throat. "No, thanks," I repeated, pulling myself out of the depths of the love seat. "About Missy?"

Enid Sievers met my gaze. "This isn't easy for me," she said. "She was Edgar's dog, really." Her eyes were nearly tearful.

I helped her out. "But she's the wrong dog for you."

Her face brightened. "That's it," she said. "That's just it. She's the wrong dog for me." Enid Sievers and her jam-packed room cried out for a Pekingese, a Pomeranian, a Maltese, a toy poodle, a Shih Tzu, any of dozens of tiny breeds. "Would you rather have a chocolate? And I have some very nice pralines that my sister just sent me from Florida." She half rose in apparent search of them.

"No," I said firmly. "No thanks. Do you think I could take a look at Missy?"

"Well, of course," Enid Sievers answered, reseating herself opposite me, "I feel terrible about this, you know, but when Mrs. Burley heard about Missy, she was so thrilled! And I realized, well, Missy will really have a better life there. So it's really better for everyone."

"We'll find a good home for her," I said.

Enid Sievers's eyes focused on some apparition behind my head, but her correction was almost sharp. "Oh, you don't need to find a *home* for her. Mrs. Burley is very anxious to have her." Now she surveyed me as if in search of signs of mental deficiency. "Mrs. Burley raises Alaskan malamutes, you know," she informed me. "And Missy is an outstanding specimen of the breed. Edgar always said so, and he was very knowledgeable."

"I'm sure he was. Do you think I could take a look at her?" *Show me the dog!*

"Well, of course," she said, but retained her ladylike pose on the couch.

I found myself glancing around. As you probably know, malamutes are among the few creatures on earth that never talk unless they have something to say. Consequently, they often remain silent for hours. On the other hand, most of them are almost ridiculously friendly. I began to feel alarmed. If, in fact, Missy were tucked behind one of the couches, chairs, or love seats or hidden under one of the dozens of tables, there must be something horribly wrong with her.

"Mrs. Sievers," I said in my firmest dog-training voice, "where *is* Missy?"

Enid Sievers gestured vaguely toward the back of the house and asked, "Or maybe you'd like a chocolate-covered cherry?"

"Thank you," I said. "Maybe later. Right now, I'd like to see Missy." Then I finally caught on. "Mrs. Sievers, would you like *me* to get her?"

"Would you? I have a terrible time with her." Her odd, vaguely mechanical voice was pitifully grateful, and she finally rose from the couch and gestured to me to follow. As I trailed after her through a furniture-packed dining room and into an out-of-date, surprisingly bare lime green kitchen, she went on about her troubles with the dog. "She's knocked me over five or six times! And I know she doesn't mean it, it's just that she's terribly strong, and, of course she's very young and *so* vigorous! And I know she misses Edgar—he used to take her for her walkies every morning and twice at night, when he was able. Edgar worshipped this dog—and I've hired a boy to walk her, and that helps, but it's not enough! And I can't let her run through the house, can I? Just imagine!"

And I did. Candy dishes emptied and smashed, porcelain figures flying, lamps crashing to the floor, tea tables toppled . . . How the hell had a malamute ever ended up in this worse-than-a-china-shop? I knew the answer, of course: Puppy Luv, that's how.

Mostly because I'd entirely dismissed Enid Sievers's claim that Missy was an outstanding specimen of the breed, I expected to see the opposite: a tiny "malamute" with some obvious Siberian husky in her; or maybe a grotesquely over-sized monster with bad hips; or simply a poor specimen, a malamute with a snap tail and coat; or perhaps a wooley. A wooley? That's a malamute with a really long, shaggy coat. Woolies are spectacularly pretty, but that coat isn't what the standard calls for, so you can't show woolies in the breed ring. Anyway, Missy wasn't one. In fact, for a pet shop dog, she was surprisingly decent looking, and she was loaded with personality.

As it turned out, she'd been confined to a large pantry at the back of the kitchen. The little room had been stripped of its original contents and furnished with a mammoth red dog bed, a set of stainless steel bowls, and a big Vari-Kennel complete with a cozy-looking fake-sheepskin crate rug. Enid Sievers had supplied me with a sturdy inch-wide leash, and I'd cautiously opened the door, but the second Missy caught sight of me, she dashed forward, wiggled all over, rubbed her head vigorously against my knees, and then veered, dashed in a couple of happy circles, and returned to me.

"Hi, pretty," I said, massaging her neck and rubbing the top of her head. "Are you a good girl?"

She plunked her bottom on the floor, flattened her ears against her head, rose up a little, gently placed both front paws in my hands, and held my eyes in hers. I was crazy about her, of course. I am a complete sucker for dogs, but especially for malamutes. And here's the damn thing, the real killer: Her color and facial markings were a whole lot like Kimi's. Gray dog, white trim with a little tan, the full mask, the whole bit. Her eyes were paler than Kimi's, her coat was a lighter gray, her tail was shorter, and her build was more delicate than Kimi's—she'd end up smaller than Kimi, I thought, with legs and feet too fine for the breed— but the superficial resemblance was there. And sweet? Missy was a born cuddler, much more submissive than either of my dogs. She rubbed herself against me like a cat. When I knelt down, she wrapped her forepaws around my neck and—I swear it's true—gave me a big hug. She didn't just rest her paws on me; she squeezed. I loved her on sight and felt a momentary rush of anger at Rowdy and Kimi, who would've welcomed her with all the joyous enthusiasm I'd display if Steve announced that, guess what, our life was about to be enriched by the addition of a new woman. Damn them, I thought. And damn the show on Sunday, too. This was one rescue malamute who'd be easy to place in a good home.

"Well," I said to Enid Sievers, who hovered timidly in

the background, "she's a sweetheart." Then, although the floor of the pantry was clean, I asked, "Is she fully housebroken?"

"Oh, yes," Enid Sievers said.

"Any, uh, bad habits? Chewing on things? Anything like that?"

"Just her toys." They littered the pantry floor: one large Nylaring, one giant Nylafloss, two plaque attackers in different sizes, three hard plastic balls, a tug-of-war toy, a big red rubber Kong toy, a chew-proof Frisbee, to mention a few. "The lady at Puppy Luv explained to Edgar that toys are very important." Well, they are, of course. But two or three hundred dollars' worth? "And," she added as if transmitting a piece of insider information, "water must always be available. That's very important for Alaskan malamutes."

"Yes," I said. Missy's water bowl was full. "Mrs. Sievers, has Missy come in season yet? Has she had her first heat yet?"

As you've probably guessed, Enid Sievers wasn't exactly a real dog person. Her pale, fine skin turned from ivory to pink to scarlet. I heard her catch her breath. Her voice was faint and controlled. "Not that I've noticed," she said. "But I'm not . . ."

I tried to dream up a probe that wouldn't embarrass this woman. *Notice any bloody vaginal discharge? Any swelling of the vulva?* In fact, it seemed to me that there was some. "Um, have there been any, uh, red spots on the floor?"

She peeped a response: "No!"

"Okay, well, don't be surprised if there are. It's perfectly normal. Look, we'll be glad to take Missy. She's lovely." Missy dropped to the floor, rolled onto her back, and eyed me. I scratched her chest and rubbed her tummy. Enid Sievers probably thought I was mad. "But," I said, "uh, I can't take Missy today, and neither can Betty Burley. If it's okay, I'll come back for her on Monday, and I'll drive her out to Betty's. Is that okay? Can you keep her for the weekend?"

Enid Sievers said that it was no problem at all. Remember that, would you? Remember that. Then I asked whether she had Missy's papers.

"Those are very important documents, you know," she informed me. "Edgar said that those were valuable documents. Missy's papers meant a lot to him." Her tone became reluctant, stubborn. "I don't think Edgar would like me to part with them."

You do any purebred rescue? If so, you're not surprised, are you? The papers had more sentimental value than the dog did. You're used to it. I've seen people abandon the dog, but insist on keeping the collar and tags. Honest to God. Anyway, if Enid Sievers had been someone other than who she was, I'd have pressed hard for those papers. I'd read about the sale of AKC papers to puppy mills. I'd heard that papers are auctioned off. Blue money, right? AKC papers. But Enid Sievers? Never. If I'd wanted to sell or auction a dog's papers myself, I wouldn't have known where to begin. Enid Sievers certainly wouldn't, either. Besides, I'd be back on Monday. I could try again. In the meantime, I asked to look at the papers. I said that I was curious about where Missy had come from, who her parents were.

While Enid Sievers was digging the documents out of a drawer somewhere, I sat on the floor of the pantry, dug my fingers into Missy's coat, stroked her muzzle, and talked softly to her. "You're perfectly safe and happy here," I said. "You're just a little bored and lonely. And I'll be back for you in three days. And then Betty and I will find a wonderful family for you, and you'll go on long walks every day. And you won't have to be alone any more. I promise. I hate to leave you, but I'll be back. And then everything will be much, much better." Yeah, I know. Spaying. All purebred rescue dogs are spayed or neutered before they're placed or immediately afterward. But why worry her with details?

Then Enid Sievers returned, and I gave Missy a big hug, shut her in the pantry, and followed her mistress back to that overstuffed, cloying living room. Enid Sievers hesitated a moment, clutching a manila folder against her bosom as if I might snatch Missy's papers and take off, but then handed it to me. I took my old place on the love seat, put the folder on the coffee table in front of me, and opened it. I was a little surprised to find that besides the familiar white, violet-lettered AKC registration slip, the folder contained an AKC-certified four-generation pedigree, for which Edgar Sievers had paid fifteen dollars in addition to the registration fee. According to the registration slip and the pedigree, Missy was Princess Melissa Sievers, a wolf gray and white Alaskan malamute female whelped eight months earlier. The breeder's name was Walter Simms. I'd never heard of him, and neither the registration slip nor the pedigree gave his address. I assumed that he was a Kansas farmer who'd found hogs unprofitable, or maybe chickens. Did you know that in Kansas alone, puppies are a forty-two-million-dollar-a-year business? Yeah, forty-two million. A year. According to something I read somewhere, there are more dogs in the chicken coops of Kansas than there are chickens. Jesus. My eyes reached the bottom half of the pedigree, the section that showed Missy's maternal line. The names staggered me.

Enid Sievers must have read my expression. "It's *very* impressive, isn't it," she said. "There are a lot of champion dogs there. The lady at Puppy Luv explained to Edgar that Missy was really a show dog, you know. All of her dogs are."

Without asking Enid Sievers's permission, I reached into my purse, pulled out a notebook and pen, and began to scrawl down the names on the pedigree. Those on Missy's sire's side sounded like puppy mill names to me: Sir Snowy II,

Caesar the Great. But her dam? Ever hear of Icekist? Icekist is the kennel name of Lois Metzler. I knew Lois. I ran into her at shows all the time. Betty Burley knew her, too. Lois Metzler was no chicken farmer in Kansas. She was a reputable malamute breeder, and her kennel was right here in Massachusetts.

Remember that business about spotting one of your infant relatives in the window of a shopping mall baby shop? Remember about taking that feeling and toning it down? Well, in the case of Lois Metzler, forget that. Take that feeling and let it rip until it blasts your chest open. A dog from Lois Metzler's lines for sale in a pet shop? I would have sworn it was impossible. So, I thought, would Lois. No wonder Missy was decent looking. After all, she came from Lois's lines.

6

SOMETIMES I IMAGINE MYSELF at a meeting held in the pale yellow cinder-block assembly room of a church basement. Rows of brown-painted metal folding chairs face a podium. In these chairs sit men and women with the brave, ravaged faces of recovering addicts. It is my turn to testify. My left hand clutches spasmodically as I grab at a nonexistent leash. I step forward and face the audience.

"My name is Holly," I say. "And I am a dogaholic."

What I really need isn't Dogaholics Anonymous, but Dog Spenders Anonymous, a self-help organization devoted to squelching the compulsion to throw away money on canine paraphernalia. Just put me within spending distance of the concession booths at a dog show, and the urge overwhelms me. How does anyone resist? If your dog does great, well, naturally, you have to celebrate. If he does miserably, you both deserve a little consolation, don't you? And if you don't even have a dog entered that day? If you're stewarding? Or just wandering around? Well, then, you don't even have a ribbon, never mind a trophy, to take home, do you? After all, this is not just anywhere, is it? This is a dog show. No one leaves empty-handed.

Thus, Sunday afternoon found Rowdy and me studying leashes in the depths of the Cherrybrook booth at the Shawsheen Valley Kennel Club's annual AKC dog show and obedience trial. The show site was the Northeast Trade Center, which is just off Route 128 in Woburn and not in the Shawsheen Valley, but clubs have a hard time finding places to hold shows, especially indoor shows. Except when transfigured by several thousand gorgeous show dogs, the Northeast Trade Center is an unprepossessing structure that looks like an abandoned single-story, flat-roofed post-World War II factory. As a show site, though, it's not bad. Dogs are, of course, allowed, and the interior space is open and fairly large. Also, the location is convenient, and the place is easy to find. In fact, if you've ever taken Route I-95 through Massachusetts, you've passed it, because I-95 is what everyone around here calls 128, America's Technology Highway. Even if you're coming from out of state, you can't miss the site: Just take the Woburn exit, Route 38, turn into the shopping mall, follow the little road that runs parallel to the highway, and you'll end up in the parking lot.

As I was saying, having once again failed to qualify in Open—yes, once again, the long sit—Rowdy and I were prowling around the Cherrybrook booth in search of consolation. So far, I'd accumulated a beautiful new rolled-leather collar that Rowdy didn't need, an identical but slightly smaller collar that Kimi didn't need either, a fourteen-ounce container of Redi-Liver treats (for the unbeatable price of thirteen dollars and thirty cents), a bottle of coat conditioner, and (at a mere eight dollars and seventy-five cents each, less than half the pet shop list price) two large-size Nylafloss dental devices.

I was fingering a handsome bright red leash that hung with hundreds of other leashes in all colors, widths, lengths, and materials, when a tiny, wiry woman with a mobile face and a head of short white curls popped up next to Rowdy like an elf materializing at the side of a tame wolf and said, "Rotten luck!"

Betty usually wears bright-colored warm-up suits that make her look like a heavily wrinkled but exceptionally agile stretch-suit-clad infant. That afternoon, though, Betty was spiffed up for the breed ring: tweed suit, lacy white blouse, patterned black stockings, black flats. You might guess that Betty Burley would own one pampered apricot toy poodle or an adorable little Pomeranian, but as I've mentioned, she's been breeding, showing, and rescuing malamutes for decades.

"Thank you," I said. "I don't feel too bad about it. I know he can do it. Right now, it's mostly a matter of being patient."

If you know anything about obedience, you'll realize that since Rowdy was in Open, the obedience class you enter for a C.D.X., Companion Dog Excellent title, he already had his C.D. The obedience ring has always been a struggle for him. He got his C.D. with scores that are nothing to brag about, and, although he loved the jumping and retrieving in Open and was capable of better scores than he'd achieved in Novice, the problem we faced now was qualifying at all. In breed, though, Rowdy is a natural. Anyway, one legacy of Rowdy's career in conformation is his adoration of breed handlers, all of whom carry liver and other goodies to bait their dogs in the ring and most of whom, Rowdy had discovered, could be coaxed into doling out treats. So at the sight of Betty Burley, he posed himself in a flashy show stance, caught Betty's eye, slapped a winner's grin on his face, and wagged his tail hard enough to send the Cherrybrook leashes flying like colorful banners blown by a strong wind. Also, I suspect that Betty reminded him of Kimi.

"This is a good-looking dog," Betty said. She has the big malamutes—M'Loots—that you see in the Midwest and other parts of the country, not the smaller Kotzebues you see here in New England. Rowdy isn't pure Kotzebue, and he's a big boy—standard size—but I was surprised and happy to hear Betty admire him. He didn't look like Betty's dogs, and most breeders like the type they raise themselves. "You better keep your eye on him today," Betty added as she reached into one of the pockets of her wolf gray suit. When I'd nodded an okay, she fed Rowdy one of those disgusting-looking chunks of dried liver for which dogs will do anything, absolutely anything, even behave themselves. "He'd go with anyone."

"I know," I said. "I didn't even bring a crate. I'm just keeping him with me. Nothing's happened, has it? I mean, here?"

In case you've spent the last few years exiled on some barren no-mail, no-dog-show island, let me explain. The militant wing of the animal rights movement, having evidently decided that love and protection are exploitation, had recently begun to release dogs from their servile state of bondage. In other words, they'd been going to shows and "liberating" dogs from their crates. Sound familiar? Yes, indeed, the American policy in Vietnam: To save the village, you have to destroy it.

Anyway, as I've suggested, Betty Burley, who is a tiny woman in her midseventies or so, looks almost nothing like a malamute, but when she answered my question about the animal rights extremists, her rather almond-shaped brown eyes blazed exactly the way Rowdy's do whenever he spots that cocker spaniel that's kept on a clothesline trolley a few blocks from my house. "Nothing's happened yet," said Betty, fingering a gray show lead, "but they've been turning up at a whole lot of shows. There've been incidents all over the country."

"It scares the life out of me." I clutched Rowdy's collar. "And here? With that shopping mall and then 128? Betty, *where* are your dogs?"

"In their crates, but it's okay. Lois is keeping an eye on them. So did you talk to that woman? The one that called me?"

"Yeah. Enid Sievers. I went over there Friday. I'm going to go pick the dog up tomorrow and drive her out to you, if that's okay."

Betty nodded. Her white curls shook. "What's she like, what's her name, Missy?"

"Yeah. Missy. For a pet shop dog, she's really quite decent looking, and she's *really* sweet. It's just, really, it's just a bad match. I mean, the husband got the dog from Puppy Luv, and then he died, and this woman is the last person who could cope with a malamute, and when you consider that, the dog is amazingly well behaved, housebroken, nondestructive, very submissive. She needs to be spayed, but that's about it."

"Great," Betty said.

"Uh, but there is sort of a problem," I said reluctantly. "It's about her papers." I examined a thin braided-leather lead.

"You get them?"

"No. But I got a look at them. There's sort of a problem." I rested my hand on Rowdy's head and began to rub him gently. "I don't exactly know what to do about it. I don't even know . . ." Without thinking, I raised my hand to cover my mouth.

Betty guessed immediately. "AMCA breeder?"

The first provision of the code of ethics of the national breed club, AMCA, the Alaskan Malamute Club of America, is this: "No member shall knowingly be involved in the sale of puppies through pet shops or any other type of wholesale outlets, including mail-order houses, dog agents, or federally licensed dog dealers or individuals or institutions involved in research." Just in case anyone misses the point, the second provision goes on to forbid the sale of litters for resale.

"She must be," I said. "Yeah, I know she is."

Betty's wiry body stiffened. "Not—"

I interrupted. "No, not you." I peered through the curtain of leads to make sure that no one was hanging around to overhear. "Lois Metzler," I murmured.

Betty folded her arms across her chest. "Look, Holly, if you don't mind me saying so, you're new at this," she said firmly. "Take any pet shop dog you want, and go back far enough, and what you find is a reputable breeder somewhere there. It can happen to anyone. How far back?"

A woman and a stunning Afghan hound, a snood on his head to protect his ears, appeared on the other side of the display of leads.

"Betty, could we, uh . . . let's move somewhere else, huh? Where we can talk."

Rowdy followed me to the Cherrybrook counter, where I paid about half what the same collars, treats, conditioner, and chew toys would've cost at Puppy Luv. Then Betty, Rowdy, and I made our way through the narrow, crowded aisles between the baby-gated rings to the cafeteria, bought some of that poisonous dog-show coffee, and stood at the vacant end of a long, high counter.

"From what I can tell," I said, "Lois sold a bitch to a puppy mill. I'm sure she didn't mean to, but Missy's dam is Icekist. Do we tell her?"

"Who'd Lois sell to? Who's the breeder?"

"Some guy I've never heard of. Walter Simms, his name is. You ever hear of him?"

Betty shook her head and said definitively, "He's not from around here."

"Probably in Missouri," I said. "Minnesota. Iowa. Whatever."

Although I didn't know where Walter Simms was, it seemed to me that I knew who he was. I could see his face, fleshy, ugly, and brutal. His nose was like a pig's, with open nostrils that spouted clumps and tufts of white hair. His laugh was ugly, too, and rotten teeth fouled his breath.

I cleared my mind. "The other names, on the sire's side, all sound like puppy mill dogs, and there's a whole lot of inbreeding."

"Puppy mills do that. Look, Holly, I don't know how well you know Lois." Betty paused. "She breeds a lot of litters."

"I've heard," I said. "Betty, do we tell her? Or . . . ?"

"You never know." Betty stretched up an elbow and leaned on the counter. "And if it happened once, it could happen again. She's got to do a better job of screening. It's not just her. We all do. But, you never know, maybe she can try and buy the bitch back. It's been done before. You end up paying two or three times the purchase price, but you get your bitch back."

"It'd be worth it. It'd be worth anything."

"Yeah," Betty agreed. "You want me to tell her?"

"Yes," I said with no hesitation. "It might be—"

"She's going to want to talk to you. She's going to need to see the papers."

"Rowdy, get over here," I said. In search of crumbs, he'd snuffled his way to the end of his six-foot lead. "Good boy. Stick around, huh? Anyway, I don't know if I can get the papers, but I can show her the pedigree. I don't have it with me, but I copied it down. This woman, Enid Sievers . . .

Look, I know this sounds crazy, but she wants to keep the papers. They have sentimental value or something. They belonged to her husband."

"People'll buy them, you know. Puppy mills will. What's she . . . ?" I could see Betty envisioning Enid Sievers as a sharp, sneaky character with connections in the canine underworld.

I smiled. "Enid Sievers is just not that kind of person. I really don't think we need to worry about that. She's, uh, sort of vague. I mean, I think she really is the kind of person who'd give up her husband's dog and insist on keeping the papers. She struck me as being sort of, uh, out of touch with reality."

Betty didn't trust my judgment. "She tell you about the husband?"

"She mentioned him. Edgar."

"She tell you that he knew he was dying when he bought the puppy?"

"No." Dog-show coffee is bad enough to make anyone choke, but I'd barely sipped mine. "You mean . . . ?"

"Yeah. I do mean. From what she says, he walked into that goddamned Puppy Luv, told 'em all about how sick he was, he always wanted an Alaskan malamute, it was his last dying wish, and then he walked out with the dog. You like that?"

"That's sick," I said. "He bought a puppy when he knew . . . ? And with a wife like that?"

"Yeah, well, you're young," Betty said. "Except for dogs, it'd be a pretty sick world out there. And even with them. Look, I've got to get back to my dogs. You coming with me?"

"Sure," I said, following her, "if you want. Unless it'd be easier . . ."

"Yeah, maybe it would," Betty said. "Give me ten minutes or so, would you? We're set up over there against that wall. See where that deerhound is? In back of there and a little to the left."

As soon as Betty left, a group of four or five people I didn't know approached the counter, spread out their lunches, and began talking about the same thing that was scaring everyone else at the show. Before I tell you what they were saying, I want to make sure that, in case you're a newcomer, you understand something about show people: This is not only the most diverse group of people you can imagine, but one of the least violent, philandering, or otherwise trouble-prone groups you'll ever encounter. We're too busy training and grooming dogs, cleaning out kennels, whelping puppies, driving to shows, and earning our dogs' keep to get into mischief. We aren't any more morally upright than anyone else; we just don't have time.

With that preface, let me now report that a heavily muscled, bristle-headed guy leaned across the greasy linoleum counter, pointed a sausage-shaped finger at a plump, vigorous elderly woman, and growled, "One of them releases a dog of mine, and I'll give 'em a lesson in liberation. I'll liberate 'em back to the fucking Stone Age."

7

ACCORDING TO A COUPLE of recent surveys, the two most popular dog names in America are Lady and Max. Other favorites include Brandy, Shadow, Duke, Bear, Rocky, Princess, and Bandit. Food names are trendy now—Sushi, Twinkie. We seem to be naming our dogs after what we devour. If so, the next *à la mode* canine appellation in Cambridge is going to be Baby Greens. In Cambridge right now, if you aren't going to serve a mixture of tiny, tender collard leaves, kale, beet greens, endive, and radicchio barely sautéed in hot olive oil, you might just as well proclaim your total rejection of fashion by dishing up a totally passé quiche Lorraine or beef Stroganoff. If we are what we eat, the residents of Cambridge are fast becoming infantile and wilted.

The point about mixed baby greens, though, is to illustrate the mysterious but intimate connection between people and dogs: At the exact moment the tiny leaf craze hit Cambridge, a parallel phenomenon sprang up in dogdom, namely, the lamb and rice fad. Every major manufacturer of dog food is now scrambling to get lamb and rice on the market. A couple of years ago, when everyone in Cambridge was dining on fresh pasta and warm goat cheese, the only dogs in America who'd so much as sniffed lamb and rice were allergy-prone canines on bland diets. Now, all of a sudden, you're apt to be accused of endangering your dog's health and well-being if you're feeding him anything else. Why lamb and rice? Well, why baby greens? And, more importantly, what's the connection? I mean, if the latest human food fad had been something Greek or Middle Eastern, you could understand it: a use for the leftovers. As it is, the human-canine bond is mysterious indeed.

Without entirely abandoning my obsession with this miraculous interspecies link, let me return to the subject of dog names. Lois Metzler grew up in Nashville, Tennessee. Icekist, her kennel name, wasn't twangy or southern, and her dogs were New England Kotzebues, but their names reflected Lois's origins in the country music capital of the world: Icekist Cheating Heart, Honkytonk Angel, that kind of thing. Lois was a Hank Williams fan, of course. Cheating Heart, one of the dogs she'd brought to the Shawsheen Valley show, had gone Winners Bitch that morning.

Ordinarily, then, Lois Metzler would've been in a moderately good mood, and she probably had been until Betty Burley broke the news about Missy. I'd given Betty ten or fifteen minutes alone with Lois. Rowdy and I had wandered around collecting free samples of lamb and rice dog food at the Iams and Natural Life booths. Rowdy had attempted to augment our stock of free samples: He'd tried to snatch a mouthful of trail mix from one of the open bins at a concession stand that sold cashews, jelly beans, dried apricots, and other nuts, fruits, and candies for people, but I'd managed to haul him away in time. Then we'd plowed through the crowds to the area by the wall where Lois and Betty were set up.

Lois Metzler must've been acquainted with the theory that the handler should disappear in the ring to allow the dog to put himself forward, but I guess if you're five feet ten inches tall and weigh as much as three or four Alaskan malamutes, disappearance isn't a realistic goal. Today she was dolled up for the breed ring in a tentlike red dress with abstract splotches of gray and black. Her head was bullet-shaped, her shoulders were massive, she had thick arms and legs, and around the middle she was just plain fat. Despite her own bulk, she kept her dogs lean and fit, and I'd always thought she was a good handler. She moved lightly and had a knack of getting her dogs to show well even in hot weather and in overheated halls when everyone else's dogs looked bored and lethargic.

When Rowdy and I approached, Lois lunged toward us, reached out, grabbed my arm, and said in a deep, scratchy, and rather loud voice, "You know, you're new in malamutes. This is some kind of mistake."

I wasn't eager to handle the rolls of fat that made natural circle bracelets at her wrist, but I wanted her hands off me. Rowdy sat at my side and took an intelligent interest as I calmly and silently removed Lois's damp palm from my thin wrist. Rowdy does not like people to grab me.

"Shit, I'm sorry," she said. She lowered her voice and scratched the back of her neck. "How many people've you told about this?"

"Just Betty," I said. "I'm not a blabbermouth. I don't like gossip. I only told Betty because I didn't know whether to tell you. I didn't know if you'd want to know. She said you would."

Lois Metzler had short, bristly gray-brown hair. Her pallid February skin was draped across small, blunt features.

The pink powder blush on her cheeks, the blue powder shadow on her eyelids, and the traces of red around her lips had the paradoxical effect of draining her face of all color. For a second, I thought she was going to faint.

I gestured toward the folding chair by the big crates that held her dogs. "Lois, do you need to sit down?"

"No!" she said fiercely. She straightened her shoulders and added with a hint of anger, "You know, I screen my buyers. This could happen to anyone, absolutely anyone."

"I know it could," I agreed. "That's the point. It *could* happen to anyone. I'm not blaming you, and neither is Betty."

Like a dog responding to his own name, Betty Burley appeared at Lois's side. They made a funny-looking pair, Brobdingnagian Lois, Lilliputian Betty, but dogs care nothing for outward appearance. Rowdy barged into the center of our circle and nuzzled at Lois's hands. She absentmindedly dug a treat out of her pocket and watched Rowdy wolf it down and lick her hand clean. For a few seconds, no one said anything.

Lois broke the silence. Her voice was hoarse, sad, and belligerent. "Which puppy was it?" Her eyes stayed on Rowdy, almost as though she expected him to answer the question.

He didn't, of course. I did. Same thing, more or less. "The dam is named Icekist Sissy."

Lois's eyes were blank. "Doesn't mean a thing to me."

In case you aren't a specialist in AKC regulations, let me explain that Lois meant *Sissy*, not *Icekist*, which was her registered kennel name and couldn't be used to register a dog from another breeder. Supposedly, puppy buyers aren't obligated to use the registered kennel name prefix. In practice, though, virtually any reputable breeder will insist that you use it, and most will enter it on the puppy's registration application, thus leaving you free to choose the rest of the dog's name. Why? When your pup goes on to take Best in Show at Westminster, the breeder wants—and deserves—the credit, of course.

"I copied down the whole pedigree," I said. "I should've brought it with me. I meant to. I'm sorry. Call me tonight or whenever. Maybe you can find out where she is."

"I screen my buyers," Lois repeated. "I educate them. They have to visit. Everybody visits at least twice. I don't ship to people I don't know."

"Stop it!" Betty ordered her.

"What are you supposed to do?" I added. "Move in with people? Live with them for a month before you'll sell them a dog?"

"Maybe," Lois said. "Maybe that's what you have to do. That or something else." Color began to return to her face. "Puppy Luv," she said bitterly. "God damn. You know something? I'll find out who did this. And I'll get my bitch back, too. Count on it."

"Good," I said. "Lois, if there's anything I can do . . ."

"I don't know," she said. "I have to think. I have to do some follow-ups. I don't know yet. But thanks, Holly. I'll call you." Then with a note of angry confrontation, she asked, "Hey, what does this pet shop bitch look like?"

"Pretty," I said. I described Missy and added, "Nice temperament, too."

"I'd take her," Lois said, her eyes on Betty, "but I haven't got room now, you know. I've got two litters on the ground. I'd like to help, but I'm full up."

The merest flicker of annoyance crossed Betty's face. "I'm taking her. Holly's driving her out to me tomorrow. But the next time you get someone looking for a pet puppy . . ."

You probably don't need a translation, but just in case: A *pet puppy* means one who isn't of show quality and can't go to a show home. Let me add that a pet-quality puppy from a good show kennel is precisely what to look for if you ever buy a purebred puppy that you aren't going to show. You'll get the benefits of buying from a responsible breeder—genetic screening for hereditary conditions like hip dysplasia and eye disease, selective breeding for good temperament, the permanent availability of a knowledgeable person who cares about the dog, and the comfort of knowing that your dog's parents are healthy, safe, happy, and well-fed. And, of course, a pet pup usually costs less than a show pup. But please consider a rescue dog first. I mean, puppies chew everything, and they wake you up at night. They leave puddles and messes all over the floor, and before long, they turn into dogs, anyway.

Back to the Shawsheen Valley show. Lois, Betty, and I had retreated to the area where they'd set up their crates, chairs, and grooming equipment. In muted bellows, Lois was explaining that she'd love to take Missy but didn't have room, and Betty Burley, who had no extra kennel space, either, was making Lois feel really guilty about not helping with rescue. Rowdy was sniffing through the wire mesh door of the crate that held Lois's bitch, and I was standing there with my knees and thighs locked together.

Dog people learn to read body language. Before I'd even asked Lois or Betty to keep an eye on Rowdy for a few minutes, Lois glanced at me, assessed my posture, and said, "Holly, do you have to go to the bathroom?"

"Yes," I said instantly. "Could you take Rowdy?" I handed her his leash. "I didn't bring a crate. I'll be right back."

"Take your time," Lois said. "It'll take me a while to pack up. I'll be here another ten or fifteen minutes."

Like a lot of other indoor show sites, the Northeast

Trade Center had a No Dogs Allowed sign outside the rest rooms, but at the Shawsheen Valley show, there was also a guard whose task seemed to be the enforcement of that stupid rule. I might've been able to sneak a Yorkie or a chihuahua into the ladies' room. But a malamute? Also, since Rowdy isn't neutered, he was obviously no lady. Anyway, I hurried off and discovered the usual, namely, that there was no one outside the men's room, but six or eight women ahead of me in line for the ladies'. This phenomenon does not, as commonly supposed, constitute proof that the world is designed by and for men. In fact, all public rest rooms are planned by radical feminist architects whose hidden purpose is to convince women that if we ever expect to compete with men, we'd better learn to hurry up. Unfortunately, the women ahead of me had failed to get the message, and it was at least ten minutes before I headed back to retrieve Rowdy.

Lois was easy to find. The grooming table that had stood by her crates was now folded up and resting against the wall, and she was tucking a slicker brush into her tack box. Her dogs were resting quietly in their crates. Rowdy was nowhere in sight.

I looked around and asked, "Where's Rowdy?"

"Your cousin came and got him," Lois said, without looking up. "Didn't she find you?"

My cousin?

"Janice?" I asked. My cousin Janice shows wirehaired fox terriers, but she's an incredible moocher. If she'd been going to Shawsheen Valley, she'd have invited herself and five or ten dogs to stay with me. On arrival, she'd have announced that the dogs were overdue for their shots. I was still seeing that vet, wasn't I? He wouldn't mind writing her a prescription for Panacur, too, would he? All this gratis, of course. If Janice had taken Rowdy and gone off in search of me, I

thought, it could only be because one of the fox terriers re-
quired major surgery that Janice wanted Steve to do for free.
Then my heart leaped. "Leah?" I asked eagerly. "Long curly
red hair? Where'd . . . ?"

But Lois was shaking her head. "Uh-uh. Dark hair.
Long." She paused, obviously fishing for a euphemism.
"Damp looking."

Oily? Janice has light hair, and one good thing to be said
about her is that she *is* clean. My heart began to pound, and I
broke out in a sweat. Yes, a sweat. Sure, horses sweat, men
perspire, and ladies glisten, but a lady who's lost her dog is
an animal.

"Where did they go?" I yelled at Lois and added, as
though I'd been unclear the first time, "Which way did they
go?" If Lois had been a dog, I'd have grabbed the scruff of
her fat neck with both my hands and administered a hard
shakedown. As it was, I glared at her and spat out: "Lois,
God damn it, you have just *given* Rowdy to some stranger!
Where are they?" Don't ask me how I expected her to know.
Then the obvious finally hit me: Lois had no idea. "For
Christ's sake," I pleaded, "help me! Help me look for him!"

My ears pounded with the words of advice I'd offered my
readers again and again: Never leave your dog unattended at
a show. Never. But I hadn't left Rowdy unattended. I'd left
him with Lois Metzler, a malamute breeder, a responsible
person, someone who knew as well as I did that vicious,
greedy people will steal show dogs. Dognappers will hold
them for ransom. Puppy mill operators will match them with
AKC papers and breed them. Wolf hybridizers won't care
about papers, but they'll sure go for a malamute, especially
an obvious stud like Rowdy, beautiful and wolflike, gentle and
friendly. And the liberationists, the animal rights lunatics!
I'd heard all the rumors and had passed along the warnings.
Rowdy would be easy prey, swishing his tail, making eyes,

playing up to everyone. An unknown crated dog could've turned protective, might've growled and bitten, but Rowdy would've been a no-risk steal. And, to someone who knew nothing about dogs, Rowdy would have looked so damned *natural,* as if he could fend for himself once he'd been freed from the bonds of human exploitation. Released. Turned loose. Manumitted. Liberated. Right next to I-95.

In my sprint for the nearest exit, I shoved past a massive Kuvasz, barely missed crushing a brace of Maltese, crashed into a blessedly forgiving Newfie, and narrowly missed tripping over a darling Cairn and plunging down onto a German shorthaired pointer. In my terror, I fixed on a mad idea: Why hadn't I just dashed off to Sally Brand? Rowdy belonged where'd he never be lost, on my skin, under it, permanently inked and linked to me. What did it matter where? On my back, on my arm, or inside my ear like the ID number on a French dog.

As I neared the cafeteria, though, I spotted a crowd of people and dogs in an area away from the show rings, and I heard what I'm now convinced are the most beautiful words in the English language. They aren't *cellar door,* of course, and they aren't what my fellow writer, Dorothy Parker, said, either: *Check enclosed.* If your partner and soul mate has vanished at a show, the most beautiful words in the English language are *loose dog.* "Loose dog!" voices called out. "Loose dog!"

One of the worst and best things about being a supposed expert on dogs is that your own dogs, the ones you presumably understand best, teach you over and over again that you know nothing at all. I pushed and squirmed through the crowd around the concession stand. From Rowdy's point of view—evidently situated in his stomach—he'd done the obvious. Before I caught sight of him, I heard the trail mix crunch under my feet. The guy who held Rowdy's leash was a jovial, ursine young Rottie-owner I'd noticed now and then in the obedience rings. I'd always liked his happy, easygoing manner with his dogs, and I liked it now with Rowdy. The two of them made me think of some corny children's movie about a bear and wolf who become pals. They beamed at one another, the man obviously proud to be the hero who'd caught the loose dog. Dogs do get loose at shows by accident, of course. Exhibitors sometimes forget to latch the crates, and there are a few notorious canine Houdinis who've figured out how to escape from anything. Once loose, though, most of those dogs are terrified: disoriented, bewildered, scared silly, sometimes outright panicked. Not Rowdy, though. The opportunistic show-off had grabbed the chance for an unexpected feast and was now reveling in his role as the center of everyone's attention. When he caught sight of me, the tempo of his tail quickened to allegro, and he burst into song. No exaggeration, either. Song. *Woo-woo-woo-woo.* In case I haven't already bragged about Rowdy, let me tell you that he has a truly spectacular voice. Objectively speaking, the dog should attend the New England Conservatory of Music instead of the Cambridge Dog Training Club. You really should hear him. Anyway, I won't swear to the following, but I will wager a small bet on it. I'm not positive, of course, but I think it's possible, and his song definitely carried a note of triumph, at least to my ears. Grinning and wagging and wooing there in the center of the crowd, Rowdy sure acted and sounded like a dog who knows he's just gone Best in Show.

8

EVERY EXHIBITOR AT SHAWSHEEN VALLEY, myself included, had sat through plenty of hellfire-and-brimstone preaching about the evildoings of radical animal liberationists. If Rowdy had been killed, my brethren in dog worship would have joined me in praying for the salvation of his soul, and, while we had God's ear, we would've whispered a few words of advice about the appropriate final destination of blackguards who commit crimes against dogs. But with my domesticated wolf returned to the fold, we were as thrilled as a congregation of ardent revivalists who've just witnessed sin itself in flagrante delicto right there in the middle of their own camp meeting—witnessed it, yes, but been left unsullied.

Twenty or thirty people asked me how it had happened, and, although no one said it, I was willing to bet that every single one of those people was thinking the same thing: *Don't you know better than to leave your dog unattended at a show?* Despite everyone's tactful silence on the matter of my apparent irresponsibility, I kept defending myself. "I left him with a friend, and she got conned, I guess," I'd say. "He was with someone I know. I don't know what happened."

When Rowdy and I finally reached Lois Metzler, who'd quit smoking a couple of years earlier, she was flopped in her folding chair taking big, wheezy drags on a cork-filtered cigarette, but she looked more in need of oxygen than of nicotine.

"Holy Christ," she greeted me.

"It's okay," I said. "Really, Rowdy's fine. He was at that damned concession stand with all the nuts and candy and stuff. The worst thing that'll happen is that he'll vomit up a mess of trail mix."

"Jesus," she said.

"It's okay," I repeated. "It's over, okay? But could you, uh . . . Lois, I still don't know what happened. Some woman came up and said . . . ?"

"Faith stopped by," Lois began.

Faith Barlow handles Rowdy in breed. He associates her with liver and glory. At the sight of Faith, he sparkles all over.

"And?" I prompted.

"And so we said hello, and Faith gave Rowdy a treat, and she asked where you were. And so I told her, and she said, 'Yeah, well, there's a big line, so don't expect her back soon.' So I said something like, 'Well, that's okay.' "

"And?"

"And Faith left, and this girl came up."

The story we pieced together was that the dark-haired stranger had probably overheard Faith and Lois, and thus picked up my name and Rowdy's. She'd learned that I'd be gone for a while, and just as Faith was leaving, she'd stepped up to Lois, claimed to be my cousin, and strolled off with Rowdy, who, like most malamutes, is always so delighted to make the acquaintance of yet one more fascinating and possibly food-bearing member of our species that he'll go with anyone. If the stranger had been a dog, Lois would, of course, have supplied a minutely-detailed description that would've enabled me or anyone else unhesitatingly to spot her in a crowd of thousands. As it was, I was able to establish that the stranger was a dark-haired female between the ages of fifteen and fifty who wore black or navy clothing and looked "damp." Damp, for God's sake. I'd driven to the show through a gray winter drizzle. Most of the dogs had been blown dry for the ring, but "damp" fit at least half the people there.

At that point, Mary Kalinowski, Shawsheen's show chairman, appeared. Trailing after her were a couple of morose security guards and four or five dressed-up people wearing show officials' badges. Ever worked on a show? Well, *worked* hardly says it. It's like giving a wedding with two or three thousand guests. The planning begins at least a year in advance, and, as the date draws near, the momentum builds, the tasks multiply, and the people in charge, especially the chairman and the chief steward, start waking up in the night and scrawling notes to remind themselves not to forget the final five or ten thousand details that will make the show run smoothly, which is to say, without incident. The officials' faces were tight, bleak, and determined. What had just happened to Rowdy was, of course, an Incident. The officials intended to investigate it.

If I'd had any hope that they'd succeed in wringing out of Lois a decent description of the dark-haired "liberator," I'd have stuck around. As it was, I gave a succinct account of my part of the story and offered the only excuse to leave that anyone at the show would've understood or accepted, namely, that although Rowdy appeared to be in good spirits, he was more sensitive than he looked and needed to go home. In truth, of course, Rowdy has the unflappable self-confidence of the truly fearless. I'm the one who's more sensitive than I look.

Even so, Rowdy did a convincing, if unwitting, job of backing me up. He began by seating himself next to me and staring at my face the way I wish he'd always do in the obedience ring. Then he stood up, shuffled his feet around, and started a soft, high-pitched whine. When that didn't work, he pranced around and burst forth in an uninterrupted series of sharp yelps and loud *woos* that drowned out human conversation. This apparent trauma-victim behavior drew the sympathy of the officials, none of them malamute people, and Lois Metzler had the grace not to translate. Shall I? Rowdy unconditionally refuses to use a so-called exercise pen. He was pleading to go outside.

"I'm sorry," I shouted over the din, "but I have to get him out of here!"

Mary Kalinowski and the other officials clucked and nodded, and Rowdy and I beat it to the obedience rings, where I grabbed the gear I'd left there, and, with Rowdy acting as a sort of canine siren to clear our route, we sped out of the building and into the parking lot's ash gray fog, thick with the musk of auto exhaust from the departing vans, RVs, and big-breed cars like mine, as well as the diesel semis roaring by on 128. About halfway across the lot, thus halfway to the distant parking space where I'd left the Bronco, I spotted Faith Barlow's van. Did I say that my Bronco might as well have DOG PERSON lettered on the doors? Well, forget that. Faith's silver van all but did. DOG PERSON actually appeared only on one bumper sticker on the back fender, but painstakingly hand-painted on both of the wide sides of the vehicle were identical teams of gray-and-white malamutes pulling artistically rendered sleds driven by identical parka-clad Eskimos. The rear doors stood ajar, and Faith herself was leaning in and rearranging her crates and equipment. At the sight of Faith, Rowdy gave himself a massive overall shake evidently meant to fluff up his coat. Then he trotted straight up to her, walked himself into a four-square show pose, and raised his beautiful big head and eyes to Faith's pretty, dimpled face.

Faith has looked about forty for the ten or twelve years I've known her. Her wavy, easy-care hair remains in perpetual transition from blond to white. The mist had given her a mass of ringlets that managed not to look juvenile or silly, probably because she has great skin. Fact: Dog saliva happens to contain a powerful cosmetic ingredient that prevents lines and wrinkles, cures acne, and promotes a healthy, glowing blush. The hitch is that it has to be scoured on three times a day. Anyway, when Faith turned and caught sight of Rowdy, she bent from the waist, and he gave her complexion the full treatment. Am I making this up? No. Honestly. You should see Faith. Ponce De Leon and all those people were wasting their time crossing the Atlantic to muck around in the swamps. The true location of the fountain of youth is a dog's mouth.

"You heard what happened?" I asked Faith.

"Yeah," she said. "They catch her?"

"No, and I don't think they're going to. Among other things, Lois doesn't even seem to remember what she looked like."

"Lois is so unobservant," Faith said scornfully.

Breed people are *so* competitive. When Vince Lombardi said, "Winning isn't everything. It's the only thing," he wasn't talking about football. He meant dog shows. Anyway, Faith Barlow's eagerness to beat Lois Metzler extended beyond the conformation ring. Lois was unobservant? Well, Faith wasn't.

"She's about twenty, give or take a year," Faith said

definitively. "Long dark hair plastered with some kind of gel. She had on a long skirt, kind of a dark paisley pattern, and a navy pea jacket, sort of a throwback-to-the-sixties look. Bad skin. No makeup. And she's short, maybe five one or two. Oh, and she was wearing a, uh, backpack—what do you call it?— like a little backpack. Rucksack. It was green, sort of loden. Dark green. Didn't Lois . . . ?"

I gave a sigh of exasperation. "Lois didn't tell me any of that, and she didn't tell the officials, either. Or she won't. They're probably still talking to her. Could you?"

"I have to go back anyway." Faith waved toward the trade center. "I'm just getting something. I'll tell them. But probably it's too late. If she has any sense, she's long gone."

"But it's not too late for next time. There'll be other shows. People like that—"

Faith slammed the van door shut. Then she finished my sentence, but not quite as I'd intended. "People like that ought to be shot," she said. "They ought to be shot on sight."

9

IN THE FOGGY EARLY DARKNESS of that Sunday afternoon, Route 128 glowed red with the brake lights of the backed-up cars and trucks headed toward Boston. Instead of swinging onto the highway to await the inevitable multivehicle collision, I decided to take the back way, Route 38, all the way to Medford, where I could pick up Route 16 to Cambridge. I followed 38 over 128 and into the center of Woburn.

Woburn. You ever hear of a parts match? It's a conformation fun match with categories for best head, ears, tail, that kind of thing. The point of a parts match is that every dog has at least one good feature. Cow-hocked or not, he has a great muzzle. Roach-backed? Sure, but with a spectacular coat. As I pulled to a stop at a red light in the center of Woburn, I was wondering what category you'd need to create in a parts match for small cities that would let Woburn win best anything or, for that matter, worst anything. I'd just awarded Woburn first place in the Most Ordinary competition when my peripheral vision registered something moving to the right of the Bronco. The object in motion turned out to be a gloved thumb. Attached to it was a small, drenched person stationed on a traffic island near the stoplight.

My only excuse is that my perception must've been slowed and distorted by the residual images of a parts match. Best size in a toy breed? Very short. Itchiest headgear? She wore one of those pointy-topped Peruvian hats with rows of cream white stick figures knitted into the brown wool. The ear flaps were knotted under her chin. Long, dark, sopping hair dripped onto her forehead and streamed over the shoulders of her navy pea jacket. In the dusk, the day pack was a dark lump. I wondered whether it had been safe for women to hitch rides in the sixties and how someone could imagine that it was still safe for anyone, male or female.

The light changed to green, and my mental processes finally shifted into first. Green. Sixties. Pea jacket. Very short.

I leaned over, unlocked the passenger door, opened it, and yelled, "Get in!"

She did. I wondered why. Rowdy, safe in a Vari-Kennel behind the wagon barrier, wasn't visible, but the crate and barrier certainly were. Also, despite my persistent and repeated application of every commercial deodorizing product marketed to dog owners, as well as a few dozen folk remedies, the predominant odor in the Bronco wasn't Outright or cider vinegar but distilled essence of dog. Especially on that cold, wet day when the windows were closed and the heater was blasting, she must've smelled it the second she approached the open door. Yet she got in. Why? If she'd bolted from the show the second she'd released Rowdy, she must've been out in that chilling weather for thirty or forty minutes. I guess she got in because she was cold, wet, and very young.

Massachusetts drivers being the charitable souls they are, every car behind me had begun to sound its horn the second the light turned green. As soon as I heard her pull the door shut, I stepped on the gas.

"You owe me thirty-five dollars," I said flatly.

"Do I *know* you?" The voice was young, clear, and educated, with a hint of a British accent, and not Harvard educated, pseudo-British, either, but real British, in other words, genuinely foreign. But just a trace.

"You owe me thirty-five dollars," I repeated. "For trail mix. After you let go of his leash, he went to a concession stand that sells trail mix and candy and stuff. It has open bins." I assume that I sounded cheerful. I was. In fact, I was having fun. I'd wanted to get one these people alone for a long time. "He didn't actually eat thirty-five dollars' worth, thank God, but he grabbed a lot of mouthfuls and threw them on the floor, which is what he does when he steals food. You wouldn't know that, of course, because you don't know anything about dogs, never mind malamutes, but he does. His name is Rowdy, by the way. He's an Alaskan malamute. Anyway, what Rowdy didn't eat or toss on the floor he probably drooled on or whatever, and the guy was nice about it, and we settled for thirty-five dollars."

The Bronco was very warm by now. The wipers made a cozy swish back and forth across the windshield. And the car smelled homey, too, of course.

The indignant young voice broke the near silence. "You're kidnapping me! Stop this car and let me out this instant!"

"Actually, I'm rescuing you. You'd've got into any car that stopped, so I've probably rescued you from rape and murder, and those dog people back there would hang you from the nearest grooming loop. I've practically plucked you off the scaffold. Actually, one of them was going to strangle you. I think I've got that right. And someone else definitely wanted to shoot you. Actually, what she said was that you ought to be shot on sight. But I didn't shoot you, did I? I'm not even taking you back there."

"You're holding me in this car against my will! And that's kidnapping. You could get in a lot of trouble for this." Childish? That's how she sounded.

"You were hitching. I picked you up. You're lucky. I happen to be a nice, peaceful person. Let me introduce myself. My name is Holly Winter. I live at two fifty-six Concord Avenue in Cambridge, Massachusetts, which is where we're going, in case you wondered. I'd offer you my hand, but I need it on the steering wheel right now, so why don't you just tell me your name, and we'll save—"

She interrupted with a self-righteous announcement: "I am not going anywhere with the kind of person who keeps an animal locked in a cage."

"Actually, you are," I said. "Right now, that's what you're doing, but the word is *crate*. Question: Why is Rowdy in a crate? Why isn't he *free*?" I answered for her. "So if I slam on the brakes, he won't be thrown against the windshield. That's why the wagon barrier's there, too. Double protection."

"You couldn't let anything happen to your valuable *property*, could you?" she snapped.

"He *is* valuable," I said. "He is one of the most important people in my life, and, in case you wondered, I am not joking. So is Kimi, my other dog. Hey, while you're at this, have you ever considered releasing children?"

She didn't answer.

"Really," I said. "I mean it. I'm serious. A lot of people would be less pained and, uh, jeopardized, in a way, if you went around liberating their children instead of doing stupid things like this. I mean, for a start, children can at least *talk*.

Not babies, of course. You'd go for preschoolers, I guess. On the other hand, there are these old statistics. . . ." I paused and explained. "I write about dogs. That's what I do. I'm a dog writer. That's why I know this stuff. Anyway, in 1982, Americans spent one point thirty-two billion dollars on pet accessories, and in the same year they spent only two hundred and twenty-two million dollars on toys for children under the age of eighteen months. Okay? So which would people rather lose?"

"Oh, for Christ's sake," she said.

Finally. I felt delighted. "The point is," I said, my voice suddenly cold, "that the quality of the bond, if you want to call it that, is not very different. Love is love. It sounds corny, but that's what this entire dog thing is about: absolute, unconditional love. And if Rowdy had been killed because you 'liberated' him, I would have been absolutely and unconditionally glad to see you dead. I might not actually have murdered you, but I'd sure have wanted to. I might even have done it. But since no harm came to him, thank God, I am taking a constructive, civilized approach to the situation."

"Stop this car!"

"No," I said, peering out to check a sign that pointed the way to Arlington. "Of course not. You haven't even met Kimi yet. Do you have any other questions?"

She said nothing.

"Well, I do," I said. "First of all, are you from A.L.F.?"

A.L.F.? Animal Liberation Front. The militant wing of animal rights extremism, the Irish Republican Army of animal liberation, but, oddly enough, British. Really, that's true. Her accent was what made me ask, of course.

"No," she said. "It was my own symbolic act."

"Rowdy is not a symbol. He's my dog. And if you think it was okay to let him loose indoors," I went on, "you're wrong. A dog fight would have been almost as bad. And he could have wandered out. It wasn't likely, okay, but it could have happened. What you did was not just symbolic, you know. It was directed against *my* dog."

"Ownership is not something I choose to recognize," she said smugly.

"Well, you may not, but Rowdy and Kimi do," I said.

"Ownership is exploitation," she mouthed. It's a stupid cliché, I know, but she was very young.

"Fine," I agreed. "But it goes both ways. What you probably don't know is that dog people joke about it all the time. 'Congratulations! You are now owned by an Alaskan malamute.' But it's no joke! We honestly are owned. *I* am. And, believe me, the interspecies relationship is voluntary. It has been from the beginning. People didn't force wolves to come into the cave, you know."

"Is that dog part wolf?" she demanded.

Well, asking that question seemed to me to be the only intelligent thing Gloria had done so far, and I gave her a thoughtful answer. Gloria. Yeah, before long, she told me her name. Gloria Loss. We talked about her even more than we talked about dogs. She was eighteen years old, and she lived in Cambridge. Until a year ago, she'd been a day student at a private prep school just outside Boston, a place that specializes in troubled kids without embarrassing their parents by advertising itself that way. The British accent came from four years in England. Her father was a professor of linguistics, and Gloria and her mother had gone to England with him when Gloria was eight. When they'd returned to America, the father had immediately turned around, gone back, and moved in with one of his students, and Gloria had seen him only twice since then.

"What does your mother do?" I asked.

"Personal growth," Gloria answered, as if it were a form of full-time employment. "Energy healing," she added.

"Healing modalities. Right now, she's trying to clarify her desires. She used to do Feldenkrais. You wouldn't know what that is. Awareness through movement, they call it."

I didn't have the heart to explain why I knew exactly what the Feldenkrais Method is, even though I knew it mostly by another name, TTouch. What is it? New Age massage and movement, a healing touch for dogs. Dog owners use Feldenkrais to heal those they love. Gloria's mother evidently did, too. Gloria herself had never owned a dog or cat. She'd once had gerbils that had reproduced and promptly eaten their newborn offspring.

At a stoplight, I glanced over at Gloria, who'd removed the ugly Peruvian cap and sat hunched in the seat, her knees drawn up in a fetal curl. Even in the dim light from the dashboard and a nearby streetlight, her face was painful to look at. She had the kind of acne you practically never see anymore, certainly never on children of privilege, children whose fathers are professors, who've traveled abroad, whose mothers can afford to pursue personal growth instead of working for a living. I felt furious at the parents who'd neglected this poor kid, who'd turned her loose to develop into a mangy stray. By the time we reached the intersection of Alewife Brook Parkway and Mass. Ave., which is to say, Cambridge, I was feeling disappointed and chagrined. I'd thought I was capturing Satan himself. What I'd caught was, at worst, a minor imp.

I didn't even bother to press her about why she'd released Rowdy. She'd already told me herself. "It was my own symbolic act," she'd said. The sight, sound, and scent of two thousand show dogs, each one groomed, pampered, and adored? Two thousand beautiful dogs, each one loved and cared for? And there she'd been, ugly Gloria. Of course it had been a symbolic act. When I'd stopped to pick her up in Medford, I'd intended to beard one of those satanic animal liberationists in my own woofy den. Just force one of those bastards to meet my dogs and spend some time with us! Training is cruelty? Let the son of a bitch watch Kimi stubbornly refuse to go indoors until we've done our obedience work. And the joyful grin on Rowdy's face when he finds his dumbbell and soars back over the high jump? Or let anyone, absolutely anyone, just hang around with us, listen to us, watch us, learn who we really are, *homo sapiens, canis familiaris,* two species delicately evolved in unison, biologically distinct, behaviorally meshed, the only two species to keep one another as companion animals. People keep cats and birds, too, of course, but dogs are more loyal to us than we are to them. We are uniquely theirs. Without us, there would be no dogs. Without them, we would be less human than we are now. No one should miss this transcendent miracle. No one but Gloria Loss, who didn't need to learn that my dogs and I loved one another more than anyone had ever loved her.

Fifteen minutes after we'd crossed Mass. Ave., Gloria stood awkwardly in the bright light of my kitchen. Faith's description had been accurate, and so had Lois Metzler's: Gloria was short, dark, and damp. Her hair had been treated with some oily gel or mousse that forced her thick locks to fall depressingly forward and downward. The paisley skirt Faith had mentioned was, in fact, the bottom half of a long, unflattering dress in shades of mustard, black, and navy. It dripped onto heavy hiking boots that had absorbed the rain. The raw, inflamed lesions that covered her face made it hard to see past her skin to the person inside.

The beauty of dogs, though, is that if Gloria had had two or three heads, each as repulsive as the first, Rowdy and Kimi would have welcomed her with the same enthusiasm they now displayed. They'd both had a brief trip to the fenced-in yard, and now Rowdy, who had, of course, already met Gloria, was sprawled on his back on the floor, his mouth open in a toothy smile, his legs wiggling foolishly in the air in anticipation of chest-scratching and tummy-rubbing that Gloria failed to offer. Kimi sat neatly in front of Gloria and kept lifting her right forepaw, but Gloria missed or refused that invitation, too.

"He wants you to rub his belly," I translated. "And she wants to shake hands."

"This is an undignified way to make animals act," she told me.

"I didn't teach Rowdy that. It's just something malamutes do. Lots of dogs do it, but it's a malamute specialty. And there's nothing undignified about shaking hands. Pawing at people is a spontaneous behavior. They do it for attention. They do it for lots of reasons. And they happen to like learning to do it the way she's doing it now, at least when they get a civilized response in return." Kimi's pretty eyes were puzzled. I was annoyed. "Damn it, give her your hand! She doesn't understand why you're ignoring her." Then I paused and said, "Never mind. I'm going to feed them. You'd better get out of the way."

I fastened Rowdy to a leash at one end of the kitchen, Kimi to a leash at the other end. Then I dished out two helpings of premium chow and fed the dogs. Gloria almost certainly disapproved, but if I don't tie up the dogs, the one who finishes first tries to steal the other one's food, and we end up with a mess of kibble scattered all over the linoleum and a snarling tangle of dogs.

When the dogs had finished eating, Gloria, who'd taken a seat at the table, said, "They're still hungry. You didn't give them very much."

As I unhitched the dogs, I said, "It's concentrated food. I use a measuring cup. They both have a tendency to put on weight, so the main thing is not to feed them too much. In terms of health, overfeeding is almost as bad as underfeeding. Um, would you like something to eat?" I didn't wait for an answer. "I'm hungry. I'll make us both sandwiches. And then we need to have a talk."

My cheese sandwiches are a lot better than the ones you buy at dog shows. In other words, mine aren't soggy, they don't taste as if they'd been made a month in advance, and the cheese is identifiable as such. As you probably know, in addition to producing dog and cat food, the big pet food companies manufacture monkey chow, ferret food, and stuff like that, with only one obvious omission. Hills Brothers, Iams, where are you? The market is here. I'd buy it. I'd be delighted. No more wondering what to fix, no more pans to scrub, no more checking to make sure you've included the four food groups? I mean, I'd want to go out to a restaurant once in a while for a little variety, of course. But most of the time? Just dish up the Purina People Chow, and I'd be perfectly happy.

In the meantime, Gloria and I ate cheese sandwiches and continued the discussion we'd had in the car.

"Could I get something straight?" I asked. "How did you get to Woburn?"

"Hitched," she said, with an air of empty, precocious sophistication.

"But how did you know to go there? Where did you get the idea?"

She chewed, swallowed, and said, "At a meeting. It's a . . . I don't belong. I haven't joined. I just go sometimes and listen." Then her high voice took on the self-righteous tone I'd heard earlier. "It's a group of people who care about the planet."

She made it sound like some place other than where I lived. There's no mirror in my kitchen, but I'm sure that my mouth took on the pseudosmile dogs make when they're about to vomit.

I said, "And these people want us to share it without exploiting it. And with all living creatures without exploiting them. Right?"

If Gloria had been even a few years older than she was, her expression of astonished recognition would have been funny.

"Look, Gloria," I went on. "You picked the wrong person's dog. I happen to be interested in Antarctica. I probably know more about it than you do and probably more than these people do, either. I am very concerned about it, and the way I got interested in it was exploitation, and, not only that, exploitation of dogs. So I understand about abuse of the environment and abuse of dogs, and I'm just going to tell you that my relationship with my dogs is not abusive and certainly not exploitative."

"You bought them, didn't you?"

"No, as a matter of fact, I didn't, but I would have. I've bought dogs. I've paid for them."

"At pet shops." Gloria bit defiantly into her sandwich.

I dropped mine on my plate and slammed my fist on the table. "Absolutely not! I won't spend a dime in one of those goddamned places. As a matter of fact, one of the main things on my mind right now is what to do about a pet shop. You know this place, Puppy Luv?"

Her jaw was locked. She nodded.

"There's a malamute puppy there. I won't buy the puppy because I will not give these bastards any profit, I will not create a market, and I will not contribute to their damned industry. But I'm still worried about the dog. Do you know where those puppies come from?"

"Puppy mills," she said.

"Yes! Now if you really want to do something about animal exploitation, and if you ever want to get seriously active, *those* are the places to go after. I mean, that's *real* exploitation. If you want to *get* somebody, get those people, not me. And not people like me, either."

I controlled the urge to show her the puppy mill tape. It's strong stuff; it gives me nightmares. I was still angry at her as well as sorry for her, but not that angry.

"Anyway, we have business to take care of," I said abruptly. "You owe me thirty-five dollars."

"I don't have any money." Her eyes were wide and childish. "Besides, I didn't touch the trail mix. Your dog did."

I just could not help laughing. "I thought he wasn't mine to own! If I don't own him, I'm not responsible for his debts, am I? Anyway, I am, and I paid, and the only reason I had to pay the thirty-five dollars was that you let him loose."

We got into what may seem like a petty quarrel. Although Gloria had dropped out of school, she didn't work, and when she'd said that she had no money, she'd been describing her chronic state, not temporary empty pockets. Her mother, Gloria told me, provided room, board, and nothing else. If the Massachusetts economy had merely been in a recession, as the newspapers kept claiming, I'd have tried to talk Gloria into finding a job. But even if there had been jobs out there, what did Gloria know how to do? If I wanted to be paid, I'd have to employ her myself. I own this house, or I will eventually, and I do most of the maintenance and repair. I can paint, spackle, cure dripping faucets, replace broken glass, and repair garbage disposals. I do my own housework, and I shovel my own walks and driveway.

"Do you have a heart condition?" I asked.

"No," she said.

"Good. The next time it snows, be here at seven A.M., and you can start working off the money. I work at home, but my tenants don't, and people start going by here early. I want the sidewalks clear. Or maybe I'll think of something else you can do. In the meantime, I need to ask you a personal question." Please understand that I could not stop myself. I couldn't look at the poor kid another minute and keep quiet. "Gloria, have you ever been to a dermatologist?"

Involuntarily, I'm sure, she dropped her head and hunched her shoulders in an obvious effort to cover her face. Worse, she blushed furiously, and the addition of yet more red did nothing for her complexion.

"Have you?" I persisted.

She managed to shake her head.

"You need to see someone," I said. D.V.M.'s are, of course, more in my line than are M.D.'s, most of whom I don't trust, but when I'd first come to Cambridge, I'd caught a persistent and disgusting case of ringworm from one of my cats, and a good dermatologist had cured me. I liked her a lot. Framed pictures of her family rested proudly on her desk: four English cockers, very handsome dogs. "I know someone good," I said. "I'll make the appointment for you."

"I don't have any money," Gloria said.

"Then we'll both pray for snow. In the meantime, don't worry about it. And don't go to any more dog shows, either."

Gloria smiled. Amazingly, she had beautiful, perfectly even white teeth, a smile out of a toothpaste commercial. Life is a parts match, right? It's a parts match. Everybody wins.

10

THE FRIGID TEMPERATURES OF Sunday night glazed Cambridge in a layer of ice as hard and slick as the coating on a candy apple. When I let Rowdy and Kimi into the yard for their first brief outing of the day, they slid, lost their footing, and had to dig in their nails and scramble to make it back up the stairs. Footing bad enough to take the ground out from under a malamute usually means a productive work day for me and a long snooze for the dogs. They stretch out on the kitchen floor, and I sit at the table drinking cup after cup of sweet tea and covering page after page of yellow legal pad with my illegible scrawl. In case you haven't guessed, the whole point of being a writer is that you get to stay home with your dogs. And, of course, the article about Sally Brand wasn't finished. There was a lot more to say than I'd covered so far. For instance, I'd assumed that Larry Wilson's brace of pec-flex-tail-wag poodles must be Sally's masterpiece, but when I'd mentioned Larry, Sally had informed me that hula girl tattoos like his had been out since World War Two. The poodles had been a technical challenge, she conceded, but, all in all, they lacked artistry. Please don't pass that along to Larry. Or the poodles, either, of course.

Despite the ice outside and the literary temptations of tea, dogs, and words in my cozy cream-and-terra-cotta kitchen, it wasn't a writing day. I was due on Enid Sievers's raspberry doorstep at ten-thirty, when I'd promised to pick up Missy and drive her to Betty Burley's. Before collecting Missy, I intended to stop at Puppy Luv, where I meant to follow Betty's advice: to stay calm, to introduce myself, and to persuade Diane Sweet to let me leave some material with the malamute puppy's papers: my own name, address, and phone number; information about training; and the national breed club's booklet about the Alaskan malamute. The booklet about the Alaskan malamute would present a problem because the section entitled "On Choosing a Puppy" explained, among other things, that pet shops buy puppies wholesale from people who don't know and usually don't care whether the pups are free of hip dysplasia, chondrodysplasia, and other genetic faults. Chondrodysplasia causes skeletal distortion throughout the body, grotesque deformities of the joints and limbs. A male and female may be carriers who show no signs of the disease themselves but whose puppies sure do. Puppy mills don't screen for it, and neither do backyard breeders. And then there's progressive retinal atrophy. Seizures. Day blindness. Anyway, I suspected that Puppy Luv wouldn't be eager to pass along a booklet containing that truthful but damning paragraph about pet shops, and, with considerable reluctance, I'd glued a blank sheet of paper over that page of the booklet and laboriously printed in some information about the Cambridge Dog Training Club. The result looked patched up, but I was hoping that Diane Sweet would simply thumb through the booklet and accept it.

Actually, I was hoping that Monday happened to be Diane Sweet's day off and that someone else would be in charge at Puppy Luv. If you're afraid to make a fool of yourself, you have no business owning a dog, but it's one thing to make a fool of yourself with someone who loves you no matter what and quite another thing to confront someone like Diane Sweet and admit that you've been a total jerk. And I had been. On Friday, instead of maturely striding in, presenting myself as who I am, and making a reasonable request, I'd acted childish. Too many baby greens lately. So instead of costuming myself as someone else, today I dressed in honest, self-revealing L.L. Bean—flannel-lined jeans, flannel shirt, heavy parka, Ragg socks and mittens, boots with good traction—and set out in my cold Bronco.

At my first glimpse of the seedy strip mall, my heart raced and fell. I'd expected the parking lot to look as icy and empty as the center of the Boston Garden before a Bruins game. In fact, the glare was so bright that I wouldn't have been surprised to see a Zamboni machine chugging away, but the area directly in front of Puppy Luv was packed with cars. *God damn*, I thought, *Valentine's Day*. In the yearly cycle of the American pet shop, summer is a time of hibernation. Pet shops do most of their business between Labor Day and Easter. Christmas, the period of greatest activity, was past. Easter was distant. Despite the cheerful display of hearts and clichés I'd seen in Puppy Luv, I hadn't expected this pre-Valentine's burst of business.

Four of the cars, however, turned out to be police cruisers. A few others were official vehicles, too. Some apparently belonged to the innocently curious or genuinely worried, the rest to the truly ghoulish. Yellow crime-scene tape cordoned off Puppy Luv. Stomping his hefty way out of the pet shop was my friend and neighbor Kevin Dennehy, who's a Cambridge cop. I pulled the Bronco into a space near the hardware store a few doors down from Puppy Luv, killed the engine, got out, and watched Kevin, who did something unprecedented.

In case you've never met Kevin, I should tell you that he's a big, burly guy, shorter than Steve, but about twice as wide. How someone who works out at the Y and who runs, too, can sustain that ever-enlarging gut, I don't know, but Kevin manages. By the time he's thirty-five, Kevin is going to have a real beer belly, even though he isn't allowed to keep beer in the refrigerator at home or drink it in the house. He can't keep or consume meat there, either, because his mother is a Seventh Day Adventist, a vegetarian as well as a teetotaler. Consequently, Kevin owns a corner of my refrigerator. That's how I happen to be an expert on his consumption of flesh and Bud. Rita, my second-floor tenant and resident shrink, says that in granting Kevin access to my kitchen but not my bed, I am fostering his prolonged dependence on his mother by encouraging him to transfer a libidinal cathexis from one Oedipally unavailable object to a symbolic substitute. That's a direct quote. Honest to God, that's how Rita talks. Also, Rita places particular emphasis on the *refrigerator,* but I'm too embarrassed to tell you what she says about it.

Anyway, as one who knows more than Kevin himself does about how much he drinks, I'll swear that his consumption is what Rita calls "socioculturally normative." Furthermore, the hamburger and bologna in Kevin's corner of my refrigerator were fresh. All this is to explain that when Kevin stomped out of Puppy Luv, staggered to the edge of the concrete walk, bent over the fragile barrier of crime-scene tape, and vomited, it probably wasn't because he had a hangover or a case of food poisoning.

Nor does he have a weak stomach. Nor, in general, does he dislike dogs. On the contrary, he's fond of them. Even so, when I went tearing across the ice, skidded up to him, and solicitously placed a mittened hand on his beefy shoulder, he dragged himself fully upright, trained his bloodshot blue eyes on me, and said with a note of unmistakable accusation, "Oh, Christ. *Dogs.*" Kevin has the fair Irish skin that goes with his red hair, but he runs outdoors even in winter, so he usually looks pale but healthy, not sickly white with green undertones.

"Do you have any more to bring up?" I asked. I'm used to ministering to nausea victims, of course. Rowdy and Kimi will eat *anything*.

The dogs like company when they're retching. I always wrap my arms around their poor heaving ribs, murmur words of consolation, and save the recriminations for later. ("Garbage in, garbage out, you big dope. What did you *think* was going to happen?") But Kevin was an ingrate. Although my practiced eye told me that he did, in fact, have more to bring up, he choked it down, glared at me, and said bluntly, "Go home."

"Okay," I said. "But just tell me . . . Kevin, are the puppies all right?"

"Jesus Christ!" He dug his hands into the pockets of his unzipped parka. "Holly, a woman's dead. A young woman. A pretty woman. And what you want to know is . . . What *you* want to know is . . . ? Christ, am I hearing this right?"

"Look, Kevin, I'm sorry, but I do want to know. I'm sorry about the woman, but I need to know. Are the puppies all right?"

Kevin Dennehy huffed himself up, locked his jaw, and said between clenched teeth, "Sure, Holly. Everything's just hunky-dory in there. Your little darlings are all rounded up and tucked in their beddie-byes. After a nice meal, of course.

Tore open every bag of dog food in the place, ran riot, peed, puked, crapped, and . . . Holly, you ever thought about what a medical examiner has to do? What the guy has to do, all day, every day? You ever thought about that?"

"Not in great detail," I said.

"Yeah, well, keep it that way," Kevin advised. "You'll sleep better. But you don't need to know a lot to reach the conclusion that it takes a whole lot of bad smell to do *that* to a medical examiner." Kevin's eyes darted to the ground. He shuffled his feet as if he wanted to kick something over the wet mess visibly steaming on the icy pavement. "The poor bastard was sicker than me."

"Kevin, nausea is nothing to be ashamed of," I said.

"Would you not keep looking at it?" He raised his eyes upward toward the cold sky.

"Diane Sweet?" I asked.

Kevin stared at me.

"Because of the malamute." I answered his unspoken question. "That's why I'm here. I was in here the other day because somebody told me there was a malamute puppy. I heard there was a malamute for sale here. And there was. So today I was going to—"

"Well, you're not," Kevin grumbled.

"Kevin, what *happened?* The person is, uh . . ."

"Yeah. Diane Sweet. She owned the place, her and her husband. A hard-working lady. Last night she's working here all alone. It's late. Guy forces his way in."

I looked at the plate glass and at the door, both festooned with valentines.

"Through the back," Kevin said. "She's working late, guy busts his way in, she puts up a fight. Cash drawer's empty."

"How did she . . . ?"

"Best guess is first he tries to shut her up, and then that

doesn't work, or maybe she struggles a lot, and he doesn't like it. So he grabs her by the throat. Or maybe it works the other way around. He grabs her by the throat, she puts up a fight, maybe she—Anyway, then he ends up wrapping the plastic around her head, and like they say on the dry cleaner's bags . . ."

"And the puppies were— The puppies were all turned loose? Why would . . . ?"

"Screw up the evidence," Kevin said. "Jesus." He blew out hard. A small white cloud rose from his mouth. "The worst mess, Jesus. I don't know how those guys are ever going to—"

"Were they loose there all night? What time—?"

"Couple of hours. When she didn't come home, the husband started calling, and then he came over. I've been here all night."

"Look, Kevin," I said. "I'm sorry, but the fact is, overeating like that is no joke, and some of those puppies weren't in great shape to begin with. You really ought to get a vet to come and take a look at them. Steve would do it. For an emergency like this, I know he would. Maybe he can—"

Kevin's face was tired and angry. "Can he raise the dead, Holly? That's all we need in there right now. We need a guy that can raise the dead. And then, after that, when that poor woman's back on her feet breathing again, I'll worry about the dogs."

"Kevin, if something happens to one of those puppies because you didn't—"

"Like I said, Holly, go home. I don't want to see you back here. Go home."

"Kevin, I'm sorry she's dead, but that woman must have had a lot of people who hated her. You think this is a dirty business now? Well, it was always a dirty business. There are probably five hundred people in Cambridge who bought sick dogs from Diane Sweet, maybe more. And every one of them must've found out what her so-called health guarantee really meant, which was not a damn thing. She didn't care where her puppies came from, and she didn't care where they went, and she didn't care what happened to them, because nobody who runs a pet shop gives a damn. They care about one thing, and that's profit. Diane Sweet had enemies. She deserved them. So I'm sorry she's dead, but I'm not sorry she's out of business, and there are going to be a whole lot of people who agree with me."

"I got work to do," Kevin said coldly. "Go home. It's not just dogs that make me sick. It's you. Get out of here. You make me sick."

11

When I stood on Enid Sievers's doorstep, my cheeks were still as raspberry as the paint on her house. Maybe nobody had chosen that color after all. Maybe a good friend had looked the house in the eye and said, "You make me sick." Did I deserve Kevin's disgust? Maybe. While I waited for Enid Sievers to answer the bell, the medical examiner who'd been sickened by the stench in Puppy Luv was probably cutting into the body of its proprietor. I wondered whether Diane Sweet's tongue still remained that peculiar shade of loud pink. My stomach turned over.

Enid Sievers opened the door. She wore lavender. Her eyes focused on a spot above my head. "Oh," she said vaguely to the spot, "I was going to call you."

As on my last visit, she invited me in, ushered me to the love seat, took a place opposite me, demurely crossed her ankles, and offered me candy. This time it was Russell Stover chocolates with cream centers. I declined.

"Mrs. Sievers," I said. "I'm in sort of a hurry?" Why did I make it sound like a question? It wasn't. It wasn't even the truth. "If I could just get Missy . . . ?"

"Missy isn't here," she said, exactly as if she'd already told me so and was irked at me for having forgotten. Then her face took on a weirdly coquettish little smile. "On Friday, my *friend* called. The gentleman I see." *Friend* and *gentleman*. She uttered the words with smug passion. I had the sense of someone revealing an unexpected and wondrous secret.

"Yes?"

She delicately cleared her throat. "When I go away, you see, the boy who walks Missy will usually come in and feed her." As if to allay my presumed concern for the security of her home, she added, "He's perfectly trustworthy. I give him a key. He's perfectly reliable."

"So . . . ?"

"He'd gone skiing! He'd already left. He'd gone on a bus with a group from church." As if his destination mattered, as if it were evidence of betrayal, she added, "To Stowe! That's in *Vermont!*" Her voice was mildly outraged. The heretofore trustworthy and reliable boy had done the inexplicable. "So my *friend* phoned Mr. Coakley." She sounded as if she expected me to recognize the name. I didn't. "And that's where she is." She folded her hands in her lap.

"And where is . . . ?"

Enid Sievers drew herself bolt upright and said sharply, "This is all very painful for me, you know."

I dipped my chin in a nod of fake sympathy. You know what happens to hypocrites? According to Kevin Dennehy's mother, the earth opens and swallows them up. I listened for an ominous rumble. There was none.

Enid Sievers went on. "And once she was there, it seemed easier to leave her. If I'd brought her back here, I'd've just had to give her up again, wouldn't I? After all, I have myself to consider, too." She raised a thin hand to her lavender bosom. "This is very painful for me."

It seemed to me that it was more painful for Missy to be kicked out of the only home she'd ever known than it was for Enid Sievers to get rid of a dog she didn't want, but for a change I kept my opinion to myself.

"Where is Mr. Coakley?" I asked bluntly.

"Westbrook." Once again, she spoke with the annoyed tone of someone who is forced to keep repeating herself.

"Westbrook, Maine?"

"No, no. Massachusetts."

My mental map of the commonwealth is probably somewhat different from yours, unless, of course, you show your dogs around here. Westford: northwest of Boston, the 4-H grounds, Minuteman Kennel Club, temperament testing. Westboro: near Marlboro, Wachusett and Worcester County shows. West Brookfield: agility training, lots of other canine activities. Weston: Weston Dog Training Club, Charles River Dog Training Club. Westfield, Westminster, Westport, Westwood? Westbrook: beyond Route 128, before 495, maybe forty-five minutes.

"Mr. Coakley breeds dogs," Enid Sievers added.

"Malamutes?"

"Oh, lots of different kinds," she said brightly.

Shit! I almost yelled it out loud. Two breeds? Sure. The husband has bassets, the wife has bloodhounds, man, woman, and dogs met at a tracking test. Happens all the time. Three breeds? His German shepherds, her collies, their Belgian sheepdogs. Okay. But *lots?* Lots makes me suspicious.

"What kind?" I asked.

"Poodles," she said. "Little balls of fluff." She cupped her beringed hands to demonstrate. "And something called a, uh, Pomeranian?"

"Yes."

"Darling! And these adorable little white ones all covered with curls."

"Bichon. Bichon frise." Curly lap dog.

"Yes! And Pom-a-poos! Isn't that cute?"

I almost wept. If the dying Edgar Sievers just had to have a dog, why not one of the little breeds? And not from Puppy Luv and not from someone who had lots and lots, either. I wasn't very responsive. I said I'd better be going and asked for Mr. Coakley's address and phone number.

Enid Sievers rose, made her way between and around a few dozen mismatched pieces of furniture, and began rummaging around in a delicate little desk with a fold-down front.

"And," I said casually, "it would probably be best if I take Missy's papers. They really should go with her."

Enid Sievers looked up, darted a glance at me, and addressed the air over my head. "Missy's papers meant a lot to Edgar," she said reverently. "I really don't think he'd want me to just give them away like that." Enid Sievers resumed her rummaging.

"Here it is," she said. She leaned over the desk, evidently copying down the information on a notepad shaped like a daisy. Then she straightened up and, as she began to make her way back toward me, said hesitantly, "And, um, this reminds me. My friend suggested . . ." She cleared her throat. "Missy's doghouse?"

"Her crate? The Vari-Kennel?"

Enid Sievers brightened up. "Edgar paid a substantial amount of money for it," she said proudly. "My friend thought that Mrs. Burley might like to buy it from me. For Missy? Or maybe you'd like it? I could give you a *very* good price."

"Maybe," I said. I didn't need it myself, but Malamute Rescue did. "How much would you . . . ?"

"My friend says that half of what Edgar paid would be very fair. To both of us. Eighty dollars."

"So half is forty," I said.

"Miss Winter, you must be joking! These things are *terribly* expensive! Edgar paid a hundred and sixty dollars for that house. And that's not counting tax! So I really couldn't let it go for—"

I'd had enough. "I hate to tell you," I said, not hating it at all, "but the standard price for a number five hundred Vari-Kennel, which is what that is, is about eighty dollars, including shipping, maybe less. New. That's in the discount catalogs." I softened up. "But it's in good shape. Maybe if you advertise, you'll find someone who'll want it."

A lot of good it did me to soften up. Enid Sievers pursed her lips in a sour pout. I'd insulted Edgar's memory, I guess. I resisted the temptation to inform her of the probable markup on Missy. The crate would seem like a bargain by comparison.

Enid Sievers handed me the slip of paper on which she'd written the information about Coakley. I glanced at it. Have you ever heard of "spidery" handwriting? Hers looked like the web: little interconnected squares linked in a complicated design, evidently meant to trap something, too.

"I'm sure Missy will be very happy with Mrs. Burley," she said as she trailed me to the door.

"I'm sure she will," I replied. Let Betty Burley explain that she wasn't adopting Missy. And while she was at it, let Betty talk this woman out of Missy's papers, too.

12

If I'd met Bill Coakley in what turned out to be the dirty flesh, I'd have hated him on sight. But I didn't have to wait. I hated him on sound.

"Is Mr. Coakley there?" I asked.

The voice was ripe with fake heartiness. "Don't see nobody else around, so that's got to be me, don't it?"

A chorus of high-pitched yapping almost drowned the reply. It came from his end of the line, of course. Rowdy and Kimi were dozing on the kitchen floor, and, in any case, malamutes don't yap. They let out an occasional yip when the situation warrants it. They can bark, but seldom do. Sometimes they howl. They also speak their native language: *Rrrrlll? Rrrwwww. Woo-woo-woo-woo.* Talking, it's called. It is, too. Once you're used to it, it's as plain as English. Anyway, whatever Coakley's dogs spoke wasn't English and wasn't Malamute, either.

I tried to project my voice. "My name is Holly Winter. I'm calling about the malamute you're boarding."

"Gotcha," he said.

"I'm the person who's supposed to pick her up. I'm from Malamute Rescue. I wanted to make sure you'd be there."

"Well, we're always *here*. We ain't got nowhere else *to* go."

"Then I'll be right out. I'm in Cambridge. I'm leaving now."

"Slow down," he said, as if I sounded hysterical. "Just slow down."

"Is there some problem?"

"No problem at all. Your friend come this morning and took the dog."

"Betty Burley?"

"If you say so."

"I *don't* say so. I'm asking you. Who picked up the malamute?"

"Your friend, what's-her-name. She come and got the dog already. She come and got her this morning."

Of course, it seemed just like that damned Enid Sievers, with her silly conviction that Betty Burley was adopting Missy. Enid Sievers hadn't bothered to let me know that Missy was no longer with her and that I shouldn't go there to pick her up. She also hadn't bothered to tell me that Betty was going to Coakley's. I thanked Coakley, hung up, and called Betty.

"Picked her up?" Betty said. "*I* didn't pick her up."

"Well, who did?" I asked. "Has Enid Sievers called you?"

"I haven't talked to her since whenever it was. Friday. Who *is* the guy? Coakley? Give me his number. I'll straighten this out."

Beta dogs, those of subordinate rank, must feel that same sense of comfort when an alpha takes charge. Betty had been dealing with this kind of mess for years. She could handle it. Not fifteen minutes after we'd hung up, she called back.

"He says the owner came and got her," Betty reported.

"No, she didn't," I said. "Enid Sievers left Missy there for us to pick up. She decided it was easier. Also, she wouldn't give me the papers. And she tried to sell me a crate."

"Yeah, well, she probably left the board bill for us to pick up, too," said the voice of experience. "But if she did, you'd think this Coakley . . ."

"Yeah, you would," I agreed.

"I don't like the sound of this. I'd feel a lot better if the bitch was spayed."

"She definitely isn't," I said. "I'll bet anything that Edgar wanted her to be able to fulfill herself. As a woman, right? He sounds like the type. Anyway, Enid Sievers has this crazy idea that you're dying to adopt Missy, and I don't know what she thinks I'm doing, but she doesn't like me. Maybe if you call her . . . ?"

Betty agreed. While I waited for her to call back, I had a sudden inspiration about tattoos. Here's what it was, and it's a good idea. It didn't solve my own problem, of course, but it's the world's first surefire plan to cure anyone of buying a dog on impulse ever again. Here's how it works: Pick out the puppy you want. Hand over your cash, check, or credit card. And stop right there. Don't put that hand back in your pocket. Let it rest on the nearest comfortable surface. Any place will do. Any place at all. And relax. This won't hurt a bit. Sally Brand knows what she's doing. Oh, you don't *want* the puppy's portrait permanently embellishing your wrist? Your back? Chest? You don't want the tattoo at all? Well, then, I guess you don't really want the dog after all, do you? Great scheme. No permanent commitment, no dog. Absolutely simple.

Betty called back.

"She says that Coakley just called her," Betty said. "He's telling her he found the dog a good home."

"I don't believe that," I said. "I mean, I believe you. I just don't believe he—"

"Yeah. This woman is . . . She's on some other planet, if you ask me, but it does, uh, it does seem like she told Coakley she was giving the dog away."

"So he took one look at her and decided—"

"Yeah. That she didn't know which way was up."

"Jesus," I said. "Neither do I."

"You and me both. We should've taken that dog. We shouldn't have waited."

"I should've taken her on Friday," I said miserably. "Why the hell did I leave her there?"

"It seemed all right," Betty said. "Didn't it?"

"Yes. It seemed fine. I mean, how was I supposed to know she had this gentleman friend? All she talked about *then* was the dear departed Edgar, for God's sake, her husband. She didn't seem like . . ." Enid Sievers had seemed sexless. My mistake, of course. No one is immune to passion. "God damn. I am so sorry. I should've just grabbed Missy and got her out of there. Shit! Rowdy didn't even qualify on Sunday. I should've taken Missy and kept her with me and stayed home. And, Jesus. It gets worse. The puppy at Puppy Luv?"

"It's—"

"I think she's okay. I'm not positive, but I think so. But the woman's dead. Diane Sweet. The woman that runs the place. She was murdered. Someone broke into Puppy Luv last night and murdered her."

Almost all real dog people are world-class talkers. Maybe it's because we're used to the constant presence of beings who love the sound of our voices. Maybe it's because we have a lot to say: whose dog went B.O.B. where, whether that second testicle has dropped yet, how many points the new bitch needs to finish. The fact is that we're exceptionally chatty. The most expensive item on any real dog person's budget isn't dog food, club memberships, vet bills, entry fees for shows, the cost of hiring handlers and groomers, or anything else obviously dog-related. It's the phone bill. Always, always. For what I pay to NYNEX, I could campaign a specials dog. You know what that is, right? A dog with a championship who's entered in Best of Breed. Am I running on? Well, I hate to say I told you so, but . . . Maybe if we'd been two bird-watchers, stamp collectors, or fanciers of Vietnamese potbellied pigs, the silence on the line would have been normal. Maybe it wouldn't. I don't know. But I assure you that dog people never let the air go dead.

"Holly?" Betty finally said. "Are you thinking . . . ?"

I hadn't been. If I'd been thinking about anyone, it had been Gloria Loss, and she'd barely crossed my mind. Betty didn't know Gloria Loss, though. But Betty and I both knew Lois Metzler.

"Forget it," I said. "Lois was upset, naturally, but . . . Look, I don't know the details, really, but I think it wasn't . . . It just wasn't a woman's crime, I think. What I heard was that a *guy* broke in. It did cross my mind that it might've been someone who'd bought a puppy that turned out to be sick. You know? Someone had humongous vet bills and tried to get Puppy Luv to pay, something like that. But Lois? I mean, yeah, of course she was . . . Her reputation and everything?"

Betty, the human Kimi, overrode me. Alpha and beta. "You know what my mother always used to say? She used to say it all the time. It drove me and my sisters crazy. 'Remember, girls, your reputation is priceless.' "

"Everyone's mother used to say that."

"Everyone's mother was right," Betty said.

My own mother, Marissa, was positively vituperative on the subject. She banned any behavior even remotely suggestive of such gross improprieties as double handling, altering a dog's natural color, sneaking food into the obedience ring, and stepping on the toes of a competitor's dog. Fortunately, she considered human love affairs a personal matter, governed by the American Kennel Club only in the sense that "all participants should be guided by the principles of good sportsmanship both in and outside the ring." At least I think that's what she thought. She died quite a long time ago. There was one . . . Well, I'm not sure what she meant. The remark was a direct quote from the AKC Obedience Regulations, but Marissa definitely said it about people, not dogs. What Marissa said was that smoothness and naturalness should be given precedence over military precision and peremptory commands. Make of it what you want. Myself, I think it's good advice.

13

As I've mentioned, Weston, Westford, West Brookfield, and lots of other Wests and Brooks appear in big gold letters on the Dog Lover's Map of Massachusetts, but Westbrook doesn't have a show site, kennel club, obedience club, or canine activity center. No one goes there for tracking tests, agility training, sled dog racing, sheep herding, lure coursing, flyball, or Newfoundland water trials. So far as I knew, there'd never been so much as a show-and-go held in Westbrook. With one exception, it wasn't a dog town at all. The exception was a business shamelessly named Your Local Breeder. I'd seen its ads in the 'Dogs, Cats, and Other Pets' section of the *Globe*'s classifieds: *"Never buy a dog from a pet shop! Come to us first, Your Local Breeder!"* Puppy Luv advertised there, too: *"Adorable AKC puppies! Not from puppy mills! More than twenty breeds to choose from!"* Below each come-to-us pitch there'd be a list of breeds and prices. Although I'd tsked and sneered at the ads, I'd never visited Your Local Breeder for the same reason I'd never entered Puppy Luv until last Friday: The list of breeds had never included the Alaskan malamute.

Yes. As if it mattered. As if it did.

As I was saying, although I'd never stopped at Your Local Breeder, I'd driven through Westbrook from time to time on my way to and from real dog towns. The prettiest sections of the town had rolling hills thick with pines and maples, and leisure farms with saltbox houses, red barns, stone walls, white corrals, and brown Morgan horses. A few of the original working farms survived as side-of-the-road vegetable stands and garden supply centers, but most of the once-agricultural acreage was now given over to Acorn and Deck houses, Royal Barry Wills capes, and brandless, nameless neocolonial split-level hybrids inhabited by commuters who willingly traded the long daily round-trip to Boston for clean air and green trees. A few areas of Westbrook looked like the ugly parts of most New England towns. My own home town, Owls Head, Maine, has its share of hovels set in mud amidst flocks of filthy, squawking geese, broken-down cars, and the rusted remains of doorless refrigerators and irreparable kitchen stoves. Westbrook did, too. And, even viewed collectively, how beautiful can a McDonald's, a Burger King, a Pizza Hut, a Wendy's, a Stop & Shop, three gas stations, and a used-car lot really be? How distinctive? Westbrook's fast-fill strip looked like a thousand others.

The turn for Coakley's was a right at the first set of lights after the third gas station. His house was picturesquely situated a quarter of a mile off the main drag, just beyond what had started out as the town dump and had evolved into a sanitary landfill. A thin row of sickly hemlocks and a ragged, tilting snow fence failed to screen the landfill from the road. Coakley's house was a seedy-looking cedar-shingled cape progressing toward hoveldom, which is to say that it did have lots of frozen, rutted mud, a dented old maroon Chevy sedan with no tires, and a harvest gold refrigerator-freezer with no doors, but it lacked the geese. The only dog run, if you can call it that, was a small chicken wire enclosure that fenced in a pile of rough plywood and the carcass of a dead chicken. The plywood was apparently the raw material for a doghouse that no one had ever gotten around to building or the remains of one that had tumbled down. The chicken? Killed by Missy?

At the shabby front door, Bill Coakley greeted me in the same jovial tones I'd heard on the phone: "Hope you come about a dog, 'cause I ain't got a lot else since the wife kicked me out."

Although the room into which he led me was almost devoid of furniture, the racket of dogs and the stench of God-knows-what would've been enough to fill the Astrodome. How many dogs? It was hard to count. Poms, Yorkies, toy poodles, Shih Tzus, mini dachshunds, and mini schnauzers were packed into cages, boxes, and orange crates stacked precariously on top of one another. A makeshift cardboard pen occupied a far corner of the room.

The superabundance of little dogs certainly contributed to the odor, but its principal source may well have been Bill Coakley. One of the amazing things about Coakley was that he wasn't very old. He couldn't have been more than thirty. I mean, you'd think it would take longer than that for anyone to accumulate so much dirt. His yellow teeth were thickly encrusted with plaque or oatmeal, maybe both. His hair looked as if he'd coated it with cooking oil before standing out in a sandstorm. The layer of dirt left its base color an open question to which Coakley himself, not having bathed for years, might not even know the answer. I mean, how does someone like that apply for a driver's license or a fishing license or any other ID? (*Color of hair, sir?* the clerk asks. *Geez, ma'am,* he replies, *your guess is as good as mine.*) Anyway, eye color was obvious—red—and it probably goes without saying that his hands and nails were . . . well, let's let it go. Suffice it to say that if Bill Coakley had been found dead, the coroner wouldn't have needed to open him up and examine his stomach contents to discover what he'd eaten lately. Dried egg coated his mouth. A long strand of spaghetti clung like a stray hair to one shoulder of his army-surplus khaki shirt.

"Mr. Coakley," I said firmly over the din of the dogs, "I'm Holly Winter. I called about the malamute. Betty Burley did *not* pick her up, and neither did Enid Sievers, the owner. Now I want to know—"

Coakley didn't wait for me to finish. "Found *that* little lady a good home," he said. Then he moved purposefully toward the pen in the far corner of the room. The light was dim. A brown haze hung in the air. Maybe once, a long time ago, this had been a living room. A battered couch remained. Like everything else in the house, including the walls, the floor, the ceiling, the air, Coakley, his clothing, the dogs, and a large, ugly cat asleep on top of a stack of crates, the couch was dirt tan. "Woman sees my usual ad in the paper, calls, stops in about a dog. One of my pups." His tone was indefinably inventive. "And she says, 'Ain't that a pretty husky you got out there,' and I says, 'Sure is.'"

"Meaning the malamute," I said. "Missy."

Coakley bent over to retrieve a large plastic bowl from the cardboard pen. Inside the enclosure swarmed about two dozen tiny puppies, Yorkies, Poms, and what I think were Pom-a-poos. "Got my chores to do here," he said. "Breeding dogs ain't easy. It's a lot of work."

Shall I spare you the food dish? Let's make a deal. I'll skip Coakley's ears, but you have to hear about the dish, which was a big avocado green spill-proof plastic bowl thickly lined with a hardened brown substance that I hope—but won't promise—was old dog food. Solidified dribbles clung to the outer sides. Coakley handled the thing with no evident revulsion or even reluctance and—this is the really disgusting part—plunged it unhesitatingly into an open bag of dog food unprepossessingly labeled Generic. The clunk and rattle of the kibble against the dish touched off a renewed frenzy of little-dog yapping and yelping. Four or five dirt brown food moths rose lazily from the bag of dog food and hovered in the dusty air. Their larvae probably had a higher protein content than the food did.

The clamor eventually subsided enough for me to speak. "*Where* is the dog now?" I demanded. "That dog belongs—"

I never heard Bill Coakley sound anything but cheerful. He did now. "Don't have to do nothing but turn around, and there's some woman's hollering at me." Happy sounding as ever, he launched into the details. "Lady from the IRS. *They're* after me. The wife, she's still after me, and that old battle-ax from the Humane. You ever get in tax trouble, let me tell you, there's one thing you gotta—"

When he lowered the dish into the puppy pen, the noise of the dogs cut him off. The little ones in the pen scrambled and fought for their foul dinner. There were so many of them that it was hard to distinguish one from the other. I wondered why anyone would buy a dog from a place like this. Kind, ignorant people must look around and think, "My God, I've got to get this puppy out of here." Or did people imagine that filth promised a bargain? But the puppies were cute, of course. Damn, they were adorable. You wanted to scoop one up, take it home, clean it up, and give it the first decent meal of its life. *You* did? No, I did. Yes, even me. They were almost irresistible.

"I'm in a hurry," I said. "I'm here for that dog, and I want her—"

"I'm telling you, ain't I? The lady come and took a look at her, and I says that the lady that owns her can't keep her no more and if you want her, she's yours, and the lady says, sure. I didn't even get nothing out of it. I done it for the dog." He looked me directly in the eyes.

Bill Coakley, canine benefactor?

"Okay," I said. "So just give me her name and—"

The ugly cat, a blatantly unneutered tom, chose that moment to plummet from its perch on the crates, traipse across the floor, and head straight for me. Its sudden dive precipitated a renewed outburst of yipping, to which Coakley and the cat seemed equally deaf.

"Handsome bugger, ain't he?" Coakley remarked genially.

I tried to feel sorry for the cat. As you probably know, cats require a higher protein diet than dogs do. That's why dogs love cat food, of course, and why a cat fed on dog food is malnourished. My hunch was that the handsome bugger ate the same food-moth chow the puppies did. Its large belly hung from a swayback. Its ribs showed. The yellow-tinged farinaceous glop that dripped from its eyes looked a whole lot like the stuff on Bill Coakley's teeth. The poor thing's ears were ragged, and its head was scarred. Also, it undoubtedly had fleas. Cats are supposed to be standoffish, right? Sure, but there's something about communicable diseases that makes them super friendly. This one sauntered up and rubbed against my legs. I bent down and stroked its bony spine.

"Handsome bugger," Coakley repeated proudly.

It may have been the cat's name. I didn't ask. Instead, I again demanded the name of the woman who'd taken Missy. I don't know why I bothered. I was far from sure that she existed.

Coakley picked up the cat, gave me a plaque-ridden

grin, shrugged, and said, with what felt like a hint of stubborn defiance, "Got it around here somewhere."

That's when I'd had it. "That dog is the property of Alaskan Malamute Rescue," I announced. Did I sound ridiculous? Maybe. Maybe not. I'm used to ordering around creatures a whole lot tougher than dirty Bill Coakley. "I want her back, and I want her back fast. You get that dog back, or I'll have the MSPCA and every other animal welfare organization in Massachusetts in here so fast you won't know what hit you. Do you understand what I'm telling you? You get that malamute back here, or I close you down." Then I stomped out.

I meant to do it anyway, or I meant to try my damnedest. I knew how to start. I knew the people to call. But first, of course, I had to have Missy back. Do you understand? I just *had* to.

14

A HALF HOUR AFTER STOMPING out of Coakley's, I had my feet planted on the concrete aisle that ran down the center of the raw-looking pale beige cinder-block kennel building at Your Local Breeder. I guess I'd expected a magnified version of the dump I'd just left. What I found was a semirural pet shop with large indoor-outdoor runs instead of fiberglass cage banks and, more importantly, with litters of puppies for sale as well as individual pups of different breeds.

I was studying the four little black cocker spaniels asleep in the run in front of me. New to dogs? The smallest member of the AKC's sporting group, the cocker spaniel is . . . But you know what a cocker is. Of course you do. Everyone does. It's one of the most popular breeds in America, the quintessential show dog and the quintessential pet shop dog, too. The great publicist of the breed, Ch. My Own Brucie, was the only cocker ever to take two consecutive Best in Shows at

Westminster—1940 and 1941—but his wins in the ring were the least of his triumphs: The U.S. population went Brucie-mad and cocker-mad. Trendiness is, of course, the doom of a breed. The indiscriminate mass production of cocker spaniels —a Brucie in every home—meant the proliferation of congenital problems: hip dysplasia, von Willebrand's disease, blood clotting diseases, and, especially, inherited eye diseases like progressive retinal atrophy and so-called juvenile cataracts, which aren't necessarily juvenile, but are definitely inherited. Dedicated cocker fanciers eventually rescued the breed. Cockers used in breeding are supposed to be tested for cataracts at least once a year, and some, like active stud dogs, twice a year. One of the silky little black cockers I was watching opened his eyes, yawned, and rested his head on his forepaws. His eyes looked fine to me, but that's the damn thing about inherited cataracts: A veterinary ophthalmologist can diagnose the disease up to two years before it's visible to the rest of us.

When I'd marched into the pet supply shop at the front of Your Local Breeder, a bland-looking, sandy-haired young man in a plaid flannel shirt said, "Hi. May I help you?"

"Yes," I said as I scanned a display of leather leashes and a stack of overpriced Kennel Cabs. "I'm interested in dogs." So, okay. Maybe it was a bit of an understatement, but it was no lie.

By comparison with Diane Sweet, the sandy-haired guy had no talent for sales, or maybe he lacked training. All he did was lead me past a couple of closed doors and into the kennel area. He didn't put a puppy in my arms or assure me that I'd recoup the purchase price of a bitch the first time I bred her. He didn't pretend that the puppies reacted to me in some astonishingly special way. He didn't offer a puppy at cut rate, and he didn't suggest a buy-on-credit plan. He didn't do a thing except leave me alone with the best sales representatives God ever created.

Which breeds, right? Was yours there? Okay. Mini dachshund, mini schnauzer, Doberman, Dalmatian, Lhasa Apso, Shih Tzu, poodle, collie, sheltie, and Norwegian elkhound. So far so good? Westie, Yorkie, English springer spaniel, Brittany, basset, chow, German shepherd, and Rottweiler. Look, wouldn't you rather *not* know? Well, okay. The cockers, of course. A Boston terrier, who looked healthier than the one at Puppy Luv. One Kees and a lone Scottie, too, a half-grown male with a twisted rear leg. A litter of Siberian huskies not a day over five weeks old. A Siberian is pretty close to a malamute, huh? When I first caught sight of those little balls of gray fluff, my heart began to race. Then I took in the high-set ears, the fox tails, and the blue eyes, and I felt a surge of sick relief. Disgusting, right? Breed doesn't matter. Puppies aren't fully immunized until they're four *months* old, and at five weeks, any puppy needs frequent, loving social contact with people as well as protection from the diseases of other dogs. But relief was what I felt. I know. I *am* ashamed.

Anyway, having finished my meditation on My Own Brucie and the fall and rise of the cocker spaniel, I made my way past the open door of an office and back to the pet supply showroom, where the plaid-shirted young guy was perched on a stool behind the checkout counter talking into the receiver of a beige wall phone.

"Yeah," he said. He paused, listened, and said, "Yeah." Then he repeated the gist of his previous remarks, listened for a good half minute, and again said, "Yeah," but added, "We breed all our dogs here." After he'd said "Yeah" a few more times, he hung up.

"I couldn't help overhearing," I said. "You breed all these puppies here?"

"Yeah," he said. His face was empty of expression.

I waited for him to elaborate. He didn't.

"Do you have any, uh, Alaskan malamutes?" I asked. "There aren't any. . . ." I gestured toward the kennels.

His voice was as flat as his face. "Nope."

"Well, do you ever?"

"Not now," he said.

The door to the office I'd passed closed with a sudden bang, and a sharp female voice rang out: "Ronald, go and sweep the grooming area! And then clean the water bowls, and I mean *wash* them and fill them. Don't just add water."

Ronald started to speak. "Mrs. Coakley—"

My face must have registered surprise, but Ronald and the woman were glaring at one another, not looking at me. *The* Mrs. Coakley? But maybe not. Her standards of personal hygiene seemed perfectly ordinary. Her short, straight black hair had a clean gleam, someone had ironed her soft-red chamois shirt and tan cords, and her black Reeboks looked new. Despite her pinched mouth and close-set eyes, she had a pretty face, with delicate features and high cheekbones. At a guess, she was in her late twenties.

"Ronald, just *do* it!" she commanded. Then she turned to me and extended a small, tidy hand with neat pink-buffed oval nails. "We don't happen to have malamutes at the moment," she said in a gracious talking-to-customers tone, "but we have some darling little huskies."

Dog people, of course, say *Siberians.*

"I just wondered," I said. "Uh, Ronald—"

"Ronald is on his way *out.* Good help is not that hard to find. The sign goes up today." Mrs. Coakley's head bobbed with assurance. The big brass button earrings on her ears danced like marks of emphatic punctuation. "I can get you a malamute," she added. "I can get you any kind of AKC puppy you want. Or if it was a rare breed you wanted, I can get that, too."

The temptation was great. *A Karelian bear dog?* I wanted to ask. *A Catahoula leopard dog, a Leonberger, a Löwchen? How about a Chinook? Can you get me a Chinook?* My heart sank. *A Chinook?* I love the breed. Her answer could well be yes.

"Actually," I said, "I was out this way because of a malamute. I heard there was one for adoption. But by the time I got there, the dog had already been given away."

If Mrs. Coakley had been a horse, she'd have reared up. "I know all about that. That was my ex-husband that had that dog—"

"Bill Coakley."

"Let me tell you something. Bill *sold* that dog. You don't *give* away a dog with AKC papers."

True enough. Sometimes, no one will take the dog as a gift. Ask anyone who does purebred rescue.

"Oh," I said.

"Besides," Mrs. Coakley added, "that wasn't a puppy. You want a dog that will *bond* with you, don't you? You want to be special to your own dog. And puppies are so cute. It's a shame to miss that."

"Of course," I said.

"You know, scientists have proved that if you don't start out with a puppy, dogs'll never recognize you as their owner," Mrs. Coakley informed me.

Rowdy wasn't really mine? Neither was Kimi? The news would come as a big surprise to them.

"I'll think about it," I said, zipping up my parka.

Mrs. Coakley smiled. "You do that, and you call me anytime and let me know just what you want. Here, let me give you a card."

She stepped behind the checkout counter, fished around by the cash register, and handed me a business card. I glanced at it. Her first name was Janice. Janice and Bill Coakley. I tried to imagine them as a couple. I tried to hear people saying things like, "Hm, how about having Janice and Bill to dinner on Saturday?" Their Christmas cards? "Best wishes for the holiday season. Janice and Bill Coakley." It seemed to me that instead of inviting them to dinner, everyone would've said, "Ick! What did she ever see in him?" And if Bill Coakley had so much as brushed his fingers against the Christmas cards, people would've opened the envelopes, taken one whiff, and said, "Boy, you don't even need to look inside to tell who sent this one." Had Janice and Bill both started out clean? Grubby? And the divorce? Maybe they hadn't fought about soap and water at all. Maybe they'd fought about money. Maybe they'd fought about dogs.

15

KEVIN DENNEHY HAS SPENT most of his life in Cambridge. So far as I know, he's never been west of the Mississippi. It's possible that he's never been west of Worcester, Massachusetts. Lately, though, he's taken to wearing boot-cut jeans and yoked shirts with pearl snaps, not because he actually wants to cultivate a cowboy look but because Walker's Western Wear is one of the few stores in Greater Boston that sell clothes big enough to accommodate Kevin's increasing bulk. At six o'clock on Monday evening, he was dressed for a remake of *Red River*, but all he was doing was burning onions at my kitchen stove.

Rita, who's my second-floor tenant and a friend of Kevin's as well as mine, had taken him to task a week earlier. She'd insisted that if he didn't start living differently, he'd end up just like his father, dead of a heart attack at the age of forty. What she'd had in mind hadn't been a radical change in diet. Rita's a psychotherapist, not a nutritionist. Besides, the meatiest food his mother ever cooks is gluten-flour mock spare ribs. Also, Kevin's a runner who averages forty or fifty miles a week. No, what Rita had been pushing was some kind of stress reduction seminar at a local holistic-spiritual-East-West-mind-body outfit called Interface. Rita had even unearthed a course catalog and tried to press it on Kevin. Unfortunately, though, he'd flipped it open to a page that listed a weekend workshop in which participants would travel to a forest in western Massachusetts where they'd track animals in the wild and learn to identify them by their spoor, in other words, their tracks and droppings.

"Spoor!" Kevin had hollered. "You know what *spoor* means?" He'd turned to me. "You get this? You really *get* this? If I don't want to die of a heart attack, I'm supposed to go out in the woods and stick my nose in raccoon shit? Jesus Christ. I don't believe it." Then he'd pulled himself together, taken a big swig of Budweiser, and said, "Pardon my French."

That's presumably what led to Rita's next piece of advice, namely, that if Kevin would substitute a glass or two of red wine for the beer or milk he usually drank with his meals, he'd be doing his coronary arteries a big favor and, at the same time, reducing his emotional stress.

"Hey, hey!" he'd said. "Hold that Bud! Bring forth the Chateau le Classy!"

But, to my amazement, he had apparently taken her suggestion seriously. At any rate, that Monday evening, instead of showing up with his usual ground beef and Bud, he'd brought a package of chicken thighs and a half-gallon jug of Gallo red burgundy.

"Distressed grapes," Kevin said, quoting Rita. He picked up a glass tumbler that Rowdy had won at a match, took a gulp, and swallowed the wine. Then he upended the package of chicken on the blackened onions. Steam hissed and smoke rose. Rowdy and Kimi, stationed on either side of Kevin, lifted their noses as if to heaven. *"Distressed* grapes," Kevin repeated. "Make 'em suffer, and then when they hit your gut, they're mad as hell. Start out with all this fat clogging everything up, and you pour these little guys in, and they blast it out." His beefy hand brought the glass to his lips. He drank, gave a satisfied smile, and added, "Just like Drāno."

The wine in my mouth began to burn my tongue. "Your stomach must be feeling better," I said.

"Could've happened to anyone." He vigorously forked the chicken thighs. "Spoor'll do that to you, you know. It's physical. You can't help it. You know, I was thinking about that today, you know, trying not to put my foot in it, and suddenly it comes to me that Rita's idea of how you clear out the old system . . . Well, it struck me . . ."

"Rita didn't mean . . . She didn't even mean the tracking course. She meant, uh, relaxation, deep breathing, that kind of thing. Your job *is* stressful, Kevin. That's all she meant. I mean, take today."

"I'm all right," he insisted, flipping the chicken black side up.

"No one says you aren't! The point is that you can't do what you do without feeling the strain. That's all. Rita wasn't blaming you."

Once the chicken thighs had an ebony crust on both sides, Kevin dished out equal portions for himself and for me. With the dogs following his every move, he picked up both plates, lumbered to the table, and added the final fillip: He stuck one massive thumb over the top of the Gallo jug, raised and tipped it, and dashed liberal splashes of wine over the half-raw chicken and cremated onions.

A huge grin filled the most Irish-looking face in Cambridge. If red hair can smile, Kevin's did. "Frog food. *Coq au vin,"* he declared proudly as he sank to his seat. Kevin's accent is quite good. His high school French teacher was a woman from Paris. I wished that she'd taught home ec. Kevin lifted his fork, held it poised, and gallantly commanded: *"Après vous."*

Rowdy and Kimi eyed me hopefully. Kimi will steal toast right out of the toaster—if you aren't vigilant, she'll take half-chewed food out of your mouth—and Rowdy's not much better. Some pretext to get up and leave my plate unguarded? Damn the splintery chicken bones. You do know about that, don't you? Chicken bones can puncture a dog's intestines. And undercooked—yuck, let's face it—uncooked chicken? Swarming with salmonella. I dug in. Better me than my dogs. Dog saliva splattered to the floor. Kevin and I discussed the murder of Diane Sweet.

"She was a very hard worker," Kevin said. "The idea was that the husband, John, did the business part, and Diane did the dogs and helped the customers. But the long and the short of it is—this isn't what John Sweet'll tell you, but it's not hard to figure out—is that she's good at everything, and he's good for nothing. The fact of it is, what he did, when you come down to it, was he lived off his wife, and now all's he does is ask when we'll be out of there so's he can open the shop up again. Guys like that make me sick." Kevin took a forkful of onion cinders, chewed pensively, and, studying my face, said, "Now, Holly, I want you to tell me the honest-to-God's truth. Is this the best chicken you ever ate?"

"Amazing." Time to change the subject. "Kevin, look. If Diane Sweet was working hard—"

"Eight A.M. every day, before the place was open, nights, weekends. Open seven days a week, and she worked eight.

She stayed there after it was closed, paid the bills, cleaned up, washed the dogs—"

"Well, you better believe the puppies need a bath when they get there." You may have observed that I have a slight tendency to preach about the evils of pet shops. I'd always gone easy on Kevin, though. No matter how emphatically I'd damned the puppy mill industry, not the puppies, Kevin would somehow have felt that I was bad-mouthing Trapper, his late and very deeply lamented dog, who'd come from a pet shop. "Pet shop dogs come from puppy mills," I said. "The puppies come from mass breeding operations, and then they're sold to brokers, who are the people who make the big money in this, and they're shipped all over the country."

He ate some chicken and said dismissively, "Yeah, yeah, like on that Connie Chung thing, but not Puppy Luv."

Connie Chung's exposé of the puppy mill industry, "The Price the Puppy Pays," was on TV a couple of years ago. The only thing wrong with the program was the title. The ones who really pay the price are the stud dogs and the brood bitches. The puppies get out.

"Oh, come on," I said. "Puppy Luv's no different. Yeah, maybe now and then they buy from a few local people, but that's the exception. If you saw Connie Chung, you already know that."

He speared a piece of chicken and pointed his fork at me. "You're wrong."

"I hate to tell you, but I'm not. Look, the thing is that the dogs aren't responsible. I'm not blaming *them*. And there isn't necessarily anything wrong with them. It's a matter of probabilities. If you buy from a pet shop, the odds are against you. With Trapper, you lucked out. But the fact is—"

"Naw, it's not that," Kevin said. "Puppy Luv gets them from here."

"If *here* is Logan Airport," I said.

"Naw. That's what Diane Sweet was doing last night. She was getting a delivery from a local guy. The guy brought the puppies, and he left, and she never got to wash them. This is a local guy."

I'm hard to convince. "Well, then, it was a local distributor," I said, "someone who picked them up at the airport and took a cut of the profits. Just because she didn't go to the airport herself . . ." I'd been cutting big pieces of chicken and swallowing them whole, unchewed and thus untasted, or that was the idea. A raw lump seemed to stick in my throat.

"Like I said, Holly, *local* dogs."

"Did you see their papers?" I rested my fork on my plate and drank some wine. "Kevin, are those puppies all right? You know, a lot of the time—"

"Here we go again," he said. "Like I told you, the puppies were all over, and the whole place is the worst mess you ever saw. The material evidence is . . . it's the lab's mess now, and it's going to take weeks. But it's all under control, and the dogs are all right. And do me a favor and don't ask if your malamute's there, okay? It's there, and it's not going anywhere, at least not until our guys have finished."

"Did I—?"

"You didn't have to," he said. "Aren't you going to finish that?"

A lone chicken thigh remained on my plate. "I'm getting pretty full." I faked a martyred smile. "And you didn't give yourself very much." Before he could object, I stabbed the thigh and transferred it to his plate. "Kevin, uh, Diane Sweet was strangled?"

"Manual strangulation. But now it looks like it was a definite second choice. You know these, uh, what do you call 'em, dog beds. Big pillows, wrapped in plastic, like that dry cleaner's stuff, and it looks like what happened was that the perp grabbed one of them and held it over her face and started to smother her. One of these, uh, dog beds is missing the plastic, and the M.E. says there's traces of this, uh, plastic film in her mouth. And a piece of it got caught on one of her earrings."

"But . . . ?"

"Too slow, and he got tired of waiting. Or she fought harder than he counted on. This was a young, healthy woman. She dug in her fingernails. There's plastic under them and on her face and around the head."

"But, Kevin, wouldn't it be harder to strangle her? Without the dog bed over her face, she'd be able to see. It just seems . . . I don't know. Without something over her face, wouldn't she sort of have more leverage?"

"Yeah, but she'd been fighting him off. She couldn't have had much strength left. It was an awful way to go. Pretty woman, hard worker. It's a damn shame. She never should've been there all alone. This good-for-nothing husband never should've let her do that." Kevin gnawed thoughtfully and added, "Unless . . ."

Rita maintains that what keeps Kevin single is his relationship with his mother. She's wrong. The truth is that he fears for his life.

I knew what Kevin was going to say. I beat him to it. "Well, I *was* wondering about the husband. Except . . ."

"Yeah, the goose that laid the golden egg," Kevin said. "But if you ask him, John Sweet, he was the head honcho, and all's his wife did was the scut work, is what it boils down to."

"Did the Sweets, uh, not get along? Did they fight?"

"Not so's the employees and the neighbors noticed, not the ones we talked to so far. Sounds more like they both went their separate ways, and his separate way was staying home watching TV and letting his wife support him, and her separate way was running the pet shop, working all the time so's he could—"

I'd had about all I could take. "Kevin, I know . . . Look, Kevin, nobody should have to die like that, and I'm really sorry, but no matter how hard Diane Sweet worked, she was in a very dirty business. It's like what your mother's always saying: Satan finds work for idle hands to do. That's whose work Diane Sweet really did, you know. Plenty of people make a good living selling pet supplies and food, and doing grooming. Diane Sweet didn't have to sell puppies."

"If you'd've seen—"

"If I'd seen her body, I'd probably feel sorrier for her, okay, but I still wouldn't think that running Puppy Luv was a good thing to do. Kevin, in Kansas—"

"I'm going to say it again. The puppies they got there didn't come from Kansas, and they didn't come from the airport."

"Then where did they come from? Kevin, if what we're talking about is Kansas in Massachusetts, I want you to tell me where. In a way, you know, this is my business. I *am* a dog writer. Maybe there's something I can—"

"Not on your life," he said. "Some of these people . . . Well, they're not nice people."

"You see? They aren't nice people, and Diane Sweet was one of them. Kevin, compared with the dogs on the average puppy farm, this chicken we just ate had a beautiful life." I looked down at my blackened plate of greasy bones. "And," I added, "if that's happening around here . . . Hey, Kevin, are you, uh, assuming that if it wasn't the husband, then, uh, what happened was that she basically interrupted a burglary? Not interrupted, but that someone broke in, and she was there? Because, Kevin, Puppy Luv is a storefront. It has big windows. A burglar would've had to be pretty stupid to think the place was empty. Wouldn't a burglar look in the front before he broke in through the back?"

"The theory is she was out back where they do the grooming. There's a cubbyhole of an office there and a stock room, bunch of little rooms in the back."

"Maybe," I agreed, "but think about the people she must've dealt with. In terms of buying the puppies, you said it yourself. They're not nice people. Also . . . I tried to tell you this morning. Kevin, with Trapper, you lucked out, but—if you don't believe me, ask Steve, if you want—Diane Sweet sold a lot of dogs that ended up getting sick and costing people a ton of money. And breaking their hearts, too. It could've been someone who bought a dog from Puppy Luv and had some kind of nightmare experience, someone who really hated Diane Sweet. Anybody would've had the sense to make it look like a robbery. The point is, Kevin, that running a pet shop isn't like running a bakery or something. It isn't neutral. Dogs get hurt, puppies get hurt, and the people who buy the puppies get hurt. And on the other end, the brokers make a whole lot of money, which means . . . Well, I'm not sure how, but I guess it means they've got a lot to lose. Anyway, there was money and pain on both sides. And Diane Sweet was right in the middle."

" 'Caught in the middle,' " Kevin intoned dramatically. He carried our plates to the sink and put the bones down the garbage disposal.

"Laugh if you want, but it's true. Except the ones who usually get caught in the middle are the dogs. Diane Sweet was an exception."

Kevin squirted a stream of generic liquid detergent into the sink. Suds billowed. "I hate to be the one to tell you,

Holly, but you're a dog snob. You ever owned a mutt in your life?"

"That is *not* fair! Kevin, I take pains . . . I don't even use the word *mutt.*"

He grunted.

"I've never owned an Akita," I said. "Or an English setter or a Keeshond. I've never owned a Border collie. Yet. There are hundreds of—"

"Liar," he said.

"Okay! I like purebred dogs. I like goldens and malamutes and Border collies and a hundred other breeds. I like . . . maybe this will sound stupid, but I like *who* they are. And, yeah, I like the way they look, how beautiful they are. But that just makes me a dog person. Or one kind of dog person. It doesn't make me a snob. And for your information, dog people are the least snobby people in the world." About people, anyway. About dogs? Well, that's complicated, but don't judge us too harshly. I mean, has there ever been a truly classless society?

Kevin looked up from the sink, but he said nothing.

Silence is evidently an effective interrogation technique. I blundered on. "I could own a mixed breed."

"Big of you."

"It's not like that! And besides, one of the things about pet shops is that what they're selling *is* dog snobbery, if you want to call it that, only they're ripping people off, because when most people see the signs for AKC puppies, they think they're getting show dogs. I saw an ad somewhere that said 'AKC certified puppies,' for God's sake, which is just bullshit, because all the AKC certifies is pedigrees, not dogs. And if you see the pedigree of a pet shop dog, well, if you know about dogs, all it looks like is the pedigree of a puppy mill dog. And people are paying a lot more at these goddamned pet shops than they'd pay a good breeder. Look, I've got a pedigree here that'll . . . Let me show you."

I went to my study, dug out the copy I'd made of Missy's pedigree, put it on the table, and made Kevin leave the dishes and look at it. You too, of course.

"What this is, is a family tree," I told him, "only you read it from left to right. It's the ancestors of Princess Melissa Sievers." I put a finger on Missy's registered name. "She's a malamute."

"Geez, no kidding," Kevin said.

"Yeah, no kidding," I said. "She came from Puppy Luv. Now just look at the top half, above her name. That part's her sire's side. Yukon Duke. Her father. Okay? And above and to the right of his name is *his* sire, Sir Snowy the Fourth. And below and to the right is his dam, his mother, Stupid Little Sally. Classic puppy mill names. Especially that one. Obviously. Poor . . . anyway, the bottom half of the pedigree is her mother's side, Icekist Sissy, and on her side, these are all famous kennel names. Famous, uh, if you know anything about malamutes. Anyway, for Puppy Luv's prices, you ought to get the bottom half of this pedigree, but what you get is the top half, in other words, a puppy mill dog."

You *do* know how to read a pedigree, don't you? Start at the top right. Oh, and remember that the AKC is a dog registry, not a spelling checker. Anyway, start at the top right. Sir Snowy II and S and S Queen of the Artic—yeah, Artic. These people can't even spell—produced Sir Snowy III, who was bred to a bitch named LJS Artic Lady (Caesar the Great *ex* JJs Molly). Got it now? Yes, indeed, Sir Snowy IV and Stupid Little Sally had the same sire, Sir Snowy III. And the breeding of Caesar the Great to LJS Artic Lady? Well, look for yourself.

Well, when Kevin absorbed that part, his exhausted face

Sir Snowy II
Sir Snowy III
S And S Queen of the Artic
Sir Snowy IV
Caesar The Great
LJS Artic Lady
JJs Molly
Yukon Duke
Sir Snowy II
Sir Snowy III
S And S Queen of the Artic
Stupid Little Sally
Caesar The Great
LJS' Queenie
LJS Artic Lady
Princess Melissa Sievers
Ch. Malsong Needa Hug
Ch. Icebound Peak Experience, CD
Ch. Icebound Follow Your Bliss
Ch. Icekist He'll Have To Go
Kotzebue Kearsage of Beaufort
Beaufort Kotzebue Belle
Ch. Happy Daze of Kaktovik
Icekist Sissy
Kaltag Sitka's Kaktovik
Ch. Kotzebue Kaltag of Kaktovik
Kaktovik Pandora of Kaltag
Ch. Icekist Family Tradition
Beaufort's Bering Bounder
Ch. Icekist Honky Tonk Angel
Ch. Icekist You Win Again

showed the only color I'd seen there that day. "This has got to be some kind of a mistake," he said with cold moral outrage.

"If it's any comfort to you, puppy mills are notorious for lousy records," I assured him. "The dam's pedigree is accurate. Those are reputable breeders."

I filled Kevin in on a little background. Ch. Icebound Peak Experience, C.D., was owned by a psychiatrist and his wife, but maybe that's obvious, and if you know anything about malamutes, I don't have to mention that Ch. Happy Daze of Kaktovik was bred by Helen Drummond, whose dogs all have names like Hurricane Drummer, Halcyon Diamond, that kind of thing. The Kaktovik dogs are pure Kotzebue, the line of mals that originated at the Chinook Kennels in the nineteen thirties, and, if you're a historian of the breed, you'll realize that the names of two of the Beaufort dogs, Kearsage and Belle, pay homage to two dogs killed in Antarctica on the Bird expeditions. Pandora is another thirties sled dog name, of course.

"Kaktovik Pandora of Kaltag was never shown," I told Kevin, "but she contributed a lot to the breed." I explained how. In detail.

Just as I was about to launch into a fascinating, if somewhat lengthy, description of Lois Metzler's foundation bitch, Kevin interrupted me by pointing to Missy's paternal line. "These two," he said. "These LJS ones."

"Yeah," I said. "If there are any genetic problems there . . ."

"Six toes," Kevin said.

"I've never heard of . . . but, yeah, that's the idea. On the maternal side, it isn't just that these people show their dogs . . . I mean, that's part of it, but the really important thing is that these breeders know their pedigrees back to

Adam and Eve, and they understand genetics, and they screen. But with these puppy mill dogs, there could be anything, hereditary blindness, you name it, which is why this bitch, Missy, shouldn't be used in breeding. The breeder, Walter Simms, whoever he is, is obviously some guy in Missouri or somewhere who doesn't know OFA from CIA . . ."

By now I could see Walter Simms clearly. He was a big, lazy, stupid man with a beer belly that hung out over the unbelted waistband of his drooping pants. His unbuttoned shirt revealed a white-haired chest with small female breasts. He stood, feet apart, in the barnyard of a sprawling farm in the Midwest. Behind him, the huge burning sun of Iowa or Missouri was sinking below a flat horizon.

"Me, neither," Kevin said.

"What?"

"CIA."

I started to explain OFA and CERF and stuff—Orthopedic Foundation for Animals, Canine Eye Research Foundation—but Kevin spread the fingers of his left hand, pointed to the names of two dogs, and said, "These two." He tapped on the pedigree.

"Yeah, you already . . . yes. They're half sisters. Bred to the same stud." I moved Kevin's fingers to the left. "And these two, Sir Snowy the Fourth and Stupid Little Sally—God, I hate that name. Anyway . . . well, it's very close."

"Close!" he said in disgust. He lowered his voice. "What this is, is incest."

"It's really not the same, Kevin. These aren't people. Dogs don't know, and, besides, they *get* bred. They don't commit incest."

"Yeah, well," Kevin answered, "maybe they don't know, but if they did, you can bet they wouldn't like it." He moved his fingers back to the names of Queenie and Lady. "Especially these two."

"Malamute bitches don't usually get along too well with each other anyway," I informed him.

Kevin's fingers resumed the tapping. "Jesus," he said. "No wonder."

16

My *Boston Globe* arrives by seven A.M. On Tuesday morning, I read it over my second cup of coffee. The front page carried the usual Boston stories. Construction on the new central artery and the new airport tunnel would be slower than expected. (By whom? I, for one, expected it to take forever.) Mayor Ray Flynn's arrival at a banquet had already been delayed. On route to the dinner, the mayor spotted a homeless man asleep in a gutter and stopped to pick him up and treat him to a Big Mac with a large order of fries. Ray Flynn is a man of the people. One of those people is, of course, his boyhood friend, Police Commissioner Mickey Roache. Boston, Boston.

Lest you suppose that the *Globe* practices provincial journalism, though, let me add that the front page articles were not exclusively concerned with events that had transpired within the city limits or even within the boundaries of the

Commonwealth of Massachusetts. A tractor-trailer had over-
turned all the way out on I-95 in far-off Woburn, and in
Rhode Island—practically a foreign country, right?—jailed
racketeer Enzio Guarini (the *Globe*'s words, not mine) was
again appealing two or three of his convictions on twenty or
thirty counts of fraud, conspiracy, and like crimes. Well, okay,
get picky if you want. Sure, Guarini grew up in Boston, and
Guarini's whole family—and Family, presumably—still lived
in Massachusetts, but just exactly how did you think he made
the *Globe*'s front page, anyway?

Probably because Puppy Luv did business way out in the
distant reaches of Cambridge, the two scanty paragraphs
about Diane Sweet's murder appeared in the Metro/Region
section. According to the paper, police were "investigating
several possible leads." And ignoring the impossible ones.
This is *news*? Diane Sweet's obituary, though, reported a fact
that was genuinely new, at least to me. This editorial slipup
was undoubtedly attributable to the *Globe*'s odd but rather
frequent practice of printing obituaries at the end of the
Sports section, thus treating demise as the great final score.

What appeared wasn't one of those laudatory accounts
of Diane Sweet's fine character and multitudinous contribu-
tions to society. Instead of a eulogy, all she got was the shortest paragraph in the cramped list of death notices. Even the
usual information about funeral arrangements and memorial
donations was missing. The gap seemed to confirm Kevin's
view of John Sweet as a good-for-nothing, the kind of husband who couldn't even bury his wife without her help. He
hadn't so much as bothered to call her his "beloved" wife. In
its entirety, the notice read:

> SWEET—Suddenly, of Cambridge, February 9, Di-
> ane L. (Richards). Wife of John B. Sweet. Also sur-
> vived by a sister, Janice Coakley, of Westbrook.

Yes, indeed. Sister. Something clicked. I turned to the classifieds. In spite of Diane Sweet's murder, Puppy Luv's ad was running under "Dogs, Cats, and Other Pets," and so was Your Local Breeder's. The two ads were in boldface at the tops of adjacent columns. As I remembered, Puppy Luv's of-fered *"Adorable AKC Puppies! More than twenty breeds to choose from."* Your Local Breeder, though, could supply *"any AKC breed on request."* According to Puppy Luv's copy, *"our beautiful, healthy puppies come from local breeders, not from puppy mills."* But Janice Coakley's ad, it now seemed to me, warned buyers about her sister: *"Never buy a dog from a pet shop! Come to us first! Your Local Breeder."*

More or less the same two ads appeared regularly in the *Globe,* and I'd glanced at them before, but I'd missed what now felt like the exchange of personal accusations, sibling rivalry rather than business competition. On the basis of the ads alone, Janice Coakley seemed to be winning. The key phrase in the Puppy Luv copy, *local breeder,* Diane Sweet's big selling point, was almost a pitch for the competition; and Puppy Luv's *"more than twenty breeds"* (however adorable) couldn't beat Janice Coakley's offer of *"any AKC breed."* Also, of course, Janice Coakley was still alive.

I made my routine check of the classifieds to see whether anyone was selling a malamute—no one was—and then I walked Rowdy and Kimi around the block, came home, looked up Bill Coakley's phone number, and once again scanned the dog ads. Three separate ads gave his number, one for Yorkies (*"tiny bundles of love"*), one for Poms (*"home raised with TLC"*), and one for Shih Tzus, poodles, and "Shis-a-poos." Why puppy buyers will pay purebred prices for cross-bred dogs is beyond me. In God's eyes, every dog is beyond price, of course, but here on earth, these Pom-a-poos, Yorkie-tzus, and all the other accidental-breeding-poos are simply mix-a-Yorks, so do yourself a favor, huh? If you want an all-

American, go to your local shelter. Save your money. And a life, too.

I put down the paper, picked up the phone, and called Bill Coakley, who sounded as hearty as he had yesterday and who once again assured me that he had found Missy a good home and that I "shouldn't worry none" about her. I concluded that in the sixteen or so hours since I'd seen Coakley, he'd worked exactly as hard on recovering Missy as he had on improving his English grammar. Janice, his ex-wife, had claimed that Bill had *sold* Missy. If so, it seemed to me, he probably knew where she was.

"This is a serious matter," I said firmly. "That dog is the property of Malamute Rescue." Yes, property. A dog who's safe at home with you may share your life, but a lost or stolen dog damn well better be your property, or he's apt to become someone else's. "And," I added, "it might interest you to know that there is a reward for her return."

Ransom? Let's call it motivation. Oh, and if you don't do rescue, perhaps you imagine that the source of this proffered reward was the whopping endowment of the Alaskan Malamute Protection League—it has none—or the riches of the Alaskan Malamute Emergency Fund, that is, a bank balance that seldom exceeds a few hundred dollars. Yes, indeed, my empty pockets. By the way, while we're on this topic, you don't happen to know Robin Williams, do you? I'm serious. Robin Williams. *Popeye? Good Morning, Vietnam?* He used to own a malamute. Maybe he still does. Anyway, if Robin Williams happens to have been your first husband's college roommate or something, and if you run into him, could you mention AMPL? The Alaskan Malamute Protection League. Just sort of work it into the conversation, huh? Box 170, Cedar Crest, New Mexico, 87008. Oh, and tell him that his donation won't go to reclaim a rescue dog like Missy, lost by someone who found her inconvenient, someone who had better things to do. . . . In fact, if you think he can handle it, tell him the brutal truth: Rescue shouldn't have to mean the painless dignity of a needle instead of the mass horror of a decompression chamber, but sometimes that's what it comes down to.

So Missy's ransom, Coakley's motivation, was my responsibility. I'd lost Missy. I'd pay to get her back. Also, I kept remembering Kevin's repeated insistence that Puppy Luv used local suppliers. I'd been assuming that Missy had come from the Midwest or Pennsylvania and that the hog-faced, fat-bellied Walter Simms had represented himself as legitimate and persuaded Lois Metzler to ship him a puppy. In fact, I'd been especially ready to believe that that's what had happened because of a story I'd recently heard from another local malamute breeder, Ginny Pawson. Seven or eight years ago, a pleasant-sounding woman in Iowa had talked Ginny into shipping her a bitch. A month later, though, Ginny spotted a malamute puppy in a pet shop and managed to get a look at the papers. The breeder shown on those papers was the same woman who'd just bought Ginny's bitch. Ginny paid twice the purchase price to buy back that puppy, but she considered herself fortunate. I'd been assuming that Lois Metzler's story was what Ginny's would have been without the intervention of coincidence. Also, of course, I'd been eager to keep the horror of puppy mills as geographically remote as possible.

Local dogs, Kevin had insisted. Not from Kansas, not from the airport. Local. Puppy Luv's ad: local breeders. By Diane Sweet's standards, Bill Coakley was a local breeder; by mine, he was a puppy mill operator who'd eliminated the broker and the pet shop by doing direct sales. Your Local Breeder. Janice Coakley and Diane Sweet were sisters. Bill

Coakley had been Diane Sweet's brother-in-law. Eight years ago, Ginny Pawson had been talked into shipping a bitch to Iowa. Eight years ago, almost all breeders were more innocent and trusting than they are now. I didn't know the birth date of Missy's dam, Icekist Sissy, but I was willing to bet that Lois Metzler hadn't sold her any eight years ago. I could find Icekist Sissy's age by consulting the malamute studbook, but it didn't really matter. The point was that Lois had sold Icekist Sissy recently enough to have been wary about shipping a puppy to an unknown buyer in a distant part of the country. Yes, it could have happened. But the chances were good that the buyer had been local. The word kept running through my head: *local, local.*

Almost on impulse, I called Gloria Loss, whose voice was thick with sleep. When she heard my name, the grogginess turned to guilt. "Did it snow? Jesus, I'm sorry. I didn't—"

"No, it didn't . . . Gloria, I've, uh, sort of been rethinking things."

"I'm really, really—"

"I've got another plan," I said. "There's something I want you to do, instead of the shoveling. It's more . . . it's sort of more connected to your original purpose. Only this could actually do some good. All it is, is . . . all I want you to do is to collect some information. It's just a matter of keeping your eyes and ears open. What I want you to do is apply for a job. If you don't get hired, that's it. We'll . . . I'll take it from there. But if you do, we have to agree right now that all you do is look and listen. You don't actually *do* anything. Okay? And you don't, uh, express your own opinions. You just give me the information, and then I worry about what to do about it. If anything."

Gloria startled me. "Is this a job at a pet shop?"

"Yes," I said. Then a little chagrined at having been second-guessed, I added, "More or less."

"I thought from the way you . . . the way you talked about them." Her voice took on that ghastly tone of adolescent admiration. "I could tell that you had strong feelings about them. You sounded really *committed.*"

I felt myself cringe. I'm so committed that I'd never even entered Puppy Luv until I'd practically been ordered there by someone who didn't even have malamutes; so deeply concerned that whenever I'd read Janice Coakley's offer of "any AKC breed," I'd never even bothered to call and inquire. When I'd seen Missy's papers, I'd conjured an image of the breeder, Walter Simms, against a convenient horizon of Iowa corn or Kansas wheat. The golden fields were so clear in my mind that, even now, I found it impossible to force Maine pines or Vermont maples to take root in the rich topsoil and raise the skyline. "What we can do is probably very limited," I said sternly, "but it's not going to work at all unless you do exactly what I tell you to do. And *nothing* else. Okay?"

The plan I outlined to Gloria was that she apply for the unenterprising Ronald's job at Your Local Breeder. She was to call Janice Coakley and explain that one of her neighbors, someone looking for a dog, had heard she was job-hunting, knew she liked animals, and mentioned the possible opening at Your Local Breeder. The scheme had several potential hitches, of course. One was that Ronald might have kept his job after all. Another was that I had no spare car to offer Gloria and was completely unwilling to encourage her to thumb her way back and forth to Westbrook. A final problem was that Gloria's appearance wasn't exactly what any employer looks for in a salesperson; even if Janice Coakley had made good on her threat to fire Ronald, and even if Gloria got an interview, Janice Coakley might still take one look and decide not to hire her. In fact, the repellent thought came to me, unbidden and unwelcome, that *dog* . . . well, never mind. I was raised in the cult of dog worship. Some names I won't speak in vain.

The transportation problem was easy to solve. When I presented it to Gloria, she said, "My mom's away for two weeks. She left yesterday. I can use the car." Gloria went on to explain: "She's in New Mexico on a personal journey."

A personal journey. A pilgrimage to meet her birth mother, right? Or reverse the roles: her first reunion with the child she'd given up at age sixteen. Or maybe a trip to the only clinic in the U.S. that even tried to treat her rare, painful, embarrassing, degenerative, and ultimately fatal disease. But the truth, it turned out, was a whole lot worse than I imagined. In fact, Gloria's mother had signed up and actually paid an incredible amount of money to spend two weeks alone in the desert with nothing but an ample supply of drinking water and one large plastic trash bag. Cambridge.

"I hope it's at least puncture proof," I said frivolously.

"What?"

"All those cacti? Never mind. Anyway, speaking of—Gloria, if you get an interview, it'd probably be a good idea not to look too, uh, Cambridge. The image they're after is probably more sort of . . ." I fished for words. "Not, uh, academic? Not ethnic. Sort of more all-American."

"Pigtails?"

"Yes! Great idea. Exactly. Unsophisticated. Anyway, we might not even get that far, so let's not worry about it yet, okay? But if it works out, all I want you to do is collect information. I want to know where their puppies come from, okay? And Janice Coakley, the woman who runs the place, told me she could get malamutes. If you can, I want you to find out where. And who the breeders are. The names of the breeders will be on the puppies' papers. There's a name I want you to look out for: Walter Simms. And who her suppliers are. But for now, just call her. Maybe that's as far as we'll get."

When I hung up, I felt guilty about that puncture-proof crack. I'm in no position to make fun of personal journeys that seem ridiculous to other people.

17

MY RESEARCH FOR THE Sally Brand article had revealed the startling fact that between sixty and seventy percent of the members of the Yakuza, Japan's Cosa Nostra, are *irezumi*. Stunned, aren't you? Or maybe your Japanese is a little rusty. *Ire-zumi* means "insertion of ink." The *irezumi* are those who bear what the Japanese consider to be an externalization of inner reality. Well, I guess Americans think the same thing. Just look how many guys wear their hearts on their sleeves. I wondered whether Enzio Guarini had a tattoo and, if so, what it depicted, but the inner reality of a jailed racketeer fell outside my experience. Clasped hands? A Mini-Uzi? For all I knew, though, Guarini had popped into Sally Brand's on his way to jail—after all, they were both in Rhode Island— and now bore on his back, chest, or upper arm the perfect likeness of his pet chihuahua, the devoted companion that at this very moment, right here in Massachusetts . . . Bonnie, my editor at *Dog's Life,* just can't resist a story about any dog who's pining away for anyone or anything. Just on the off chance, I made a note to ask Sally Brand.

So I was working, right? I mean, this *is* what writers do, you know. Being a writer is really wonderful. Most of your so-called work consists of kicking around a lot of sticky ideas until they glop onto one another, by which time you're low on dog food and people food. So you scribble something on paper, hit the keyboard, sprint to the post office, and eventually get paid to keep staying home with your dogs. Well, it's a great life.

To return to the gummy ideas, consider the possible adhesions: local dogs, personal journeys, inner realities, families, organizations, my happy profession, and my futile effort to transplant New England pines and maples to the rich, flat agricultural acreage of porcine Walter Simms, who was, for a start, an inner reality of mine, not someone I'd actually used my resources to pursue.

If I want to find out who's who in reputable dogdom, I know quite a few people to ask, and I can also consult the membership lists of the Alaskan Malamute Club of America and lots of other clubs I've simply had to join. AMCA and the other national breed clubs are highly selective in admitting members. The dog magazines, though, don't screen the breeders and kennels that advertise puppies, so their listings are no guarantee of reputability, but there are a lot of ads placed by the famous, the infamous, and the unknown.

Then there's the matter of disreputable dogdom, which you may be surprised to learn actually has what is in effect its own organization, namely, the United States Department of Agriculture, the branch of our government that licenses puppy mills and puppy brokers. Whoops, pardon the slip, Class A and Class B dealers. Class A dealers breed animals; Class B dealers breed and sell them. Or if you're a sci-fi fan,

maybe you aren't surprised. Parallel universes? You don't believe me? Write or call the USDA and ask for a copy of the
booklet *Animal Welfare: List of Licensed Dealers.* Yes, welfare.
Ha-ha. In fairness, though, I must point out that not every
USDA-licensed dealer is a puppy mill operator or broker. A
few dealers maintain rabbit and ferret farms. Some breed
kittens. A few have names that sound above reproach. Johns
Hopkins University, for instance, is a USDA-licensed Class A
dealer. So there's no stigma, really, is there? After all, Johns
Hopkins doesn't mass-produce puppies for pet shops. Well,
then, why the USDA license? Research, of course, including
research on laboratory animals. Rats and mice? Probably.
Also, I've heard, Alaskan malamutes. No stigma, huh?

Now that I've presented an unbiased account of USDA-
license holders, let me continue. I had the booklet. I just
hadn't bothered to see whether Walter Simms was listed. I
hadn't checked anything else either. I'd asked a couple of
local malamute breeders, and I'd stopped there. And my family resources? If I'd phoned my father, I'd have told you,
wouldn't I? Of course I would. I hadn't.

So I made a big pot of tea and settled down to work. Let
me summarize the results of my research. Walter Simms
didn't advertise Alaskan malamutes in *Dog's Life, Dog Fancy,*
or *DOGworld.* His name was absent from the listings of malamute breeders in the *Gazette* and the *Malamute Quarterly.* If he
advertised malamutes anywhere, he didn't include his name
in the ad. No one called Walter Simms belonged to the national breed club or to any of my local clubs, either.

In case Walter Simms belonged to some local kennel
club for which I lacked a membership list, I checked with the
Dog Breeders' Referral Service. You know about that? Ken-
nel-club-member breeders take turns having their phone
numbers listed in the paper and answering calls from people
about where to find Skye terriers, boxers, whippets, or what-

ever. February happened to be Ray Metcalf's month. You know Ray and Lynne? They raise Clumber spaniels. We train together. Anyway, Walter Simms wasn't listed, and Ray had never heard of him.

Then I made more tea and got out the USDA booklet. If you've ever consulted the damn thing, you'll remember that the Class A dealers appear in the front section of the booklet, the Class B dealers at the back, and that, in each section, the names are listed alphabetically within each state. Consequently, you can't just look under *Simms, Walter* to find out whether he's licensed and, if so, where he does business. No, if you want to be thorough, you start with the Class A dealers, and you check through Alabama, Arizona, Arkansas, and so forth for forty-one pages of single-space type with one dealer per line. Then you do the Class B dealers. They're easier: only thirteen pages. By then, you have a headache and a heartache. In an attempt to spare my eyes and my soul, I checked the A and B lists for the New England States first, but I didn't find Walter Simms. Then I turned back to the A dealers in Alabama and went through every single state. When I'd finished the A dealers, I did the B dealers. Walter Simms didn't have a USDA license. Neither, by the way, did Bill or Janice Coakley.

Finally, feeling something like one of Enzio Guarini's soldiers, I called the don of my family, namely, my father, who lives in Owls Head, Maine, where I grew up. In the dozen or so years since my mother died, though, Buck has transformed the place. My parents raised and trained golden retrievers. Marissa was also a dedicated gardener who labored over her perennial borders. The peonies have survived, and so have some lupins, but the only day lilies left are the orange ones she never really liked. Her beloved delphiniums vanished in a few years. Buck took her death very hard. What yanked him out of his despondency was his discovery of wolf dog hybrids, which, I am delighted to report, he has now quit breeding. The last litter (Clyde *ex* Millie) was whelped a while ago, and Buck refused to sell any of those pups or any of his adult wolf dogs, either. Also, he's built a ten-foot security fence around the once-red barn. In Marissa's day, the barn was a model kennel building—she paved the outdoor runs herself—and the inside has held up pretty well, but from the outside, the place now looks like a correctional facility for canines convicted of white-collar crimes.

But the great news isn't the increasing disrepair of the place, the permanent neglect of the garden, the appearance of the ten-foot fence, or the apparent cessation of wolf dog breeding. Buck hasn't actually sworn off wolves, at least not yet, but he has finally returned to the fold, which is to say that he not only worships his half-grown golden retriever puppy, Mandy, but has rediscovered dog shows, matches, and obedience trials. He never stopped attending them, but I'm sure he'd forgotten the thrill of entering. By the way, in case you ever spot him in the ring, let me warn you that he's not the trainer and handler Marissa was. She taught him a lot, though. Also, even before the current attention-training craze (*Watch me! Ready? Ready, ready? Watch me, watch me!*), Buck understood the principle that you get what you give. "A handler always ends up with the dog he deserves." Slogan of the Royal Air Force Dog Training School. When my father trains a dog, he's so overwhelmingly *present* that no matter where the dog turns his attention, there's Buck again.

"So," I said to my father, "how are you?"

He answered like the real dog person he is; he bragged about Mandy. "This is undoubtedly *the* most remarkable obedience prospect to set paw upon God's green earth in the last decade," he proclaimed.

I refrained from mentioning Vinnie.

Buck continued. "This little Mandy character is *the* most alert, curious, bright-eyed creature . . . never takes her eyes off my face. Did I tell you how she did at her first match?"

"First place in Pre-Novice. That's really wonderful. Another Winter Wonder," I blurted out. That's what everyone called my mother's dogs, Winter Wonders—they were, too—but the words brought Marissa back so vividly that my eyes watered. I shouldn't have spoken the phrase aloud, not to my father.

To my surprise, though, Buck seemed flattered. He thanked me. Then he kept on bragging about Mandy, who is, by the way, almost as perfect as Buck claims.

"Future *DOGworld*, huh?" I said.

Stranger around here? A *DOGworld* obedience award requires earning all three obedience titles within twelve months or earning a C.D., C.D.X., or U.D.—Utility Dog title —in three consecutive trials with a score of 195 or higher in each trial. 195? You're kidding. Where are you from, anyway? Neptune? Mars? Well, welcome to Sirius, the dog star. That's 195 out of a perfect 200.

"Bernie Brown better watch himself," Buck said happily.

Bernie Brown, in case you don't already know, is a top handler and a famous obedience instructor. Needless to say, Bernie Brown does not have malamutes. In fact, a quote from one of Bernie Brown's books is tacked to the bulletin board in my study: *"Malamutes make excellent pets, but I wouldn't want to train one."* What breed does Bernie Brown have? Take a wild guess.

To avoid undermining my father's self-confidence by offering an estimate of his chances against Bernie Brown, and also to get to the point of my call, I said, "So has Jim Chevigny seen her yet? Or Marian Duckworth?"

Jim and Marian are two of Buck's oldest friends. He has a lot of friends. These two happen to work at the AKC, and they don't sweep the floors there, either.

"As a matter of fact, Marian was at the club last week," Buck said. That's the Mid-Coast Obedience Club. I was astounded. To the best of my knowledge, Buck hadn't trained there since Marissa died. "Jaw dropped open when she saw this little lady work," he went on. "Dropped open and just hung like that. You'd've thought she was waiting for the dentist."

Mandy's heeling is impressive, of course. Well, damn it, she's a golden. What do you expect? But Marian Duckworth has seen lots of perfect heeling. What had astonished Marian had certainly been my father's sudden return to apparent normality.

"Well, maybe you could ask Marian something for me," I said. "Or Jim Chevigny. Or someone else. I need a favor."

Sympathy filled Buck's voice. "It's this X, isn't it?" he asked gently. That's the X in C.D.X., Companion Dog Excellent, Rowdy's next obedience title.

"NO!" I answered more sharply than I'd intended. I softened my tone. "We're working on it. We'll get there."

"Never be ashamed to ask for help, Holly," he said. "No one knows everything. We all have a lot to learn. Now, I, for example, have given a lot of thought to that last column of yours."

Buck almost never admits to reading my column, but I know he does because he invariably drops minor corrections into our conversations. As it turned out, though, the gist of his "thought" about the column was that I lacked the spirit of healthy competition that he and Marissa had worked so hard to instill. In the column, which was about non-AKC titles granted by national breed clubs, I'd mentioned an Alaskan malamute called Clifford. Clifford, who is owned by

Robin Haggard and Jim Kuehl, is, in fact, Am./Can. Ch. Poker Flats Ace of Spies, C.D., W.P.D., W.W.P.D., W.T.D., W.L.D. Translation? American and Canadian Champion, in other words, breed champion; Companion Dog; and Working Pack Dog, Working Weight Pull Dog, Working Team Dog, Working Lead Dog. The Working titles were what the column was about; they're granted by the Alaskan Malamute Club of America, not the AKC. Buck's complaint was that I hadn't put a single one of those Working titles on either of my dogs.

"Now take this Working Pack Dog title," Buck said. "If I understand this correctly, the requirement—"

"Buck, I have other things to worry about right now. I don't really need any help putting titles on my dogs. What I need is some information about a registration. I need to know what the AKC has on a malamute called, uh, Icekist Sissy."

"Well, Icekist," Buck said. "That's Lois Metzler."

"I know. She's the breeder, but what I want is the owner, anything about the owner, like an address, and also anything about changes of ownership. Also, have you ever heard of someone named Walter Simms?"

"Simms. Used to be a fellow up near Rangeley. English setters, he had. There was one called Ranger—"

Once Buck starts to describe a dog, you have to choose between cutting him off immediately or listening for the next hour. "That was Simpson," I said. "Harry Simpson. He died in a plane crash about ten years ago."

"Harry. That was it. Never heard about it." Buck sounded alarmed and grieved. "Damn shame. That dog, Ranger, was—"

But I was able to reassure him. "The dog wasn't with him," I said. "He was alone."

"Even so, the poor fellow," Buck said, as if to accuse me

of gross insensitivity. "Abandoned like that. One day Harry was there, the next day he was gone. An English setter isn't like a malamute, you know. This Ranger was—"

"Ranger was fine. I ran into Harry's widow five or six years ago, and she had Ranger with her, and he was fine. Anyway, this is someone totally different. Walter Simms."

"Never heard of him," Buck said. "What breed does he have?"

"Malamutes. Maybe some other breeds, too. Probably. I don't know. He isn't necessarily around here. He could be anywhere. See if you can find out, would you? It's Walter Simms, with two *m*'s." I paused to give Buck time to make a note of Simms's name. Buck wouldn't need to jot down Icekist Sissy's, of course. He wouldn't even need a reminder. Buck never forgets a dog's name. "Buck," I added, "this is important. Simms is the breeder shown on the papers of a malamute called Princess Melissa Sievers. I need to know about him."

"Puppy mills," Buck said. "*That's* what this is about. Puppy mills. AKC ought to blast those goddamned places off the face of the earth."

The American Kennel Club has no individual members. Its members are clubs, each of which has a delegate. My father is not an AKC delegate. Maybe he should be.

18

MAYBE YOU'LL REMEMBER THAT at the Shawsheen Valley show, when Betty Burley and I broke the news to Lois Metzler that her line had shown up on the pedigree of a pet shop dog, Lois turned pale and acted horrified. On Monday, though, the day after the show, Lois didn't call me for the information I'd promised her on Missy's pedigree, and by midday on Tuesday, I still hadn't heard from her. I'd been on the phone for most of the morning, of course. Maybe she'd tried to reach me. I was pretty sure that if Lois had actually had a heart attack or if she'd fallen into a state of nervous prostration, someone would have let me know. Could Lois be ashamed to call, afraid that I'd blame her for not screening her buyers? Or possibly she was sick after all, and I hadn't heard.

But when I reached Lois, she sounded healthy enough, which is to say, fit enough to have taken the initiative instead of waiting to hear from me. "Oh, yeah, I've been meaning to call you," she said rather vaguely and mildly, as if she'd been neglecting a promise to pass along the name of a wonderful new brand of coat conditioner. "But I can't talk now," she added. "I've got some people coming to look at a puppy. They're supposed to be here now. But they won't stay too long. Why don't you come out here in an hour or so?" She made it sound like a summons, not a question or an invitation.

I agreed, but hung up feeling resentful. Who was Lois to order me to drop everything and drive out to her place? We could have exchanged information over the phone. Furthermore, although it was Lois whose bitch, Icekist Sissy, had evidently ended up in a puppy mill, I was apparently more eager than Lois was to find Sissy and maybe even to reclaim her.

But I was eager, and I did drop everything. Lois's place, which I'd visited before, was north of Westbrook, but about the same distance from Cambridge, that is, a drive of forty-five minutes or so. The temperature had suddenly risen to the high thirties, and with the roads wet but free of ice, I made good time. Just as I arrived, a Volvo station wagon was pulling out of Lois's driveway; the people who'd been coming to look at a puppy had apparently arrived and were now leaving.

If you don't have malamutes, you'll probably assume that when I parked, got out of the Bronco, shut the door, and followed the concrete path to the front door of Lois Metzler's many-times-expanded and thus sprawling yellow split-level, I was greeted by an eardrum-puncturing chorus of barking, but I wasn't. As a watchdog, the Alaskan malamute is less useful than the average canary, which might sing or at least chirp or peep. When my doorbell rings, my dogs don't just ignore the signal, of course. Far from it. They instantly dash forth to welcome whatever friend, burglar, or rapist is calling

on us. Unless the visitor's arrival happens to coincide with
Rowdy and Kimi's dinner time, though, the only sound they
emit is the almost inaudible swish of two wagging tails.

In a kennel situation like Lois's, a big pack of malamutes will usually manage some token growling, but her dog
runs, I remembered, were located at the extreme end of her
back yard, nowhere near the house. If she'd had near neighbors, the distance would have made sense. Malamutes aren't
silent, of course, and, like all other dogs, they have fantastic
hearing. For instance, if you so much as *think* about feeding
them, they hear the whir of your mental wheels, and they
start roaring and wooing. But Lois's house had a pond on one
side, woods on the other, and an empty pasture across the
road. In any case, I reached the door unheralded, and even
when Lois opened it and led me through a small trophy-
laden den to her bright, cramped kitchen, there still wasn't a
dog to be heard or even smelled. I mean, a whole kennelful
out there in the backyard? And not one dog in the house? Yes,
acute self-inflicted auditory and olfactory deprivation. The
only sound in the house came from a radio tuned to a country
station.

Lois, though, looked reassuringly normal, and her
kitchen was outright supernormal, which is to say that almost every object that could possibly bear the image of an
Alaskan malamute did so. Lois herself bore only one: Smack
on the front of Lois's gigantic blue denim tent dress, an em-
broidered malamute happily rested his life-size head on the
generous cushion of her bosom. The selection of breed-
adorned garments in size Queen XXL Tall is probably quite
limited, and I wondered whether that enforced near-sterility
in personal adornment might explain the population explo-
sion in Lois's kitchen. On the walls hung two malamute post-
ers, a malamute calendar, and two framed needlepoint pictures of guess what. Malamute potholders and a malamute

dishtowel dangled from magnetized malamute hooks on the stove. On the front of the white refrigerator, additional malamute magnets held sheets of lined paper from malamute memo pads. A malamute apron hung on the back door, on the floor beneath which rested a malamute door mat. Yet another malamute grinned at me from the toaster cover, and the same dog also tried to disguise the identity of a box of tissues. Piled on a counter were malamute place mats, and malamute mugs and glasses drained in the sink. You think I'm done? Switch-plate covers, doorstops, a tote bag, candles, two candy dishes, and decals on every pane of every window. Oh, and the walls were plain white. I concluded that Alaskan malamute wallpaper didn't exist. Yet. But the demand is there, of course. It's definitely there. And, in case you think I'm making fun of Lois, let me point out that anyone who was sponsoring a contest among her own body parts to decide which one would win a tattoo of two Alaskan malamutes was not in a position to accuse other people of excessive breed loyalty. Okay?

"My God," I said, tucking my Alaskan malamute key ring into my shoulder bag, "where did you find all this?" I took off my parka to reveal my new yellow malamute sweatshirt. My question, by the way, was perfectly serious. If you have chows, cockers, goldens, shepherds, Yorkies, or some other really popular breed, or if your breed is considered highly decorative—Scotties, Dalmatians, and Labs—it's pretty easy to have a generic picture of your dog on practically any object you want. A Dalmatian shower curtain with matching towels and washcloths? Of course. But just try to find a Chinese crested shower curtain, a Border collie towel, or a malamute facecloth, never mind a whole set of coordinated bath accessories.

"I hunt around," Lois said, "but, of course, half of the

stuff I see, I won't buy. The malamutes look like Siberians or God knows what else. Coffee?"

I accepted the offer and took a seat at the table, which had a couple of places cleared for eating, but seemed mainly to serve as Lois's desk. Stacks of typed pages, newsletters, premiums lists for shows, and issues of dog magazines covered most of the surface.

"That's my contract right there," Lois said as she filled two mugs from a miraculously dog-free coffee maker. As I've mentioned, Lois grew up in Nashville, and you could hear her hometown in her speech, especially in the soft way she said *contract*. "You can see for yourself. If they decide to sell the dog, I've got first refusal. They need my permission to transfer ownership, and they need it to breed. It's a standard contract."

I glanced at it. Among other things, if the pup had a serious illness at the time of purchase or if the pup developed hip dysplasia within two years, you got a new dog or your money back. Standard? Yes, for an ethical breeder. According to any standard pet shop contract, of course, under absolutely no circumstances do you ever get your money back.

Lois gave me my coffee. I will not describe the containers from which I spooned sugar and poured heavy cream. Suffice it to say they both had tails. "The one that's involved is from He'll Have to Go and Family Tradition," I said.

"Jim and Hank," said Lois, heaving herself into a seat. "Funny name for a bitch, but, yeah, that's the one. I've been on this since yesterday morning. I've been too busy to do the follow-ups I should've been doing all along, so I've been getting caught up. But I'll tell you, this is a heavy price to pay for being busy, if you ask me." A thin layer of moisture coated Lois's blunt face. Her skin and eyes were tinged with gray.

"So you've already tracked down . . . ?"

"Well, I started with the summer before last, a year and a half ago, because I always screen my buyers, always, but that was the time I might've got taken, because I had a lot of dogs at the time, and I bred three litters that summer." Her little eyes scanned my face. "And if what you're thinking is that three litters is too many, you're wrong, because I'll tell you, those dogs are doing very, very well."

Lois went on to tell me about three dogs who'd already finished—finished their breed championships—and some others who had their first majors—major wins—and so forth and so on. The record was impressive, especially for such young dogs, all under two years old. I kept nodding and murmuring approval, but all the while I was thinking of Icekist Sissy. Ending up as a brood bitch in a puppy mill is no one's idea of "doing very, very well."

Before long, I got tired of listening. Also, of course, I was impatient to hear what Lois had discovered. "About Icekist Sissy," I said. "What did you find out?"

"Yuppie couple," she said. "They called. Ames, their name was. I told them to come see the puppies, and they did, and they seemed, I don't know, okay. They both did some computer stuff, so they were gone all day, but they had a fenced yard. And besides that, they'd already put up a kennel. So they sounded all right."

Lots of breeders, including Betty Burley, who's supercareful about buyers, share that strong bias in favor of any potential puppy buyer whose yard is fenced. I'm not so sure. What does a fenced yard really guarantee except the presence of a handy place to neglect the dog?

"They didn't know anything," Lois added, meaning, of course, anything about malamutes, "but they seemed all right. So I sold them a bitch from the third litter. *And* they signed a contract."

"And then?"

"And what I know now—I talked to him yesterday—is that they both lost their jobs, cutbacks, first her, then him. They were living in Acton, but the only job he could find was in Hartford, Connecticut, so they had to move, and they rented an apartment. And that's when they sold the puppy."

"Without calling you?"

"Well, according to him, they tried, and they couldn't reach me, but you can take that with a grain of salt. They put the contract in a file drawer and forgot about it, if you ask me, even though this was only maybe two months after they bought the puppy. So, anyway, they put an ad in one of these little freebie papers, and they sold her."

"To a guy named Walter Simms," I said confidently.

Lois corrected me. "Rinehart. Joe Rinehart."

"Oh," I said. The name sounded vaguely familiar, but I couldn't place it.

"He's supposed to live in Burlington—Massachusetts, not Vermont—and I must've called twenty times, but all I get's an answering machine."

Burlington is yet another jewel on Greater Boston's now-tarnished high-tech necklace, namely, Route 128.

"Did you get an address?"

"I've got it here somewhere," Lois said. While she shuffled through a pile of puppy contracts, notes, and bills, I fumed. Burlington was about a half hour from Lois's house. What was she doing just sitting here? *Selling puppies,* I thought.

"Here it is," Lois said, handing me a slip of paper.

Beneath the face of a happy-looking malamute, Lois had scrawled the name Joe Rinehart, a phone number, and an address: 84 Sherwood Lane, Burlington.

She reached for a white Trimline phone that sat on top of a stack of *Malamute Quarterly*s on the table. "I'll give him another try now." She dialed, listened, and handed me the phone. A recorded male voice gave the number Lois had dialed. It went on to issue an unfriendly invitation to leave a message. Lois took the phone from me and hung up. "I keep leaving messages," she said.

"So let's go! Let's just drive over there. You know, it's possible that this is a different bitch, isn't it? Lois, we could get there, and this one could be fine. You aren't a hundred percent positive that this is the one, are you?"

"Ninety-nine," Lois said, but her face was expressionless, and she made no move to get up. "I'm prepared to buy her back, you know. I've reconciled myself to that. And I have to keep reminding myself, I'm not the first person this has happened to."

"Then let's go!" I said again. "People don't always answer their phones. Sometimes they just leave their machines on because they don't feel like talking. Lois, someone could be there! I mean, for all we know . . ."

She shifted in her seat. I looked at her, but she avoided my gaze. "I can't now," she said. "I've got someone coming."

"To look at a puppy," I said coldly.

"Yes, as a matter of fact. These happen to be exceptional litters. I've had a lot of interest. These people are . . . Well, it's a show home, and I've got to . . ."

I reached into my shoulder bag, pulled out Missy's pedigree, slapped it on the table, pointed to the top half of the page, and ordered Lois to look at it. "This bitch of yours is only a year and a half old, and she's probably been bred at least twice by now. The chances are very good that she's sick and half starved, and you better believe that even if she's in okay physical shape, she's a mess otherwise, because no one's spoken a kind word to her since she landed in this hellhole, wherever it is."

"I'm prepared to buy her back." Lois's voice and gaze

were strong. Fat, thin, brawny, scrawny, old, young, whatever, anyone with Alaskan malamutes has a tough streak. "You're not a breeder, Holly. You don't understand. I'll pay twice the purchase price. I'll pay more if I have to. This is one of the worst things that could happen to any breeder."

That's when I lost my temper. I stood up, glared, and yelled, "Lois, *you* are not the one this has really happened to! The one who's really suffering is this poor half-grown puppy, Sissy, and if you gave a damn about her, you'd leave a note for these puppy buyers and come with me right now."

She curled her lips inward, ran her tongue over them, and said mulishly, "I can't."

"In that case," I said, "maybe we better get something straight. If I find this bitch, you *will* take her back?"

As you may or may not understand, my question was an insult. In effect, I'd asked her whether she was an ethical breeder, and in asking, I'd suggested that the answer might be no.

Lois certainly got the point. Her little eyes blazed. "I already told you, I'll buy her back."

"And if I show up here with her?"

Lois looked down at the pedigree. I followed her eyes as they moved over the dogs' names. Then, with no warning, she thrust out her fat right hand, grabbed the paper, crumpled it, and hurled it to the floor. Neither of us spoke. In the background, the radio played a Dolly Parton song. Sweat beaded on Lois's blunt nose.

"Look, Holly, you're trying to do the right thing, but you said it yourself. After where she's been? You don't know what she's picked up there. Brucellosis, parvo, parasites—it could be anything. I just can't have a sick dog carrying something in here. One litter out there's only five weeks." Lois was absolutely right. A five-week-old puppy is horribly vulnerable to infection. But she killed my sympathy. "Besides, I'm full up. I've got these two litters on the ground, and I did a repeat breeding of Jim and Hank, and she's due in a week. I'd like to take this bitch, but how can I, even if she's healthy? I don't have room."

Any breeder with no room to take back a single dog has no business breeding another litter, never mind two or three. Lois looked up and read my face.

"Holly, like I said, you're not a breeder. You don't understand. I can't have her here, but I will buy her back. I'll take responsibility for her. I'll pay whatever I have to, and I'll pay the vet bills and whatever it costs to board her. You've got my word on that."

Fair enough? More than fair. The dog, the vet bills, the boarding? Not cheap.

"Actually," I said, "I understand completely."

And I did. I finally understood that whether or not Lois gave a damn about her bitch, she'd pay anything whatsoever to buy back her own good name.

19

EVERY GOOD BOOK ON COMPETITIVE dog obedience warns you to avoid numerous handler errors that will cost you points and may even make you and your dog fail to qualify. Handler errors? You give a voice command and a hand signal when the rules for an exercise permit either one but not both. If your dog lags, he's thereby losing himself points, but if you slow your own pace to match his, you're committing a handler error, and any decent judge will dock you points for it. Some handler errors are deliberate, of course; you decide to lose points instead of failing outright. Most are inadvertent. One accidental handler error that even the kindest or most inattentive judge can't overlook consists of failing to get the dog into the ring at all because you got hopelessly lost on the way to the trial. The cure? A good map and a detailed local atlas.

According to the map of Burlington in my *Universal Atlas*

of Metropolitan Boston and Eastern Massachusetts, which I consulted before pulling out of Lois Metzler's driveway, Sherwood and Locksley lanes were dead-end streets that ran off Nottingham Road. Now, I'm not naive. In other words, as I entered Joe Rinehart's neighborhood, I didn't actually expect to be accosted by an evil sheriff or a band of merry men, but I'll admit that I did envision something of a theme tract of pseudo-thatched-roof cottages and fieldstone minicastles set amidst tall greenery at least somewhat suggestive of a forest. Even before I turned onto Sherwood, though, it was obvious that there had been profound confusion about just what movie was supposed to be shot on this set. These oddly assorted haciendas, glass-and-cedar lodges, New England colonials, Mediterranean villas, Victorian bijou mansions, and plain old big pretentious houses had a few things in common, though. Every single one had a triple garage, and they all looked as if they'd contain opulent bathrooms and ghastly lamps.

The white neo-Georgian house at 84 Sherwood Lane came as a relief in the sense that the movie was unmistakable. The tall white columns were angular instead of round, and there weren't any oaks, of course, but the only other thing missing was a soft-sculpture Scarlett O'Hara fanning herself on the porch. I pulled into the mile-wide driveway, killed the engine, looked in the rearview mirror, and addressed the dogs. "Behave yourselves, guys, because we're in a very exclusive neighborhood."

Even before I got out of the car, I guessed that no one was home. A couple of plastic-bagged daily newspapers lay on the wet brown lawn. Every curtain was closed. Every blind was drawn. I didn't hear a sound until I got to the front door, pushed the bell, and thus caused a set of chimes to inflict on my innocent ears a blessedly muffled version of—believe it or not—"That's *Amore.*" Movie confusion, right? The Italian palace down the street probably got "Dixie" by mistake.

I made my way around Tara to the backyard, but found no sign of a dog—no kennel, no tie-out stake, not even a telltale pile on the grass. I went up a short flight of steps to a small, open porch that sheltered the back door of the house. On the floor lay a big sisal mat that depicted neither a dog nor anything else. The back doorbell produced a muted, tuneless ring of the chimes. A slip of white paper sticking out of a sheet-metal milk box by the door turned out to be a bill from the dairy. The box contained exactly what the bill said it did, namely, two one-quart bottles of homogenized milk and a one-pint carton of half-and-half. The name on the bill was Joseph Rinehart. I concluded that I had the right address and that Rinehart's dairy wasn't bilking him. Samantha Spade. The date on the bill was yesterday's. With the professional writer's mistrust of the printed word, I lifted out one of the bottles, eased off the silver cap, and plunged in my finger. Before my hand reached my mouth, I smelled the off odor, and, instead of licking my finger, I wiped it on my jeans.

Then I went back to the Bronco and drove home to Cambridge. Oh, I made one stop on the way. Emma's Pizza, Huron Ave. Blame Rinehart's chimes. The song running through my head had finally reached my stomach.

My answering machine had two messages, one from Gloria Loss, the other from my father. Both said they would call back. When Rowdy and Kimi had gobbled down their dog-show samples of all-natural lamb and rice, they eyed the rapidly accumulating pile of pizza crusts on my plate. I untied the dogs and took a handful of pizza crust. What I had in mind was a quick play-training session to work on speeding up their downs, but before I'd said a word or given a signal, Rowdy's legs went out from under him, and about a second afterward, Kimi hit the floor, too. Great. They'd both mastered a whole new obedience exercise: the notorious Drop on Pizza.

The phone rang. Gloria was elated. "I decided I'd just show up there, not call, just show up, and—"

"You didn't have directions," I said sourly.

She was breathless with excitement. "I just went out there, and I thought I'd ask at a gas station or something, but I didn't even need to. I saw the sign, and I just walked in, and the most amazing thing happened. It was the most amazing thing I've ever seen in my entire life."

"Oh," I said.

"You know how there's this sort of front room? In the front, there's like a little shop. And the puppies are in the back."

"Yes."

"Well, I just sort of walked in, and there wasn't anyone there, and then I heard people's voices in the back, so I went there. And you won't believe it."

"Try me," I said.

"This guy?"

"Ronald?"

"Yes. He was . . . I guess he was supposed to be cleaning out the kennels, only I guess, while he was, they started having a fight."

"He and Janice Coakley?"

"Yes. And you won't believe it."

"I might," I said, "given the opportunity."

"The *second* I walked in, the exact *second,* he had this sort of little shovel in his hand, and it was, uh, full. And Mrs. Coakley . . . I guess she'd just said something to him? And he just hauled off and threw it at her!"

"The shovel?"

"No! The, uh, the . . . everything that was in it!" Gloria finally found the lost word. "Pooh! He threw this gigantic shovelful of dog pooh at her." Gloria caught her breath and added, "And he didn't miss, either."

"Janice Coakley must have been a little provoked," I said.

"Provoked! I thought she was going to kill him. All I could think of was this woman that was murdered at Puppy Luv, and I thought, wow, there's going to be a whole series of murders in pet shops, and here I am—"

"But she didn't." I stopped. "Or . . . My God, she didn't, did she?"

"No, of course not. What she did was . . . It was just like a movie. She pointed her finger at him and yelled, 'Ronald, you're fired!' It was totally amazing."

"I can imagine," I said.

"So then, honestly, it was incredible. He just left. He walked out. Just like that. And so I helped her get cleaned up, and she hired me."

"Just like that?"

"Not exactly. It took a while. She was sort of upset." Gloria's voice dropped. "She was crying. It was sort of awful. And then a couple of the puppies threw up, and that's basically how I got the job."

"How?"

"I asked her if she wanted me to clean up, you know, after the puppies."

"And she just hired you? Just like that?"

"Sort of. I'm, uh, kind of on probation. I'm temporary. But it was really amazing."

Lucky, yes. Amazing? Not really. Just the work of the great semantic palindrome. You know what a palindrome is, don't you? The same thing spelled backward and forward. *Madam, I'm Adam.* And *semantic* is meaning, right? So a semantic palindrome *means* the same thing both ways. Anyway, the

truly amazing thing is that, so far as I know, in the entire
English language, there's only one example. Yes, you got it.
Divine intervention.

After I'd reminded Gloria of her tasks at Your Local
Breeder, I called Buck, who always comes through when I
really need him, which is to say, whenever I'm desperate for
help that has anything to do with a dog. Icekist Sissy's story
started as I'd expected. The breeder was, of course, Lois
Metzler, and the first owners were Mark and Linda Ames,
Lois's yuppie couple. Sissy's ownership had been transferred
to Joseph Rinehart. The surprise was that he still owned her.

"Then he must have leased her," I said. "He leased her
to Walter Simms."

Have I lost you? According to Section 1 of the AKC rules
on registration, *breeder* means the person who owned the
puppy's dam when she was bred, unless the dam was leased
at the time of breeding. In that case, *breeder* means the lessee.

My father continued. "Princess Melissa Sievers. The
breeder is this Walter Simms you asked me about. The owner
is Edgar Sievers. No transfers, nothing else."

"And Simms? Did you find out . . . ?"

"I had a hard time prying this much out of her. They're
getting more close-mouthed down there than they used to
be."

"It's okay," I said. "This is a lot. It's a big help. Thank
you."

When I hung up, those tall New England trees finally
took root. The horizon narrowed and rose behind fat-bellied
Walter Simms. A breeder like Lois Metzler or Betty Burley
might well ship a bitch across the country to be bred to the
perfect stud. Leasing might be part of the arrangement. But
Rinehart? Although he lived nearby, Lois and I had never
heard of him; in the world of malamutes, he was no one. I
finally got it. People like that don't lease their bitches to

breeders halfway across the country. Why would they? If Rinehart had leased Icekist Sissy, then the lessee, the sow-faced, female-breasted Walter Simms, wasn't some puppy farmer in the Midwest. Toto was a Cairn, of course, not a malamute, but I spoke Dorothy's words aloud to Rowdy and Kimi: "Guys," I said sadly, "something tells me we're not in Kansas anymore."

20

IF YOU'VE EVER CONSULTED the USDA list of puppy mill operators and brokers—pardon me once again, Class A and B animal dealers—you'll understand why I rechecked the damned
thing. There are so many thousands of people listed that any
one name is easy to miss. Last time, I'd started with the
nearby states. If Walter Simms's name had been there, my
fresh eyes and brain should have caught it, but, then again,
I'd expected to find it, if at all, in the notorious Big Six—
Iowa, Nebraska, Kansas, Arkansas, Missouri, Oklahoma—or
possibly in Illinois, Indiana, Colorado, Minnesota, the Dako-
tas, or Pennsylvania, anywhere but right here in New England. This time, I began with Class A dealers in Massachusetts. Simms wasn't listed. Then I turned to Massachusetts B
dealers. Walter Simms wasn't one. But Rinehart was. Like a
lot of other dealers, Rinehart had a blank to the right of his
name, under the heading "Doing business as," but an ad-

dress is evidently mandatory. Rinehart's was 688 Boston Road, Westbrook. Westbrook? Coakley. Your Local Breeder. The same. How had I missed it the first time? By scanning five or six thousand *names*. By ignoring addresses.

NYNEX information for Westbrook had no listing for a Joseph Rinehart. In an effort to spare myself the drive out there, I also tried the Boston yellow pages under pet shops, kennels, kennel supplies, animal transportation, and a couple of other headings, but neither Rinehart's name nor the address in Westbrook appeared. I wanted to stay home with Rowdy and Kimi, and, to tell the truth, I didn't want to groom them, train, or even write about them. I was halfway through Donald McCaig's *Eminent Dogs, Dangerous Men: Searching Through Scotland for a Border Collie.* I ached to lie in bed with the book in my hands and my dogs at my feet.

Reluctant and tired, I went anyway. Enthusiastic and energetic, so did Rowdy and Kimi. Afraid to drive alone at night on dark country roads? Get a dog! Better yet, get two! The song says that you'll never walk alone. As it neglects to point out, you'll never drive alone, either. Anyway, dark it was. By the time we crossed into Westbrook, the night was so black that I had trouble shaking the perception that my headlights were failing. Whenever a car approached and I courteously switched from high to low beams, the road ahead looked like an unilluminated tunnel with invisible walls. Then, as soon as the car passed, I'd put on the high beams again, not just to see where I was going but to reassure myself that the headlamp bulbs hadn't suddenly burned out.

Before leaving home, I'd consulted the map of Westbrook in the *Universal Atlas* and discovered that Boston Road was the same one I'd followed to the turnoff for Bill Coakley's just the day before, the pretty-here, ugly-there route that the stagecoaches between Westbrook and Boston must have taken two hundred years ago. Now, though, the night hid yesterday's low hills and stretches of woods, and the tiny windows of the gentrified farms shone like penlight beams in an endless cavern. It seemed to take hours to reach that bright strip of fast-food joints. Except maybe in the eyes of the CEO of McDonald's, arches have never shone more golden than they did that night.

I'd eaten an entire Emma's pizza, minus a few bits of crust; when I slowed down and peered at the McDonald's on my right, I wasn't trying to decide between a Quarter Pounder and a fish sandwich. Rather, I was looking for a street number. The McDonald's had none, but its next-door neighbor, Cap Heaven—truck caps, what else?—was number 670. Rinehart was 688. His place must also be on the right, not far ahead.

But I didn't need a street number. I'd passed the place on my way to and from Bill Coakley's. Its signs were so big and obvious that I almost missed them. Both were fastened to the same two tall, thick posts at the edge of Boston Road. The top sign read:

RINEHART MOTOR MART
Quality Pre-Owned Cars and Trucks
Sales, Service, Parts

The sign beneath had slightly smaller lettering:

Rinehart Auto Body
Expert Collision Repairs
Refinishing Specialists
Down Draft Spray Oven—Modern Baking Facilities

Baking facilities? Don't ask me. Cars aren't my specialty. Dogs are. But even after I realized that spraying and baking must have something to do with repainting automobiles, that

bottom line felt sinister, especially the word *oven*. The situation made me vaguely sick. I'd found a dealer in used cars. A
body shop. That word ate at me, too. *Body*. I kept rereading
the sign, as if repeated exposure would somehow make everything fall into place, but the words became increasingly ab-
surd and ludicrous. *Collision. Parts.* And *Pre-Owned*. My God, I
thought, when you read between the lines, it's not about used
and smashed-up cars at all. It's about secondhand dogs. Parts
and service.

After a minute or two, I came to my senses, looked beyond the sign, and realized that Rinehart Motor Mart was
exactly what it claimed to be: an auto body shop and used-car
lot, and a big one at that. The sign by the road was like a goal
post at the end of a football field so jammed with late-model
cars, vans, and pickups that I almost expected college kids to
pile out for the postgame party. But the white numbers
chalked on the windshields spoiled the effect. A big orange
sticker on a Bronco much newer than mine advertised it as a
special of the week. Another special was a long black limo
that even I was able to identify as a Cadillac. In the brilliant,
theft-deterring floodlights, I also picked out a few of the cozy
house-on-wheels vans I always envy when I see them in the
parking lots at dog shows: a Ford Aerostar, a Plymouth Voy-
ager, and a luxurious Toyota something-or-other that looked
showroom new and big enough to sleep six or eight malamutes, one lean woman, and her ardent vet in perfect comfort and near privacy.

I'd pulled to the side of the road. Now I got out and
stared, and the anomaly hit me again: I wasn't here to gather
daydream material about the perfect dog-show van, which I
could, in any case, customize in my sleep with no help from
Joe Rinehart. I was here because I'd found Rinehart's name
and this address in the U.S. Department of Agriculture's list
of Class B animal dealers in Massachusetts. *This* address?

Beyond the car lot was an ugly brick two-story flat-roofed building that obviously housed the auto body shop and the car-lot business office, but I was too far away to see whether there was a number on the door. But this *had* to be the right address. The name *Rinehart*? Not far beyond Cap Haven, definitely number 670? After this was a Pizza Hut. Anything beyond the Pizza Hut would certainly have a number higher than 688.

I could have clambered over the metal barrier and crossed the car lot to check out the building, but the floodlights deterred me. I didn't intend to steal a car, even the enviable Toyota van, and I didn't intend to be mistaken for a car thief, either. I looked around and spotted a service road that ran between the car lot and the Pizza Hut. I returned to the Bronco, pulled ahead, and turned down the service road, a roughly paved drive that took me past the auto body shop and beyond the reach of the fast-food and car-lot floodlights. Once again, the low beam of my headlights was too faint to penetrate the darkness. I switched to high beam and made out a scrubby, rutted field ahead, a few rusted oil drums, a dented blue dumpster, and, around the rear of the auto body shop, a high fence of heavy wire mesh. I pulled into the field, turned the Bronco around, and was just starting to jolt back in the direction of Boston Road when a loud engine started up and a set of bright headlights came on in the fenced-in area behind Rinehart's. I stopped the car and watched. A section of the wire fence turned out to be a gate. Someone must have opened it while I was turning the Bronco around. An oversize dark van with no rear windows—a panel truck, I guess it's called—backed out. The driver's door opened. My high beams caught the tight jeans of a young guy with a good body. Parts and service, I thought. Truth in advertising. I watched him swagger to the gate, close it, and start back to the van. He wore a baseball cap on backward and a denim jacket with fleece around the collar. He moved well, and his face was old-movie handsome. He looked a little like a definitely oily James Dean—not that I have anything against greasy vitality, of course.

But he veered to face my headlights and broke the spell. Even over the Bronco's engine and the loud roar of the van, his voice was loud, metallic, and inexplicably enraged: "Get the fuck out of here!"

Alaskan malamutes love people, of course, but every once in a while, their hackles rise at a tone of voice, a gesture, or maybe only a faint scent of something evil in the air. In the back of my car, Rowdy stirred. I could almost hear the hair rise along his back. To my amazement, he gave a single deep, soft growl. Rowdy is the friendliest dog I've ever known. He absolutely never growls at strangers. Even so, I kept the windows closed, the doors locked, and my mouth shut. I tore down that rutted service road, headed home, and didn't look back. Rowdy hadn't been growling at a stranger. He'd been talking to me. He never speaks unless he has something to say. And he never lies.

21

When I arrived home, the burly, shrouded figure of Kevin Dennehy was pacing the sidewalk. Although Kevin considers our neighborhood his responsibility, he doesn't actually walk a beat along Appleton and Concord, and if he did, he wouldn't wear a torn sweatshirt and a pair of worn-out summer shorts over a set of Lifa polypropylene long underwear topped by a ragged scarf and a half-unraveled watchman's cap and bottomed by a pair of million-dollar athletic shoes. Should you happen to notice him there, don't be alarmed—he's just cooling down after a long run.

As I was opening the tailgate, Kevin lumbered up and said, "Dog training?"

"No, for once," I said. "I've been, uh, looking at vans. A Toyota van."

"Yeah? That'll cost you."

"It's used," I said.

"Toyota, huh?"

"Yes."

"You got something against Ford all of a sudden? Or Chevy?"

"Since you mention it," I said, "I do have something against General Motors. Crash tests with dogs. You want the details?"

Rowdy and Kimi bounded onto the driveway and began sniffing around to find out who'd done what where while we'd been gone.

"You know," Kevin told me solemnly, "if you're not careful, one of these days you're going to turn into one of these animal rights nuts."

"Kevin, you know something? In China, they eat live newborn baby mice. By their standards, you're an animal rights nut, okay?"

"You're in a great mood tonight." He kicked one of the rear tires of the Bronco. "Car trouble?"

"No, not really. It's, uh, the mileage is getting up, and the interior . . ."

"Yeah," Kevin agreed. "Smells like dogs."

I corrected him. "Only in wet weather."

"Hey, what'd they offer you for it? On a trade?"

"No one looked at it," I said. "Rowdy, get your nose out of that this minute! Leave it!"

"Well, watch out," Kevin said. "Before you let 'em look at it, get it cleaned up, and don't bring up the mileage. Some of these sharks . . . Hey, where you been looking?"

"In Westbrook," I said slowly and deliberately. "Rinehart Motor Mart. Joe Rinehart."

I was playing a hunch. Missy had come from Puppy Luv. Missy's dam, Icekist Sissy, belonged to Rinehart, who had evidently leased her to the breeder, Walter Simms. Rinehart was a USDA-licensed puppy broker. If Kevin had been going over the paperwork at Puppy Luv, he'd probably seen Rinehart's name. Kevin certainly wouldn't volunteer any information about Puppy Luv's sources of dogs, but if I dropped a name, he might show some response.

Some response? Kevin hollered, swore, apologized, and then turned cold. "What did I tell you, Holly? These aren't nice people."

I rested my back against the Bronco. "No one needed to tell me that. I knew it already. You're the one who just discovered it, I guess."

"Do you know who Rinehart *is?*"

"A guy who can't tell the difference between a dog and a used car," I said. "He's a USDA-licensed puppy broker. I even know where he lives. As a matter of fact, I was at his house today. He lives in Burlington."

"So you know everything there is to know about him, don't you?"

"Maybe," I said arrogantly. "Everything that counts. Except where he is now and what he's doing with—"

Kevin interrupted me. "You know who his wife was?"

"No," I said. "I didn't even know he had one."

"Maria Guarini," Kevin said. "Maria Guarini Rinehart. The late. Died of cancer a couple of years ago."

The frigid air suddenly penetrated my parka and gloves. "Guarini," I repeated flatly.

"Guarini. Enzio's son-in-law."

"Kevin, I'm freezing," I said. "Come inside."

"Hey, I'm all—"

"I don't care if you're sweaty! Come inside. Kevin, I'm not fooling around. Come in with me. You wanted to scare me, right? Okay, I'm scared. In fact, I'm scared off. I swear, I will never so much as set foot in Burlington again, all right? But you can't take off now."

If you ever share the confines of your kitchen with a large human male who's cooling down after a long-distance run, you may find yourself remembering, as I did, that dogs sweat principally through their tongues and the pads of their feet.

"Hey, I'm stinking up your kitchen," Kevin apologized. "Let me go—"

"No. I want to know what's going on. Sit down, would you?" When I'd settled him at the table with a cold Bud I said, "Kevin, I need to know what's going on. I'm not deep into this, and, believe me, Guarini's son-in-law? I'm a dog writer, okay? I don't know anything about people like that, and I'm not exactly eager to meet them. So don't turn paternal. I just need to know, uh, where I am. First of all, is Rinehart . . . Is he a sort of slim guy, early twenties, maybe? Good-looking in a kind of greasy way? Drives a dark van, and—"

"Where'd you run into *him*?" Kevin plunked the beer can onto the table and eyed me belligerently.

"Rinehart Motor Mart. So that's Joe Rinehart?"

"Naw," Kevin said. "Rinehart's a long drink of water, and he's probably pushing sixty. Sickly-looking guy, white hair with a lot of yellow in it, combed straight back and kind of, what do you call it, crimped. You know, with these rows of waves across the top like he's been to the hairdresser."

"Well, that's definitely not . . . Kevin, tell me something. If Rinehart . . . Kevin, just how involved is the mob in this stuff? I mean, is this puppy mill and pet shop business one of their, uh, sidelines?"

Kevin flexed his shoulder muscles, gave a sly little grin, and said, "Course, this is supposed to be a deep dark secret, but the next time there's an opening for special agent in charge of the organized crime squad, you better keep your ears open, 'cause you're going to hear the phone ringing next door, and then, if I'm not home, you're going to hear them beating down my door."

"Okay! Yeah, I guess the FBI or whatever doesn't exactly delegate this stuff, but, Kevin, you do have some idea of what is and isn't run by the mob. And you obviously have some idea of who these people are. So do they . . . ? I mean, could it be some kind of money-laundering thing? Rinehart is a puppy broker, and if Guarini . . ."

Kevin shook his head. "There's nothing these people won't touch, but Joe and Enzio aren't pals. What you hear is that when Joe married Maria, he was expecting Enzio to open up his arms and welcome him into the bosom of the family." Kevin gave what I took to be a Don Corleone locked-jaw grin, embraced the air in front of him, and swooped it to his chest. "Only Enzio's no dummy, and he decided Joe was marrying his daughter for her family connections. It might've worked out all right if Joe and Maria had given Enzio some grandchildren." Kevin paused.

"But they didn't," I said.

"No kids, and according to Enzio, it's on account of Joe, and then when his daughter dies, that's on account of Joe, too." He tilted his head back and emptied the can of Bud.

As I got him another, I said the obvious, namely, "That's totally senseless."

"Tell that to Enzio," Kevin said. "Take that back. *Don't* tell that to Enzio."

"So Joe doesn't work for Enzio?"

"Like I said, they aren't pals. But, of course, Enzio's had a little trouble in his life lately. Maybe Joe doesn't work for Enzio. Maybe he doesn't exactly *not* work for him, either. To a guy like Enzio? So maybe Joe was a bastard, but he was Maria's husband, and . . . These Italians are like that." In case you happen to be a militant member of the Cambridge Com-

mittee on Political Correctness, let me implore you not to get
Kevin fired. For one thing, Kevin's best friend, Mickey De
Franco, is also his cousin, and, like most other Irish people in
Greater Boston, Kevin is part Italian himself.

"So this guy I saw tonight," I said. "When I asked you if
that was Rinehart, you didn't just say no. You said something
like, 'That's not *Rinehart.*' So it sounded like . . . I mean, I
had this feeling that what you meant was that he was someone else. Not just not Rinehart?"

Kevin stood up and stretched. "He's a tough little nobody."

"Rowdy didn't think so," I said. "When . . . I'd turned
my car around, and . . . really, I didn't do *anything* to him.
He'd pulled his van out of the back lot at Rinehart's, and he
got out to shut the gate, and I saw him in the headlights. And
so he started swearing and yelling at me to get out of there.
And Rowdy growled."

The sound of his own name would rouse Rowdy from a
coma. He'd been stretched out on the floor in a deep doze,
but now he stood up, shook himself, and padded over to me.
Have I ever mentioned what a beautiful dog he is? As maybe
you've noticed, he looks quite a lot like a famous malamute
named Inuit's Wooly Bully, who was called Floyd. Rowdy's a
pretty boy, too. I told him so.

"Probably a dog somewhere around," Kevin said. He
had a point. That van could have been packed with puppies.
When Rowdy and Kimi are in *their* car, they'll warn other
dogs away. If they spot a particularly dominant-looking canine, they'll roar, yell, and claw at the windows.

"I didn't see one," I said, "and if there's a dog around, I
notice. Besides, I could tell. Maybe you won't believe it, but
it's true. Rowdy didn't like the sound of this guy's voice."

Kevin's big face crinkled up, and he said, "Oh, yeah?"

"Yes," I said. "So what's his name?"

"Simms," Kevin said. "He's Rinehart's delivery boy. He's the guy who brought the puppies to Diane Sweet. Walt Simms. Hey, Holly, like I told you, local dogs."

Rowdy strolled to his water dish. He drank with loud splashes. The refrigerator hummed. Kimi yipped softly in her sleep. To hide my face from Kevin, I got up, filled the kettle, and put it on to heat.

"Oh," I said, smiling. Smiling? You bet. Kevin would arrest Walter Simms for the murder of Diane Sweet; Simms's dogs would somehow be confiscated; we'd get Icekist Sissy back; and we'd rescue the others, too. "Well, Kevin, if this guy was there that night, then obviously—"

"His story's, uh . . . his story checks out."

"He admits he was there?"

"Oh, yeah."

"And?"

Kevin's smile was wry. "I'll tell you something." Kevin's eyes have a wonderful clarity. They locked on mine. "You hear the craziest things in this job. Amazing things. And every time I think I've heard it all, then I hear something else."

"What did you hear this time?"

"Well, Sunday night, Monday morning, we figured what we were dealing with here was a rape and robbery."

"You didn't tell me that," I said. "My God. That really is awful. Now I *am* sorry for her." And I was, too. Yeah, I know. Murder didn't elicit all that much sympathy, but rape did. I'm not trying to justify my feelings, you know. I'm just telling you what they were. "Kevin, what the hell are you smiling about? You know, I have read and heard a lot about how the police, at least male cops, don't take this seriously, but I never, ever thought that *you*—"

"It wasn't rape," Kevin said.

I was furious. "Oh," I said, "I suppose she had on black

lace underwear, so you guys decided—Kevin, I can hardly believe this. If anybody had asked me, I would have said that more than almost *any* other cop, including women, you would be—"

"Hey, hey." Kevin raised both palms to stave off a tirade. "It all checks out. They had a regular thing going, him and Diane. Whenever Simms brought an order of puppies, uh, let's say the puppies weren't the only thing he delivered."

"You're joking. How do you know that? I suppose that's what Simms said, right?"

Kevin patted his giant hands on his even more giant thighs and made clucking noises to Rowdy, who happily went to him. "This night business hit me right from the beginning. You have to ask yourself, why would she stay there late, washing dogs? Why not wait till morning? Why not get someone else to do it? Yeah, Diane did a lot of work, but she ran the place, and she could've got one of these kids who work there to wash and brush the puppies. Only she didn't. But the main thing is, all of them knew about it."

"How could they know? I mean, they might have wondered or something, but . . ."

"One of these kids, Patty, her name is, nice kid, one time, back in December, she gets home from work and a couple of hours later, she can't find her wallet, and all her money's in it, driver's license, and she's going out. So she thinks maybe she left the thing at work, it fell out of her pocketbook, so she goes back to Puppy Luv."

"And?"

"And when she gets there—this is at the back of the store—she sees this guy Simms's van, so she figures Diane is still there, so she knocks and whatever, and then when nobody comes to the door, she lets herself in. And back there, there's this room where they wash the dogs, and that's where they keep the coffee pot, take their breaks, hang their coats, that kind of thing. And that's where this kid, Patty, keeps her pocketbook. Only she never gets that far, because when she opens the back door, she sees that the door to this dog washing room is half open."

"Grooming area," I said. "And?"

Sex embarrasses Kevin. His coloring is totally Irish, very fair, and when that Irish color rushes to his face, he turns scarlet. He looked at the floor and said quickly, "And there they were, going at it."

"On the grooming table?" I asked. It seemed like the logical place.

But Kevin gazed upward, smiled, shook his head, and finally said, "They've got a funny kind of bathtub there, for washing dogs. Not down low, like a regular tub. Up high, sort of waist high, set in the wall."

"They're always like that," I explained. "So you don't strain your back leaning over."

"Well, I don't know if that's why they were in it," Kevin said, "but that's where she says they were. Bubbles and all. In a dog bathtub. Like I said, this is a crazy job."

"They probably weren't too pleased when Patty, uh . . . or . . . ?"

"According to her, they didn't see her, never knew she was there. She just took one look and snuck out. And, uh, some of what Simms has to say confirms the whole story. And there's, uh, material evidence to support it."

"What kind?"

I could almost hear the grind as Kevin shifted to professional gear. "Her, uh, birth control device," Kevin said stiffly. "Knows what she used, where she kept it, what she kept it in. He said she was wearing it. She was. And the, uh, case was where he said it was."

"That does sound . . . yeah, I agree."

"And the rest of Simms's story checks out. He left his

last place at around ten to nine, and he got to Cambridge, to Puppy Luv, around nine-thirty. The stop before was Diane's sister's place, this one you see the ads for, Your Local Breeder."

"I've heard of it," I said.

"And at around ten after ten, the sister, Janice, calls Diane, and Diane tells her that Simms has already left. And then Simms has this sister, Cheryl, he lives with, and Cheryl swears he got home around quarter of eleven, and that fits."

"Does it? Where does he live?" I asked casually. I hate a sneak, but what choice did I have?

"None of your business."

"Near Rinehart," I guessed. "His business." I corrected myself. "Businesses. Plural. Westbrook. Then that *is* where Puppy Luv gets its dogs. From Rinehart. Believe me, from now on, I stay far away from him, okay? The whole idea of Guarini scares me. I don't want anything to do with those people. I just want to know. You've seen the paperwork at Puppy Luv. Just tell me. That *is* where the dogs come from?"

Kevin nodded, hesitated, and said with no expression in his voice or on his face, "Rinehart. Rinehart Pet Mart."

"Christ."

"Yeah, like they were cars. I wasn't going to tell you that."

"But you did," I said. "Hey, Kevin, I'm really sorry I yelled at you about the, uh, rape business. I was wrong. I mean, actually, I was right to begin with. About you. What I said tonight was unfair. I am really sorry."

"Hey, forget it."

"Thank you," I said. "So tell me. If this kid Patty knew about Diane and Simms, and all the other people who worked there knew about it . . . ?"

Kevin smiled. "Yeah. Numero uno. John Sweet. The hubby. Home watching TV. No phone calls, no visitors, no nothing. First at the scene. Cannot wait to get us out of there so he can open up shop."

"So the question really is whether Diane's husband knew about Simms. Could Patty or someone have told him?"

"Not a chance." Kevin shook his head. "At least in my opinion, not a chance. And he didn't spend a lot of time there. Yeah, it's possible he overheard someone saying something, or maybe he just got suspicious."

"Maybe just the way you did," I said. "Maybe he wondered about why she was staying so late to wash the puppies when she could've gotten someone else to do it in the morning. Or maybe . . . Kevin, you found material evidence. Maybe John Sweet found something, too." I hate to embarrass Kevin, but I asked, anyway. "Kevin, where did she keep her diaphragm?"

But Kevin didn't even turn pink. "Like I told you before, she did all the work. Very systematic. Businesswoman type."

I interrupted. "Well, where?"

"In a manila folder in a filing cabinet in her office," he said. "Right where it belonged. Alphabetical order. Under D." A look of wonder filled Kevin's broad face. Imagine a double-size, red-haired Irish-American Jean-Paul Sartre confronting a raw sense of *being*. "Like I keep saying, Holly, in this job, you wait long enough, you run across everything."

22

When Steve arrived at midnight on Tuesday, I was asleep. He let himself in. At breakfast on Wednesday morning, I thought about telling him what was going on, but decided against it. Dragging him to a pet shop had been okay, but hauling him into this mess of puppy mills and brokers? Those bastards couldn't operate without shady veterinarians to certify the health of sick puppies they've never even seen. I wanted to keep Steve completely away, totally protected.

As soon as Steve left, I called Bill Coakley and offered him five hundred dollars in cash for Missy's return. The amount—roughly four hundred and ninety dollars more than I could afford—was probably a hundred dollars less than Edgar Sievers had paid for her at Puppy Luv. Now that Missy was no longer a cute little baby, though, her market value as a pet had probably plummeted to one or two hundred dollars, assuming that someone would buy her at all.

But what was Missy worth as a brood bitch? She was eight months old, due to come in season any day now. A puppy mill operator would probably consider her a better deal now than she would have been four or five months ago because she could be bred almost immediately. He'd be spared the expense of keeping a puppy bitch alive during those useless months before her first heat. *He?* Or possibly *she?* Did Janice Coakley actually breed any of those puppies she claimed were all hers? I was relying on Gloria Loss to find out. But Janice Coakley wasn't the only Westbrook connection. Bill Coakley, her ex-husband, was pretty close to Your Local Breeder, and Rinehart's dual dealership was within walking distance of Bill Coakley's. On Sunday evening, shortly before Diane Sweet's murder, Walter Simms, who worked for Rinehart, had made a delivery to Janice Coakley at Your Local Breeder and had then driven to Puppy Luv, where he'd made his usual double delivery to Diane, Janice's sister. Well, so what? The valentine in Diane Sweet's window? Love is a warm puppy. Also, it was none of my business what consenting adults chose to do with one another in the privacy of their own grooming areas.

So, as I've suggested, the network of relationships involving Janice Coakley, Bill Coakley, Joe Rinehart, Diane Sweet, and Walter Simms wouldn't have concerned or worried me if these people had dealt only with one another and with inanimate objects. If Rinehart had brokered nothing other than used cars? If Janice, Bill, and Diane had been foisting off automotive lemons on the ignorant public? If so, Walter Simms and Diane Sweet would've ended up in the back seat of an old Chevrolet—or possibly a car wash—and I wouldn't have cared at all. But now that I'd been forced to relocate Walter Simms to my own turf? Now that all roads led to Westbrook? It seemed to me that if Bill Coakley hadn't sold Missy to his ex-wife, he'd probably sent Missy to join her mother, Icekist Sissy.

How much had Missy been worth to Janice Coakley or Rinehart or Simms? Purebred dog fancy is my home, but I live above ground; I was a stranger in this underworld. I'd heard, read, and even written about it, of course. I knew, among other things, that in this underworld, both AKC papers and purebred dogs were sold at auction—and not necessarily attached to one another, either. In purebred hell, Missy could even end up as an AKC-registered Siberian husky and the dam of dozens of AKC-registered pet shop Siberians. Am I exaggerating? A man named Bob Baker once registered a nonexistent litter of Labrador retrievers with the AKC. Baker didn't do it as a joke. He works for the Humane Society of the United States, and he did it to dramatize the point that AKC papers guarantee absolutely nothing. So, you see, people like Bob Baker had charted the slimy routes through this subterranean muck, but I'd done no more than study their maps. I was feeling my way around. My hands were dirty. I felt sick about the five hundred dollars I'd offered Bill Coakley, scared that the bribe was laughably inadequate, nauseated by this whole *business* of buying and selling dogs as commodities, angry at the AKC for accepting registration fees from puppy mills, and, most of all, disgusted with myself for having lost Missy.

I was slumped in a chair at my kitchen table mulling over these sad matters when Kimi suddenly trotted in from the bedroom, spotted a Nylabone on the floor, clamped it between her teeth, raised her head, and began a private game of releasing and catching the toy. She'd open her big jaws until the Nylabone just barely began to drop from her mouth, then she'd seize it, loosen her grip, and once again snap the toy between her teeth. The click of her teeth on the artificial bone, the slight ripple of her neck and shoulder muscles, the glamourous glint of her thick coat—Kimi and her playful joy were unimaginably lovely. She does not foresee her future or any other beyond her next meal. She is a Zen master, intensely here and now. She restores my soul.

Thus renewed, I called Jane M. Appleyard, who . . . Well, this isn't a diversion. You know what a battle-ax is? Yes, of course, a powerful weapon of war. Bear in mind, by the way, that I'm not the one who decided to call Jane M. Appleyard a weapon of war. The term was Bill Coakley's, and when he bitched about "the battle-ax from the Humane," I immediately knew that he meant Mrs. Appleyard, a breeder of golden retrievers and a vigorous force in the Eleanor J. Colley Humane Society, which is located two towns away from Westbrook. Mrs. Appleyard runs the society because such was the wish of its eponymous benefactor, a dear friend of Mrs. Appleyard's. Mrs. Colley, whom I knew slightly, was a strong-minded Radcliffe graduate who got ticked because her alma mater wasn't lobbying Harvard to grant tenure to women and who left most of her money to dogs on the grounds that Labrador retrievers had done more to advance the cause of women than Radcliffe ever would. I've shown under her son, Wilfred Colley, who judges in Open and Utility. He's a good judge, tough but fair. Just like his mother, I guess.

But back to Mrs. Appleyard, who is what purebred dogdom calls "a very typey animal." She's the quintessence of who she is—Bryn Mawr '37, golden retrievers, white linen, man-tailored khaki, practical shoes, and, of late, an ebony cane—and all of her parts fit together perfectly. Five feet seven is tall for a woman of her generation, and Jane Appleyard has not permitted age to reduce her by so much as an inch. Her large frame supports a head shaped almost exactly like a football but covered on top with silver hair hacked short by a hand that must wield a pair of grooming shears, a hand that is most certainly her own.

When she answers the phone, you can practically see her in her rich, full, low-pitched, but rather booming voice. She never bothers to say hello, but firmly and cheerfully announces, "Mrs. Harold Appleyard," as if she could possibly be anyone else. Today, as usual, a dog barked in the background. "Daisy, that will *do!*" Mrs. Appleyard commanded, then said, evidently to me, "Well, is someone there? I don't have all day. Speak *up!*"

"Mrs. Appleyard, this is Holly Winter," I said.

"Holly Winter! I was thinking about your mother just the other day. You know, dear, everyone remembers her."

I said that I did, too. Then I got right to the point. "I wondered if you could help with something. This has to do with, uh, rescue. I'm trying to find a man named Walter Simms. I wondered if you'd ever heard of him?"

Mrs. Appleyard cleared her throat. "I have indeed," she said. "I've even been out there, but the two of them won't let me back on the property, and the fact is, it's an extremely frustrating situation. We find this *all* the time. We know who these people are, we have a very good idea of what's going on, and there's not a *thing* we can do!"

"Could you tell me . . . it's his sister he lives with?"

"Cheryl. Walter is perfectly compos mentis, you know, but poor Cheryl simply isn't all there. It's a terrible story. The house . . . Well, you can literally smell it from the road. The mother died five or six years ago, and that's when things went from bad to worse."

"This is in . . . ?"

"Afton." Mrs. Appleyard's *a* was broad. "It isn't really in our territory," she added, meaning the Eleanor J. Colley Humane Society's, "but it doesn't really have anyone else, either."

"Afton's somewhere near Westbrook? West?"

"Northwest. Not too far."

"And the Simmses?"

"Well, from what I can put together, both of the parents drank." I could hear the creak of a wicker chair as Mrs. Appleyard prepared to settle in for a long story. "But things didn't go completely to pieces until the mother died. Walter would have been seventeen or so. Cheryl's about two years his junior. And then, let's say approximately two years ago, the father took off. The family had had, oh, I suppose they called it a farm, but that's a glorified term for it. And then, at some point, before the mother died, they got talked into one of these broiler businesses. A chicken farm. Some charlatan sold Simms on a get-rich-quick scheme, got him to erect one of these ghastly tin chicken-ranch affairs. Hideous thing. Absolutely enormous. What's left of it is still there. Well, *that* little enterprise didn't last very long."

"Is that where the dogs are? In this, uh, chicken coop?"

"A few of them, I assume, on the first floor. I can't imagine that there's anything upstairs. Most of the roof's gone. I never got close enough to get a look. Cheryl stood right there on the porch of the house with a shotgun in her hand and ordered me off the property."

"My God," I said. "When was this?"

"Two or three months ago. Three. The beginning of December, I believe it was. It seems that everyone in Afton knew what was going on, but it's a dreadful little place, really, appalling schools and a tremendous sense that a man's home is his castle, what one's neighbor does to his dogs and his children is strictly his own business and all that sort of rot."

"So people know, but—"

"Well, the primary concern is for Cheryl," Mrs. Appleyard said crisply. "And the authorities *are* aware of her, and I don't know how many social service agencies have tried to get involved and do something. That's how I happen to be familiar with the situation, because one of the social workers *finally* had the good sense to get in touch with us about the dogs. But now, well, it seems that concern lessened somewhat after the father was out of the picture. There'd been some suspicions about *just* what was going on there when he was around."

"Abuse of some kind?"

"Neglect, at best," said Mrs. Appleyard. "What else doesn't bear contemplation. But then the father packed up his bags and took off, and it was about the same time that Cheryl finished school. So, after that, there was a bit of out-of-sight-out-of-mind operating, and, besides, the father was the focus of the most extreme concern, and that little problem seemed to have cleared itself up nicely. And this Walter, the brother, is obviously a bad hat, but he seems prepared to provide for her, at least in the minimal sense that she's getting enough to eat and has a roof of some sort over her head. I wish the same could be said for the dogs."

"Has anyone filed any complaints? Has there been any kind of legal—"

Before I could finish, Mrs. Appleyard huffed indignantly. "In brief, we are in a perfect pickle! You can smell the place from the road, and I've heard I don't know how many second-hand stories about the numbers of dogs there, but I cannot get a firsthand complaint, and it's impossible to show probable cause because we cannot get onto the property! I am certainly not setting foot there again, not all alone, I promise you."

"But at least people are aware of it now," I said. "I guess that's a start. I'm concerned because they seem to have malamutes, or Walter does. I got involved because of a rescue dog that originally came from a pet shop. Puppy Luv. I saw the papers. Simms was the breeder. At first, I assumed he must be in Missouri or somewhere, some obvious place like that."

"The whole puppy mill industry is undergoing an adaptive metamorphosis, if you will," said Mrs. Appleyard. "Negative publicity about out-of-state puppies? Then adapt! Raise them locally, under precisely the same conditions, of course. Vermont has a terrible problem now. And New Hampshire. But the pet shops are still bringing in puppies from out of state, of course. And I wish we could assume that the puppy mills are the only source, but there have always been rumors about breeders who sell to these pet shops. They aren't supposed to, and they hope no one finds out, but it's been known to happen."

"You know," I said reluctantly, "I've heard those rumors, but I honestly find that hard to believe, except in really rare cases."

"Oh, admittedly, it's rare, but there are rumors now and again. I heard it just the other day, as a matter of fact, about one of your malamute breeders. This is someone I won't stoop to name, because I won't stoop to gossip, but this is a very well-known local breeder, a reputable breeder, except that what people have been saying for a while is that she breeds too many litters, from what one hears."

"People are always saying that," I pointed out. "Breeders always think that other people are overbreeding. But they're not doing it themselves, naturally. What *they're* doing is making an important contribution to improving the breed." Mrs. Appleyard actually guffawed. She does that. I went on. "But, um, maybe I shouldn't say this, but if the person you heard this about is Lois Metzler, it's a misunderstanding." It wasn't a wild guess. There aren't all that many well-known local malamute breeders; Lois Metzler bred at least twice as many puppies as any of the others; and everyone was, in fact, always saying that she bred way too many litters.

"A name never passed my lips," said Mrs. Appleyard.

"Lois Metzler breeds a lot more dogs than I think she should or you think she should, but I'm positive that she would never sell to a pet shop. Never. So if you hear that rumor again . . ."

"I'll let it go in one ear and out the other," Mrs. Appleyard said, thus, to my mind at least, confirming my guess that Lois Metzler had actually been the breeder in question. Then she changed the subject. "I heard that one of those animal rights lunatics released one of your dogs," she said.

"Not exactly," I said. "I happened to . . . actually, don't mention it to people, but I ended up meeting her. We had a long talk. We worked things out. She didn't really understand what she was doing."

"A dog loose indoors at a show! This was your male?"

"Yes. But nothing happened."

"If you don't mind my saying so, Holly, you're taking it much too lightly. Think of the consequences! If he'd gotten himself in a fight?"

"This person, the young woman who did it, is . . . I felt so sorry for her, and she really won't ever do it again. She's very young and sort of lost. She was basically led astray by bad companions. She really was."

"And what makes you assume that her companions have suddenly changed?"

"Well, for a start, I guess because I've become one of them."

"These animal rights people are dangerous," Mrs. Appleyard boomed. "They're convinced that the end justifies the means. They'll say whatever they think is convenient at the moment, but when it comes down to what they do, they'll stop at nothing. Absolutely nothing. Don't trust that young woman, Holly! Don't trust her!"

23

A QUICK TRIP TO THE phone book shelves of the Cambridge Public Library gave me Walter Simms's address—or what there was to it: Old County Lane, Afton. Back home again, I set to work preparing to present myself to the Simmses as a purveyor of a line of flea control products. By now I'd had enough of masquerading as a puppy buyer, and I wasn't sure that Simms and his sister did direct sales, anyway. The role of social worker or humane society representative would have been plausible, of course, but my good bullet-proof vest was at the cleaner's, and the spare isn't fit to wear in public. The sales rep of a dog chow company would have been worth a try, I guess, but I picked flea control products because I wanted something that would assuredly be of no great interest to a puppy mill operator. On second thought, maybe dog food would have done as well.

A battered storage cabinet in the basement yielded two

pump spray bottles of flea and tick killer, a canister of powder, a bottle of insecticidal shampoo, another of kennel and
yard spray, and two unopened packages containing flea and
tick collars, virtually the full line of a company called Flee-B-
Gon that may well have Flee-B-Gon out of business by now.
Its products are—or were—perfectly natural, organic, gentle,
and useless, as I'd discovered the previous August when every
flea in Cambridge seemed to have landed on my two dogs.
Steve had warned me that vitamin E and coconut oil would
be ineffective against the megainfestation, but he'd also assured me that they were harmless. If Walter or Cheryl
Simms took me up on the offer of a free sample—assuming I
got that far—at least the dogs wouldn't end up in worse
shape than they already were.

Back upstairs, I ran a damp sponge over the Flee-B-Gon
containers, and when they looked practically new, I packed
them neatly into a briefcase that ordinarily held nothing except loathsome memories of a job I once held in a place
suffering from what I believe is called "sick-building syn-
drome," which is to say that no dogs were allowed.

I didn't bother changing into anything special. I wasn't
sure what a Flee-B-Gon rep looked like, and I was willing to
bet that Walter and Cheryl Simms weren't experts on pest-
control couture, either. Besides, the thermometer outside my
kitchen window read forty-one, and what should have been
falling as snow was pelting down as premature spring rain. I
wore a yellow slicker and a pair of the world's only genuinely
waterproof boots, my yellow L.L. Bean Wellingtons. Getting
your first puppy? You can manage without the canine play-
pen, the X-pen, and the Wee-Wee Pads. It's even possible to
raise a dog without a crate. But unless you live in the Sahara,
you're going to walk the pup rain or shine, so invest in L.L.
Bean Wellies, the best two-footed friend a dog walker ever
had.

According to the atlas, Afton was beyond Route 495, Boston's outer beltway, farther from Cambridge than I'd thought. Rowdy and Kimi would be bored at home, and I'd miss their company, but their health was more important than my comfort. If by chance I got into the puppy mill, I'd leave with my boots and maybe my hands and my slicker contaminated by the multitude of the parasites and diseases that flourish in filth. Infection is a problem among the largely pampered entrants in a dog show. Some kennels maintain isolation areas where dogs live in quarantine after they return from shows. To avoid carrying diseases into their own kennels, a few extraordinarily careful people reserve one pair of shoes exclusively for shows. I don't own show shoes that never touch home ground, but I always keep Rowdy and Kimi up on their shots, I have regular checks for parasites, and I don't expose them to puppy mills. The shoes I'd worn at Bill Coakley's and at Your Local Breeder had already been soaked in chlorine bleach.

I spread the dogs' fake-sheepskin pallets on the kitchen floor, tuned the radio to a talk station, hugged the dogs, told them to be good, and set out. Then I headed out of Cambridge on Route 2. I eventually cut west and drove through the bleak, sodden landscape for what felt like hours.

My mental image of the fat-bellied Walter Simms had given way to the reality of the lean guy at Rinehart's, but I'd somehow retained my original vision of his sprawling mid-western farm. Old County Lane turned out to be a narrow but paved rural track overhung with New England maples. When I pulled the Bronco to the side of the road in front of the Simmses' place, I realized that although I'd discarded the pig-faced slob, I'd unconsciously located my revised Simms on the original's turf. But the faded, sloppy white letters painted on the dented black mailbox by the gate definitely spelled out "Simms." The name matched. The place didn't. I'd been picturing exactly what I'd seen in the films and photos of puppy mills in Minnesota, Nebraska, and Iowa, places like that. Kansas? No. I haven't seen many pictures from there, certainly no recent ones, and for good reason: In Kansas, it's a felony to photograph a puppy mill. If it weren't for the First Amendment, Kansas would probably declare it a felony to make word pictures, too. Anyway, thick New England underbrush and February-bare maples encroached on Walter and Cheryl Simms's little lot. When Mrs. Appleyard had said that you could smell the place from the road, I'd imagined a quarter-mile drive across flat fields to a big farmhouse and a collection of widely scattered dairy barns and substantial outbuildings. The Simmses' seedy little two-story dirty-white house sat at the end of about ten car lengths of rutted mud. The only large structure on the place, a long barrackslike sheet metal chicken coop in back of the house, had half collapsed from an original two floors to a single story. The side yard held an avocado green refrigerator with the doors still on, the wrecks of two wheelless cars, some little plywood shacks, several oil drums, and a flashy-looking late-model car that I was instantly able to identify as a Mustang, a Camaro, or possibly what I thought might be called a Trans Am. In any case, its color was black, and it was trimmed with red and white racing stripes.

Probably because I'd watched films of raids on puppy mills, I'd imagined driving into a farmyard, but, at the Simmses', a rusted barbed wire and wood gate blocked the entrance. Cheryl and Walter's landscape designer had cleverly repeated the texture and materials of the gate in the treatment of the fence that separated the property from the verge of the road. It, too, was constructed of sagging, aged uprights and cross pieces, and its chicken wire harmoniously echoed the reddish-brown of the barbed gate's hydrated ferric oxide. A big store-bought black-and-orange sign nailed to the dead center of the gate announced:

NO TRESPASSING
KEEP OUT
THIS MEANS <u>YOU</u>

I parked by the gate, grabbed the briefcase, and got out of the Bronco into the rain. When Mrs. Appleyard had said that you could smell the place from the road, she hadn't exaggerated; the air, in fact, smelled foul. A few dogs barked. I slammed the car door. I'd removed the bumper sticker, but should I have left the Bronco down the lane? In back of Rinehart's, I'd seen nothing more identifiable than a dark van. I reasoned that Walter Simms had seen nothing more distinctive than a large dark car. The night had been very black, and the Bronco's headlights must have reduced his night vision. He'd had no reason to notice and remember the number on my license plate. And if the Bronco looked like the property of a dog person? Well, why not? Dogs were, after all, my pretext as well as my real reason for being there.

I reached the gate and was searching for a latch when the torn screen door at the front of the house squealed open and discharged a scrawny young woman in a hot-pink nylon raincoat. She began to scream at me.

"This's private property," she shrieked. "Me and Walter don't want nobody sticking their big fat noses in our business!"

I'd heard those frantic, terror-driven tones before, but only in the snarls of fear-biting dogs. Some fear-biters strike with no warning. I considered myself lucky. I removed my hand from the gate, took a deep breath, gave a smile that cramped my cheeks, and held up the briefcase. "Ever have a problem with fleas?" I asked brightly. "Sure you do," I went on. "Let's face it. So does every other breeder." I tried not to stare at her. Sudden direct eye contact will sometimes trigger a rapid flash of teeth and a swift lunge.

"Me and Walter—" she began to bleat.

I interrupted. I'd spent the long drive to Afton composing this spiel, and I intended to deliver it. "And we're all tired of being offered easy solutions that cost a fortune and don't work." I took another big breath of fetid air. "Why don't they work? Because, Miss, uh, Simms," I said, glancing at the mailbox, "fleas are not an *easy* problem."

"Me and Walter—"

"You and Walter have tried your best, just like everyone else," I declared, "but now and then, fleas have gotten the best of you. But you're not alone. Many other top show kennels have had the same unhappy experience. And, of course, to compound the problem, most of these so-called easy solutions to the flea problem are dangerous chemicals that pose a threat to you and your animals." Inside the house, dogs were yipping and barking. A raindrop worked its way under the neck of my slicker. My merry tone was making me queasy. I swallowed and said, "But now, Miss Simms, you can join the thousands of happy breeders who've already discovered that Flee-B-Gon's unique three-step program is the safe, easy cure that really, really works." I was talking very fast. I didn't stop. "Step One? Treat the environment, because only about ten percent of fleas are on your dogs, you know. The other ninety percent are all around us." I swept my arm dramatically. "In our yards and kennels, in our animals' bedding, and even in our own carpets and furniture!" Perfectly true, by the way. "Step Two? Treat the animal. Step Three? Prevent reinfestation."

"Me and Walter don't want none," she said stubbornly,

but her tone had changed from shrill to whiny, and her eyes were on me.

"No cost and no obligation," I said, opening the briefcase. A gust of wind sprayed me and it with rain. "In fact," I added with sudden inspiration, "I'm here today, Miss Simms, to deliver the good news that you and Walter have been selected to participate in our special Flee-B-Gon Selected Breeders Program." I swear, you could hear the capitals in my voice. There is nothing, but nothing, I won't do for dogs. "Miss Simms," I said. "This is Miss Simms I'm talking to?"

"Yeah, Cheryl," she admitted.

"Well, Miss Simms, all you do is accept these samples of Flee-B-Gon products." I held up the half-open briefcase. "Give them a try. And in a month or so, let us know just how thrilled you are with them." I wiped the smile off my face and confided, rather loudly, because of the distance, "And you can use these fine products with the full assurance that Flee-B-Gon contains *no* harmful chemicals. Everything we manufacture is one hundred percent natural and organic. Why, you could drink a bottle of this kennel and yard spray, and it wouldn't do you a bit of harm. You have my personal guarantee on that."

My smile crept back. Cheryl was halfway down the muddy drive. As she approached, I tried to listen hard to the dogs. The high-pitched yipping certainly came from the house. The stench came from everywhere, including, it seemed to me as Cheryl Simms drew near, from the young woman herself. Her pale hair was thin and matted, and she had the blotched skin of someone who lives mainly on potato chips and diet soda. The hot-pink nylon protected her body from the rain, but her Reebok imitations sank into the mud. She didn't seem to notice her wet feet or ruined shoes. If it hadn't been for the dogs, I'd have felt guilty about luring her out with the offer of something for nothing.

Then the screen door banged hard. Walter Simms appeared on the sagging porch. His complexion, darker and better than his sister's, would have stood up to her hot pink, but he wore a Hard Rock Cafe T-shirt over tight jeans and high-topped sneakers. At his side, a handsome, sleek young male Rottweiler trembled with excitement. "Cheryl, what the hell are you doing?" Walter shouted at her. "Get back here!"

Cheryl cringed and headed toward the house.

Then Walter Simms turned his furious face toward me. "What the shit do you want? Can't you read the fucking sign? It says to keep the fuck out of here."

His sister was already cowering on the porch. "Walter, she's givin' stuff away," Cheryl said pitifully. "She's givin' it for free."

Walter looked exasperated. "For Christ's sake, Cheryl."

"It's for free," Cheryl pleaded. "For fleas. Walter, please?"

Walter turned toward me, stabbed a finger toward my briefcase, and demanded, "What the fuck's in that?"

"Flea powder. Spray. It's a line of flea control products."

"Me and Cheryl don't need none. Get the fuck out of here."

"That's a handsome Rottie you've got there," I said. "You know, a bad case of fleas could really do a job on him. Fleas can carry tapeworms, for one thing. And a lot of dogs are allergic to fleas. If he starts scratching, he'll tear up that beautiful coat."

"Oh, yeah?" Simms jerked his thumb back toward the source of the yipping. "Champ's around all them other dogs, and he never picked nothing up."

"Well, he could," I said, wiping the rain off my face with

my free hand, "if the other dogs have fleas. Maybe you've just been lucky so far. You take pretty good care of Champ, don't you?"

And, I swear to God, Walter Simms beamed. Like his Rottie, he was dark-eyed and muscular, and his face had the same well-developed cheekbones as his dog's. "Yeah," he confessed almost shyly. Then he turned serious. "I ain't got no money to waste on them dogs out there," he said, jerking his thumb once again, "but I don't want nothing happening to Champ. That stuff really work?"

"Yes," I lied. "I told, uh, Miss Simms. I'll leave you the free samples." I was as close to Walter Simms as I wanted to be. "I'll put them in your mailbox, okay? Is that all right?"

Cheryl threw Walter a look so subservient that I almost expected her to crouch and leave a little submissive puddle on the porch at his feet.

"Is that all right?" I asked again.

Walter looked Cheryl up and down, then said, "Yeah."

As I was stashing Flee-B-Gon containers in the mailbox, I called casually, "Hey, what's so special about Champ? I mean, your other dogs . . ."

Walter Simms looked at the Rottie and clapped his hands. The sleek black-and-rust dog gave a powerful upward bound and made a springing, muscular landing at Simms's feet. As if stating the obvious, Simms said, "Champ's not like them others. Champ's *my* dog."

24

I LEFT AFTON THAT WEDNESDAY afternoon feeling wet, weak, and cowardly. In visiting Walter and Cheryl Simms, I'd accomplished nothing. I'd smelled and heard the evidence of a puppy mill, but the only dog I'd observed had been Walter's pet Rottie. Champ looked anything but neglected. According to Missy's papers, Simms had malamutes, presumably including Missy's dam, Icekist Sissy, but I hadn't even been able to verify the presence of the breed. I'd had a small camera tucked in my shoulder bag. In retrospect, I wondered why I'd even bothered to take it with me. Had I expected Walter and Cheryl Simms to give me free run of the place to do a full-page spread for *Dog's Life*?

But if Cheryl Simms had been alone there? It seemed just possible that Cheryl might at least have opened that gate. She'd eyed my briefcase of bright containers with the greediness of a deprived child. If I'd taken advantage of

Cheryl's simplicity to buy my way in, I just might have had the chance to get a couple of photos. If so, Jane Appleyard might have had the probable cause she needed to take legal action, maybe enough evidence to get the authorities to raid the damned place and permanently close it down.

As it was? I hadn't even found out for sure that Simms had Missy. I tried to forget Missy's open, friendly trust, the eagerness of her greeting, her puppy sweetness, that full mask on her face, the markings so much like Kimi's. Until the previous Friday, only five days ago, Missy had spent a pampered life in the small and hot but clean and toy-packed pantry of Enid Sievers's overstuffed raspberry house. I tried to console myself. Although Missy's own existence had left her utterly unprepared for hardship, she was, after all, an Alaskan malamute. The breed evolved in the brutal environment of the Arctic. Some of Missy's own ancestors had survived the unspeakable cruelty of the men and the climate in Little America. An Alaskan malamute can endure almost anything, I reminded myself. Tears filled my eyes. I pulled to the side of the road. The Byrd expeditions are the stuff of my nightmares. Why in God's name had I looked to Antarctica for consolation?

When I'd blown my nose and pulled myself together, I decided that instead of heading directly back to Cambridge, I'd detour through Westbrook and stop at Your Local Breeder. Gloria Loss had been due to start work there this morning. She'd had very little time to discover anything, and Janice Coakley had probably kept her busy cleaning out kennels and scrubbing kibble off food bowls. I probably wouldn't even have a chance to talk to Gloria alone; Janice Coakley might not trust a new employee to deal with a customer. Even so, I'd already established myself with Janice as a potential puppy buyer—there'd be nothing suspect about a second visit—and Westbrook wasn't far out of my way.

When I drove up to Your Local Breeder, the parking lot by the kennel building held three cars, one of which, a charcoal gray Volvo sedan, turned out to have a Cambridge resident parking permit on its dashboard. Adhering to the back bumper of the car was a campaign sticker for a candidate for the Cambridge City Council, a radical feminist lesbian woman whose chances of election were deemed slight. Why? Most observers agreed that, given her conservative views, she didn't stand a chance. Cambridge: Berkeley with lousy weather. Anyway, maybe my luck had turned. At least Gloria hadn't quit or been fired.

Far from it. I found Gloria in Ronald's old place, perched on the stool behind the counter in the kennel supply shop at the front of Your Local Breeder. Unlike Ronald, Gloria was working. In fact, she was ringing up a sale. Although she looked far from beautiful, the change in her appearance was remarkable. She'd obviously washed her hair, which hung in neat dark braids, and, in place of Sunday's gloomy drapery, she wore a starched white shirt. Her skin was still an erupted mess of acne, of course, but she'd lost some of her neglected, hapless air.

On the opposite side of the counter stood a blond, freckle-faced woman and three blond, freckle-faced little girls. In the world of dogs, the ability to produce miniature versions of oneself, as if by parthenogenesis, is called prepotency. This was obviously a prepotent dam. With a vaguely reluctant look on her face, she was paying Gloria for a tiny, adorable Finnish spitz puppy that rested in the arms of the tallest of the three children.

"Now," the woman said to Gloria, as if concluding a discussion, "you're very sure that they don't bark?"

You know what a Finnish spitz is? Cutest breed in the world, just like a darling little fox. I'd get one tomorrow, except for one thing: yapping. As if tuned to my thoughts, the puppy launched into a series of ear-shattering yips. The woman's eyes widened.

"She's just nervous now," Gloria said. "Wait till you get her home. You'll hardly hear a peep out of her. Practically a silent breed."

The child holding the puppy said impatiently, "Mom, who *cares?* This is the one *we* want."

The next tallest little girl seconded her sister. "Yeah, Mom. You saw her. She ran right to *us*. She picked *us*."

The mother conceded. Gloria handed her a receipt and a plastic bag that must have held puppy paraphernalia. The mother gave the bag to the smallest child and hefted a twenty-pound bag of premium chow in her arms. The blond family filed out.

"For Christ's sake, Gloria," I hissed softly, "three days ago ownership was exploitation. Remember? And now, all of a sudden . . . The Finnish spitz is a totally inappropriate breed for that woman."

"They'll be nice to the puppy," Gloria said.

"They'll probably have her debarked," I whispered, "if they keep her at all. And if they sell her or give her away, those'll be three brokenhearted kids."

Gloria looked so crushed that I was sorry I'd spoken. The woman and her daughters had seemed kind and decent. Maybe they'd adapt to the puppy after all.

"Or maybe it'll work out," I added very quietly. "Are you all alone here? Where's . . ."

"At her lawyer's. Mrs. Coakley's sister just died, and she wants to know what's in it for her, or that's the feeling you get. There's an old guy around somewhere, but he doesn't know how to work the cash register."

"Do you?"

"Now I do," Gloria said. "Anyhow, Mrs. Coakley didn't have much choice. She was going to close up, but then that woman called and wanted to know if we were open, and I guess Mrs. Coakley didn't want to lose a sale."

We were open? What's this *we?* I thought. Then I had what my friend Rita calls an ah-hah experience. This must be Gloria's first real job, and, like any other kid her age, she was proud to find herself behind a cash register, taking money and handing out receipts. Even so, Gloria's rapid identification with her new employer made me uneasy. Also, I remembered Mrs. Appleyard's warning. On Sunday, Gloria had been unnaturally eager to switch her loyalty to me. Had I lost it already? Had I ever had it? I felt frightened about trusting Gloria and guilty about using her, but, as I've said, I'll do anything for dogs.

I cleared my throat and asked under my breath, "Where's this guy who works here?"

"Out back," Gloria told me. "It's okay. And I've got a lot to tell you."

"When is Janice Coakley due back?"

"I don't know. Half an hour maybe. She's getting her hair done, too."

I leaned an elbow on the counter. "Okay, but if she shows up, just start telling me about Siberian huskies or something, okay?"

"I don't know anything about them," said Gloria, suddenly childish.

"You know as much about them as you know about the Finnish spitz," I said, "and you winged that all right." Gloria smiled. I felt a pang of guilt. I still hadn't called the dermatologist to make an appointment for her. "Walter Simms delivers puppies here," I went on. "I know that now."

"Yeah," Gloria said. "A lot of them come from him. We're supposed to tell the customers that Mrs. Coakley breeds them all, but she doesn't, really."

"She breeds some of them?"

Gloria pushed her braids back. "Yeah, she's got—That's her house, out there, in back of the parking lot. That's where she lives. And somewhere behind there, maybe in the barn, I know she has some dogs. You can hear them. I haven't been back there."

"That's okay," I said. "But Simms brings most of them?"

"Some," Gloria said. "He's supposed to bring some tonight. She put in an order. That's what she does. She calls up and orders them, what breeds she wants. I heard her. It's weird. It's like someone calling up a store and ordering groceries, only it's dogs. It's really weird."

"I believe you." I tried to keep the disappointment from my voice. I'd already known that that's how pet shops order puppies, and I'd known that Simms delivered to Your Local Breeder. In hoping that Gloria would learn anything useful, I'd been kidding myself.

"Only," Gloria continued, "at least this morning, she made two different calls. Her office door was open, and I was supposed to clean the kennels, so I did the ones close to the door."

"Maybe she deals with more than one broker."

"Except they're all coming at the same time." Gloria's eyes were serious.

"That does seem kind of strange," I admitted.

"So," said Gloria, pulling herself up straight and holding her shoulders back, "as soon as Mrs. Coakley left, I went and looked."

"You looked . . . ?"

"It sounded fishy, and that's what I thought you wanted, anything fishy. So as soon as Mrs. Coakley left, I went into her office." Gloria glanced toward the back of the shop. "Back there. And the file was right on her desk, because, I mean, she'd just been making these calls, and she was going out. And it was like what she said on the phone. Like, uh, two lists. Only the other sort of strange thing was that the prices were different."

"They would be," I said. "Pet shops pay different prices for different breeds. They sell them for different prices, right? The puppies here don't all cost the same, do they?"

"No, but for the same breed, they do. Like that Finnish spitz was seven hundred dollars, and some of the others are a whole lot cheaper. Like cocker spaniels are three twenty-five. But, like, *all* the cocker spaniels are three twenty-five, only she pays a hundred for them to one guy, and a hundred and fifty at the other place."

"I don't understand," I said. "So why not just get them all from the place that only charges a hundred?"

"Because those people didn't have enough," Gloria said. "That's what it sounded like. We sell a whole lot of cocker spaniels, I guess, and she wanted, like, a litter of puppies, and she was supposed to get them Sunday, only she didn't. So the first call she made, she tried to get, like, three of them, only she ended up ordering two, and the next call, she only ordered one."

"So she got as many of the cheaper ones as she could," I said.

"Yeah," Gloria said. "Yeah, I mean, if you look at the lists and stuff, you can tell that's what she did. It's like, well, my mother'll do this when she shops for clothes. She'll go to T.J. Maxx, Hit or Miss, those places first, and then there'll be stuff she can't find discount, and she'll go to the regular places and pay full price."

Beano! Have I lost you? Well, then, bingo! But that's not what it's called at the fairs in Maine, where we still use real beans, dried ones, of course, to cover the numbers on our cards. When it comes to dogs, I've learned to temper my competitive spirit, thus malamutes in obedience, but when I'm seated on one of those old wooden benches in a Maine beano tent with three cards lined up in front of me on the oilcloth and I put the fifth bean in place to complete that straight, winning line? Well, I'll tell you, I'm a killer.

"Beano!" I said out loud.

Gloria looked mystified. "What?"

"Nothing," I said. "Never mind, Gloria, this is very helpful. You're doing great. This is really helpful." I quit leaning on the counter and began to zip up my yellow slicker. "So the first call was to Simms, right? And I bet the second one was to a guy named Rinehart."

"That's what the papers say," Gloria confirmed. "Her list and the, uh, order forms, I guess you call them."

"Simms and Rinehart," I said. "I knew who they were, but I didn't know what was going on. Now I do. Hey, Gloria? Thanks a whole lot. I think maybe you've done enough, okay? When Janice Coakley gets back, just tell her you're allergic to dogs or something, or just don't show up tomorrow."

"But, Holly—"

"I know what's going on, okay? I'll explain it some other time. I'm going now. Janice Coakley'll be back soon, and I want to get home. My dogs have been alone long enough." Through the plate glass window, I could see that the rain had started up again. I pulled the hood of my slicker over my head.

"Holly?"

"Yeah?"

"Don't you want the, uh, papers? The list and—"

I did a swift about-turn. Gloria was holding out a large manila envelope.

"Don't you want them?" Gloria's voice was hurt and puzzled. "They're just copies, but I thought . . . The Xerox machine was right there, and I thought . . . I couldn't take them, because Mrs. Coakley would notice they were gone. So I just copied them. Isn't that good enough?"

I snatched the envelope from Gloria as eagerly as Rowdy and Kimi grab liver treats. I used my hand, of course. If I'd used my teeth the way the dogs do, Gloria would have lost a finger.

"Good enough?" I told her. "It's beautiful."

"Oh, and there's one thing . . . About Mrs. Coakley?" Gloria's face took on the condescension of youth for age. "She's . . . This is sort of . . . You can tell she's sort of in love with this guy."

"The old guy who—?"

"No. This guy, Walter Simms. You can tell from how she says his name. She gets sort of smug sounding, like, '*Walter*'s bringing me some puppies tonight.' Like that. It's kind of cute, the way she says it, you know, 'Walter.' " Like she's bragging about her boyfriend. Is he?"

"I have no idea," I said.

"It doesn't matter," Gloria said. "I was just kind of wondering."

25

I'D MISSED ROWDY AND KIMI so much that when I returned
home, I made the mistake of greeting them on bended knee.
I ended up with a scratched chin, a sore nose, and a bruised
jaw. Since winning the unconditional love of these two dogs, I
have sustained more injuries than I received in all my pre-
malamute years. Take it from someone with the scarred
knees of a retired quarterback: If a happy malamute ever
makes a mad dash toward you, flatten yourself against the
nearest solid vertical object. I've been dragged down the back
stairs three times, and before I learned never to walk malamutes in icy weather, I hit the sidewalk twice. Oh, and watch
out: These dogs have skulls of steel. Knock heads with a
malamute, and you see double for three days. You *still* think
you want a malamute? Well, the breed boasts a few angels,
but most mals will steal food, raid the trash, chase cats, kill
livestock, and kiss the burglar. When mals are shedding, your

house looks like the aftermath of a sheep-shearing contest, and, with the possible exception of all terriers, they are the world's greatest diggers and the world's worst obedience dogs. But as soul mates? As kindred spirits? As an intelligent companion in a partnership of equals, the Alaskan malamute is without peer.

So I washed the scratch on my chin, forgave the dogs, let them out and in, fed them, admired them while they ate, and then made my way to the Dennehys' back door. Have you ever met Kevin's mother? If not, maybe I should warn you: Her Biblical pronouncements can be slightly startling; she favors the Old Testament and the Book of Revelation. Also, her face has a severe expression that I attribute to chronic pain; instead of cutting her steel gray hair or just letting it hang, she twists it into a knot that she bolts to the top of her skull.

Mrs. Dennehy edged open the back door, eyed me, and opened her mouth.

I beat her to it. "Behold," I said, "I stand at the door, and knock." Revelation, chapter three, verse twenty. "Is Kevin home?"

He must have heard my voice. A couple of seconds later, he loomed behind his mother. He was pulling on a black raincoat. His eyes looked hungry for escape.

I was bursting with enthusiasm. "I have a million things to tell you, Kevin," I said as soon as he stepped outside.

"You want to walk?"

"I have some things to show you first," I said impatiently. "I know what's going on. Kevin, Simms is double-dealing. He's cheating Rinehart, and I can prove it."

When we reached my kitchen, I ignored the dogs, who were bouncing around and playing up to Kevin. Before Kevin even had his raincoat off, I'd whipped out the envelope Gloria had given me and spread the three photocopied pages on the table. "There!" I said. I kept talking while Kevin pulled his arms out of his sleeves. "This one is a shopping list. Okay? They're all from this place called Your Local Breeder. In Westbrook. This is how many puppies Janice Coakley wanted, the breeds, how many of each breed. She wanted twenty puppies. Like here? One mini schnauzer, one Shih Tzu, three cockers, one Doberman. Anyway, I even know why she wanted three cockers, okay? First of all, it's a popular breed, but the line she gives her customer is that she's a breeder, right? Your Local Breeder. And apparently she does breed some dogs, but she also buys puppies and passes them off as her own. Like these cockers."

"Hey, slow down," Kevin said. He lowered himself into a chair.

"Sure," I said, but I was wired. I didn't take a seat, and the words kept tumbling out of my mouth. "Then after she'd decided what she wanted, instead of making one call to place her order, she made two. First she called Walter Simms, and then, after that, she called Rinehart. And the reason she called Simms first was to see which breeds she could get cut-rate. Discount, okay? Like take the cockers. On the first page, you can see that she wanted three, but Simms must've said he could only supply two. So she ordered those two from Simms, here on this page. And then when she called Rine-hart, she just wanted one cocker. Rinehart charges more than Simms. Like here? She's paying Rinehart one-fifty for a cocker, and Simms only charges a hundred."

Kevin was thumping Rowdy on the back and rubbing the top of Kimi's head.

"Don't you get it?" I demanded. "Just on these two cock-ers that Janice Coakley ordered from Simms instead of Rine-hart, Simms is cheating Rinehart out of a hundred dollars."

Kevin finally glanced at the pages, Janice Coakley's ini-tial shopping list and the lists of the puppies she'd ordered from Simms and from Rinehart. "Yeah, same as at Puppy Luv," he said blandly.

I could feel my face fall. "Kevin, if you knew that . . . ? Look, maybe you don't get it, because you don't see where the big profits are. A guy like Rinehart, a broker, probably only pays around forty dollars for a cocker puppy, and in theory, according to the law, he's supposed to keep the puppy for a minimum of twenty-four hours, I think, but the USDA isn't the world's greatest enforcement agency. In fact, it's probably the worst. So, say Rinehart pays forty and sells for one-fifty, he's made a hundred and ten, okay? And he's had a really quick turnover. Maybe it costs him five or ten dollars to have the puppy picked up and another five or ten to have the puppy delivered, plus he pays some vet to sign some papers, but his profit is tremendous, and it's quick, and it's not a lot of work, either."

Kevin looked damp and stolid.

I went on. "The point is that Simms is using Rinehart's setup to cut into Rinehart's profits. Simms isn't trying to do in Rinehart's business, because he can't. A pet shop needs a reliable source of a whole lot of different breeds, and the only way to get that is through a broker. Simms is small-time. He can't compete with a broker. What Simms is doing, really, is just supplementing his own income at Rinehart's expense. Simms runs a puppy mill, and, other than that, he's just a delivery boy. He's using Rinehart's van and his whole organization, including whatever vet Rinehart's bought off, to deliver to Rinehart's customers."

Kevin ambled to the refrigerator, got a beer, popped it open, and upended it over his mouth. When he lowered it, he said, "We cops aren't the brightest people in Cambridge, of course, but we can manage simple arithmetic. Course, we have to count on our fingers and all that, but . . ." He sank back into his chair.

"So have you talked to Rinehart? Because, you know, in a way, Diane Sweet was cheating him, too. So is Janice Coakley, if you want to look at it that way. For all I know, maybe Rinehart found out, and he decided to make an example of her, of Diane Sweet. Or else maybe . . . Kevin, I wondered if Diane Sweet could have told Rinehart?"

Kevin gave a strange, knowing grin. "Joe Rinehart catches a guy sticking his hand in the till, and . . ." He zipped a beefy thumb across his throat and made a gruesome sound. "And why would Diane blow the whistle on Simms? Simms was her boyfriend. And if he hadn't been? She blew the whistle, she'd've ended up paying more than she already did." Kevin looked down at the pages spread on the table. "Now you feel like telling me how you got hold of these?"

"No," I said. "Kevin, the other thing is . . . Someone suggested to me that Walter Simms might have the same thing going with Janice Coakley that he did with Diane." I paused. "Or maybe just that Janice wishes he did."

Kevin finally perked up. "Where'd you hear this?"

"From someone who couldn't possibly know about Diane and Simms. Interesting, huh?"

Kevin's blue eyes go slightly out of focus when he's mulling something over. Eventually he said, "Yeah, but she did call her Sunday night. Janice called Diane. Phone company says so and—"

"Or *someone* called?"

"Janice did. Answering machine was on at Puppy Luv. Machine picked up, and then Diane did. What's on the tape is just her saying hello and Janice saying it's her, and then Diane turned the machine off."

"What time was this?"

"Ten after ten. Call lasted two minutes."

"Does Janice say why she called Diane?"

"Checking in. Women do that." I let that pass. Kevin

continued. "She knew Diane'd be working, and she called her up to give her a little break."

"For two minutes?"

"Diane said she was busy and she'd call her tomorrow."

"Kevin, does Janice inherit anything from Diane? Did Diane leave her—?"

"One opal ring, belonged to their grandmother. Maximum value maybe a hundred bucks. And something like a sixteenth of an interest in a cottage on Lake Winnipesaukee. One of those family messes where it got left to everyone, and now no one knows who owns what."

"Those things cause a lot of family fights," I said. "Did—?"

"Yeah, but Janice and Diane were on the same side, and they couldn't've sold their shares, anyway."

"Oh." I thought for a second. "Kevin, if there's an answering machine at Puppy Luv, then . . . Her husband says he kept trying to call her, right? Did he leave any messages?"

"She didn't turn it back on. After she talked to Janice, she must've forgot. People do that all the time."

"Huh. Do you still think maybe the husband—What's his name?"

"John. Could he've gone there? Yeah. Is he strong enough? Human gorilla. Did he know about her and Simms? He'd've had to have been pretty dumb not to know. But you talk to him, and that's how he hits you, big and dumb. If he'd've known, would he give a damn? Show me the guy that wouldn't. We told him, real gentle, and all's he says is that she was raped. And he gets all broken up, and then he starts asking when we're going to get out so's he can open up again."

"Kevin, what about the stuff you sent to the lab? And the autopsy?"

Kevin tilted his chair and teetered on the back legs.

"Well, let's see," he said. "For dinner she had an eggplant sub and potato chips. She'd had her appendix out. She wasn't pregnant."

"That's all really helpful," I said. "Look. Janice and Diane were business rivals, okay? Look at their ads sometime. They competed for business. And maybe they also competed for Simms. He left Janice's, drove to Diane's. Janice called Diane, and Diane said she was busy. They hung up at twelve minutes after ten? It takes maybe forty minutes, give or take, to get from Westbrook to Cambridge. Late on a Sunday evening, maybe less. So when was Diane murdered? What time did she die?"

"Body temperature, stomach contents, doesn't mean a thing," Kevin said dismally. "You been watching too much TV."

"Right," I said. "The Westminster Kennel Club Dog Show. All the latest news in forensic science. What time did she die?"

"After the last time she was known to be alive. Before she was found dead. Hey, no joke. This is what they tell us."

"Don't they even give you a guess?"

"Ten-thirty, eleven, eleven-thirty. Give or take."

"Then Janice had time. Where does she say she was?"

"Home, like everybody else. Where were you Sunday at eleven?"

"Home."

"Yeah. Me, too."

Kevin looked as discouraged as I felt. Kevin, though, is a good cop. He really gave a damn about who murdered Diane Sweet. John Sweet? Joe Rinehart? Walter Simms? Janice Coakley? *Prove they conspired,* I thought. *Lock them all up for life.*

26

When Kevin left, I idly gathered up the three photocopied pages, crumpled them into one ball, and aimed at the kitchen wastebasket. After all the practice I've had in tossing obedience dumbbells, I should be Larry Bird, but I missed. When the ball of paper hit the floor, Rowdy and Kimi looked, twitched their ears, and decided that it wasn't worth retrieving. They were right, of course. Even so, I picked it up, separated the pages, and took them to my study.

Imagine a dog writer's study, and you'll see mine. You'd never guess that I do most of my writing at the kitchen table. The study is hot in the summer and cold in the winter, and in the spring and fall, it's either freezing or sweltering, but, as I've said, it looks perfect. Framed pictures of dogs and certificates of titles cover the walls. Match, trial, and show ribbons flutter from the frames. Tacked to a big bulletin board by my desk are scads of dog photos mailed to me by people who read my column. Danny and Vinnie's trophies rest on top of the bookcases, and the shelves below are jammed with thesauruses, style manuals, and books on obedience training, breed handling, grooming, veterinary care, the history of the genus *canis*; issues of *Dog's Life,* the *Gazette, DOGworld, Dog Fancy, Off-Lead, Front & Finish,* and the six or eight canine newsletters I receive every month; the complete works of Jack London; histories and first-person accounts of the Byrd expeditions; and everything ever written about the Alaskan malamute. The filing cabinets by the desk support an unabridged dictionary and the diehard Okidata printer that's cabled to a PC so old that if computers were licensed, mine would wear antique plates. The computer rests on the desk facing the window.

I dropped the wrinkled pages on top of the pile of new magazines, unfinished work, and to-be-filed papers that covered the keyboard. My hand-scrawled draft of the article on Sally Brand half-covered the USDA booklet of licensed puppy mills and brokers. Missy's pedigree rested on the latest issue of the *Gazette—Pure-Bred Dogs/American Kennel Gazette,* the official publication of the American Kennel Club. I felt sad and bitter. I'd been crazy about the whole idea of tattooed dog portraits. The article now hit me as shameful and frivolous, especially the stupid, cutesy title: "I've Got You Under My Skin." In Kansas alone, there were three thousand nine hundred twenty-seven USDA-licensed puppy mills and at least as many more that were unlicensed. And what was I doing? Making corny word plays about ink, dogs, and love.

What was the AKC doing? Accepting fees: litter registration fees, individual dog registration fees, and miscellaneous other fees from USDA-licensed Class A and Class B dealers and from almost any other puppy mill operator or broker who mailed in a check, too. The AKC litter registration fee? Fifteen dollars. According to most estimates, puppy mills an-

nually produce and register about one hundred thousand litters. In litter registrations alone, that's an income of one
million five hundred thousand dollars a year. My God—I was
raised to believe that His earthly address was 51 Madison
Avenue, New York, New York, AKC headquarters. And what
was my Vatican doing about the thousands of Joe Rineharts
and Bill Coakleys in this country? About the Puppy Luvs and
the clones of Your Local Breeder?

What was the worst that the AKC would—or even *could*
—do to Walter Simms? I flipped to the Secretary's Page of
the *Gazette* and scanned the notices. A man in Virginia had
been fined five hundred dollars and had his AKC privileges
suspended for five years because a county court had convicted
him of animal cruelty charges. A woman in Missouri had
received the same fine and temporary suspension for failing
to comply with the record-keeping and identification requirements of Chapter 3A of the Rules Applying to Registration
and Dog Shows. If I managed somehow to get the AKC to
inspect Simms's records? The AKC isn't even allowed to
make unannounced inspections. Simms would be warned,
and by the time the AKC got there, his paperwork might
meet the damned requirements. The AKC inspector could
report the filthy conditions to the local authorities, of course,
and Mrs. Appleyard might finally be able to get some action
going, but the process could take months or, for all I knew,
years. And then? If Walter Simms lost the privilege of regis-
tering dogs in his own name, he'd register them to Cheryl or
to Joe Rinehart or to any friend or relative who happened to
be handy. If Simms were convicted of animal cruelty? He'd
pay a small fine, maybe even go to jail for a few months, and
then he'd be back in mass-market dogs again.

I picked up the USDA list of licensed dealers and tried
to fit it on the crowded shelf of loose material where it belonged. I couldn't get it all the way in, and when I yanked at

it, a pile of odds and ends tumbled to the floor. I knelt down and started to tidy up the spilled miscellany: an extra copy of the AKC obedience regulations, a pamphlet on how to play Frisbee with your dog, a photo of Kimi and my cousin Leah the day they earned their third Novice leg, a pamphlet called "You and Your New Puppy," a few dozen premium lists and entry blanks for long-past shows and trials, a flier about the United Kennel Club, and a handful of Christmas cards I'd saved.

I sat on the floor and leafed through the cards. Most showed photos of people's dogs, but the one that caught my eye had a black-and-white drawing of a malamute under a Christmas tree. Clasped between his paws was a torn-open present, a package of dog biscuits. He held one in his mouth. A tag on the present showed the name of the dog, Cody. He's real. He was rescued by the Illinois Alaskan Malamute Rescue Association, which sold the cards to raise funds. I opened the card and read the message: *Let there be peace on earth and let it begin with us.* The temperature of the hard wooden floor under me seemed to drop ten degrees.

With *us,* right? Not with Kevin Dennehy and the Cambridge Police Department. Not with the American Kennel Club. Not with the United States Department of Agriculture, Jane M. Appleyard, the Eleanor J. Colley Humane Society, or the citizens of Afton. And *let it begin?* From the beginning, instead of restoring peace to Missy and to myself, I'd tried to find people to do it for me. Let Kevin take advantage of a brutal murder to arrest Rinehart, Simms, Janice Coakley, and everyone else involved in the evil enterprise of mass-producing dogs. Let the AKC and the USDA close the bastards down. Let the humane society and the local citizenry raise an outcry that would rouse the authorities to action.

Why does the puppy mill industry thrive? How do pet shops that sell dogs manage to stay in business? Because we all take the same attitude I'd been taking: Let there be peace on earth. Let it begin with someone else.

For the first time since I lost Missy, I felt calm. Scared? You bet. But very calm.

My first step was to call Steve, who sometimes arrives unannounced. Although a D.V.M. would have been an asset on my mission of peace, I wanted to keep him completely out of it.

"I'm sick," I announced.

"You're never sick," he said.

He was right. I tried to imagine what could possibly be wrong with me. "I must've eaten something at the show," I said.

"Three days ago? And you're the one who's always saying that dog show food—"

"Coffee. I drank some dog show coffee." At any dog show in the United States, including the posh benched shows, even Westminster, you'd swear that the pale liquid that comes out of those industrial-size percolators is yet another item in the Flee-B-Gon product line. But, as I'd assured Cheryl Simms, the stuff really is safe to drink.

"But this is Wednesday. That was—"

"Then it must have been something else. I keep throwing up. Chicken! I ate some chicken. I knew it tasted funny."

When Steve had failed to talk me into going to the Mount Auburn emergency room, he offered to come and take care of me, but I assured him that I was already feeling better and just needed to go to sleep. Alone. We exchanged our usual sweet nothings about the cute things our dogs had done recently, and I promised to call him the next day.

Then I went upstairs to Rita's and persuaded her to take care of Rowdy and Kimi in the morning. The previous spring, when I'd had a different reason to ask the same favor, Rita heard me out and ended up eyeing me as if I'd lost my mind.

Rita is a clinical psychologist. In other circumstances, I might have paused to evaluate my own sanity, but, in the sport of tracking, predawn madness is normal and necessary.

"Let me get this straight," Rita had said solemnly. "Correct me if I'm wrong, but as I understand it, you want me to let your dogs out and in, and give them breakfast, because you're getting up at four A.M. and driving an hour and a half to an empty field where you're going to take a walk so that, sometime later, a dog can come along and follow in your footsteps."

Before she'd gone on to refer me to a psychiatrist who specialized in heavy-duty medication, I explained that I owed it to the club to help and that it isn't all that easy to recruit experienced track layers. She rolled her eyes toward the ceiling and said that she couldn't imagine why not.

As you'll have gathered, Rita is not a real dog person. Tracking tests around here always take place on weekends and never in winter. A tracking test on a Thursday morning in the middle of February? But Rita bought the story and agreed to help with the dogs. As usual, she touted out a few silly rationalizations about why she couldn't walk them, even one at a time. In my absence, Rowdy might decide to take on his archenemy, an aggressive neighborhood cocker owned by people incapable of socializing a goldfish. Kimi might be seized by one of her frenzied impulses to dash around in wild circles until Rita ended up like a trussed chicken, her ankles bound by the leash. Hadn't I once remarked that the Alaskan malamute wasn't a *scissorable* breed? Well, it wasn't a *walkable* breed, either, and it was barely *feedable*, too. But I didn't protest. The yard is fenced. I just said thanks.

Then I prepared the Bronco. The back already held two large wire-mesh dog crates and two blankets. I added some additional blankets, two bowls, and a gallon jug of fresh water. Back indoors, I got out a medium-size dark gray backpack and began to assemble the items I'd need. I put a fresh bulb and two new D batteries in one flashlight and also replaced the bulb and the two AA batteries in the Mini Mag-Lite my father gave me for Christmas.

In a burgundy case on the top shelf of my bedroom closet, I found another present from Buck, a Smith & Wesson Model 60 Ladysmith, stainless steel with a frosted finish, the pocket pit bull of .38 specials, the perfect companion animal for the girl who really, really *can* say no. I'm more at home with a deer rifle or a .22 than I am with a revolver, but I'm not a bad shot. When *you* had a date to go to the movies, *I* had one to go out to the dump and shoot rats. Repulsive? Now, yes, but remember that there weren't any movie theaters in Owls Head. Also, I did learn to hit a moving target. So I added the Ladysmith, ammo, the holster (another Christmas present), a pair of wire cutters, a small camera with a built-in flash, a nylon training collar, a six-foot leather lead, and a length of gauze that would do as a muzzle.

Then I concentrated on the big problem: the noise of the dogs. As you probably know, bark-control devices are in vogue these days. The simplest kind is just a tight muzzle that holds the dog's mouth shut. But how many dogs did Walter and Cheryl Simms have? I didn't know for sure, but far too many for me to run around muzzling. Antibark collars would have the same drawback. You know what they are? Some emit high-frequency sound waves that bother a dog's sensitive ears. The others are bark-triggered shock collars, which I wouldn't have used even if I'd had the requisite supply sitting around. Write me off as a softhearted fanatic if you want, but I don't believe in giving electric shocks to dogs. Anyway, individual collars were out. High tech offered one more option, namely, a little manually-operated box that, like the collars, makes a high-pitched sound inaudible to people but very unpleasant to dogs. There's even a long-distance model marketed to desperate people whose neighbors' dogs are driving them crazy but that one, I thought, made a buzz that people could hear. In any case, I didn't own one of these devices, and, even ignoring the problem of ethics, there was a hitch: As far as I knew, the gadgets didn't work instantly. According to the ads I'd seen, they were used to train dogs to quit barking, not to provide immediate silence. Even so, if I'd had one handy, I might have packed it.

As it was, I intended to get in and out fast, and I counted mainly on being mistaken for a natural intruder, a foraging raccoon or a stray dog passing swiftly on its way. My backup plan was based on the inability of the average dog to bark and chew at the same time. I filled a gallon-size plastic bag with the small dog biscuits that I use as training treats, and in a second plastic bag I packed my secret cache of medium-size rawhide bones. Secret? Banned by Steve, who says that rawhide would be safe if Rowdy and Kimi would chew it slowly like normal dogs instead of swallowing it in big chunks that could obstruct their intestinal tracts. But the damned thing is, they love the stuff, thus the secret cache: one raw-hide bone for every leg of an obedience title. But do me a favor, huh? Don't tell Steve, and don't mention it to anyone else, either. Because of my column and all that, I'm supposed to be a model of responsible ownership. Only my all-forgiving dogs know my deepest sins.

Anyhow, whether or not I should have packed the raw-hide bones, that's what I did. Then I stowed everything in the backpack, shut it in a closet where the dogs couldn't raid the goodies, and laid out my clothes: jeans, a black sweater, my old navy parka, a tattered navy poncho, wool socks and gloves, and heavy hiking boots. When Rowdy, Kimi, and I returned from a walk around the block, I took a shower, set the alarm for four A.M., went to bed, and fell asleep. Why not? My conscience was finally starting to feel clear.

27

I DON'T GO TO FUNERALS anymore. My recent knowledge of them is entirely celluloid. I have the impression that graveside ceremonies are usually held in the rain and often attended by people who can't carry the tune of "Amazing Grace." A common convenience at Mafia burials is a large canopy to protect the lace-shrouded widow from the drizzle. At the back of the crowd lurk henchmen whose overdeveloped trapezius muscles strain the shoulder seams of ill-gotten hand-tailored suits. Male mourners exchange whispered plans to avenge the deceased.

My almost exclusively cinematic experience of funerals has probably misled me. In fact, I know it has. For example, at the real thing, the air reeks of gladioli instead of popcorn, or so I seem to recall. Also, in real life, the sad part doesn't exactly come as a big surprise, so I'll bet that no one ever has to make do with greasy paper napkins. The rest I'm not sure about.

What reminded me of movie funerals and the unanswered question of their correspondence to reality was the canopy of leafless, dripping branches that overhung Old County Lane in Afton at five-thirty on the morning of February fourteenth. Italian women did not sob in the thick undergrowth that lined the road. Hardy pioneers did not grieve for brethren outgunned by Jack Palance. Were canopies strictly Hollywood?

Oh, yeah. I didn't go to real puppy mills, either, not as a rule. I'd read about them and heard about them. I'd seen photos and films. I thought I knew. I really believed that the sad part would come as no surprise.

Back to real life. As I may have mentioned, Old County Lane was little more than its name suggested, a roughly paved country road just about wide enough to accommodate my Bronco. Like every other blacktopped surface in Massachusetts, it was randomly mined with vicious potholes. As I crawled through the darkness at a maximum of maybe ten miles an hour, they eluded my headlights and defeated the Bronco's suspension system. To the best of my recollection, the Simmses' place was about a mile after the turnoff onto the lane and about a quarter mile beyond a nondescript brown house with a large, distinctive red mailbox. I'd reset the trip meter at the turnoff. At .6 miles, the red mailbox appeared on my right. I was positive that this was the last house before the Simmses'. If I remembered correctly, what lay beyond on the right was, first, a stretch of woods, then an open field, and then a smaller wooded area that separated the field from the roughly cleared patch of land around the Simmses'. I slowed way down and trained my eyes on the right-hand side of the road. Although I couldn't have been doing more than five miles an hour, the Bronco hit a hole that threw my teeth out of alignment. I swore. Then the field suddenly appeared. I killed the headlights and pulled to the side of the road, but when I got out, I left the door open and the engine running.

Sooner than I expected, I found what I suspected would be there, a break in the tumbledown stone wall and the thin line of mixed maples and weeds that divided the field from the road, and a welcome pair of ruts left by the tires of last summer's farm equipment. Returning to my Bronco, I locked the hubs, got back in, shifted to four-wheel drive, eased into the field, and pulled to the left, out of the ruts and onto a firm, grassy area where the saplings that overgrew the wall would help to screen the car from the lane. I turned off the engine and opened the door. In the distance, a couple of dogs barked. At me? Or maybe at a skunk or a thieving raccoon or a bold individual extending the coyote's range.

Except for the voices of the dogs, the silence was absolute. I tried not to break it. At least to my own ears, my efforts failed. To load the Ladysmith, you press the thumbpiece forward, thus unlocking the cylinder so you can turn it. You put the rounds of ammunition in the charge holes, and you turn the cylinder back into the frame until it locks. The procedure doesn't normally sound like grapefruit-size hailstones falling on a tin roof. And, yes, I know it's unsafe to carry a loaded revolver, but what was I going to do? Protect myself with an unloaded firearm stuffed in the bottom of my backpack? By the way, even though Buck had the holster specially made for me, it was a stupid present. Underarm might have been okay. But did he really expect me to swagger around like Annie Oakley with a gun on my hip? I left my parka unzipped, but when I pulled the tattered old poncho over my head, the fabric swished and moaned like a high wind. The car door closed like a clap of thunder.

But once I was moving across the furrows and tussocks of the field, my inaudible footsteps seemed to deaden the air like white noise. At the edge of the field, I pulled out my two-D-battery flashlight and, using my hand to shade the beam, flipped it on. Ahead of me lay a low stone wall, the traditional New England marker of boundaries. This one, though, like the one that bordered the lane, hadn't been mended for decades. Good fences? But who reads Robert Frost these days? Walter and Cheryl Simms were no one's idea of good neighbors, anyway. The Norway maple, the kudzu of the rural Northeast, had sown itself thickly on both sides of the wall. On top, rusted strands of old barbed wire waited to snare and trip the unwary, but it didn't get me. As I've said, I grew up in Maine.

The woods beyond the wall were so dark that it would have been easy to believe that the sun was waiting for the first of April to rise briefly and, even then, only as a mean joke. Ever been in the woods around here? Well, if not, forget the postcards of model sugar bushes in Vermont and the travel brochure pictures of groomed forests in state-owned park land. When I say *woods,* I don't mean a Christmas tree farm or a spruce plantation, either. I mean thick brush, impenetrable clumps of alders, fallen logs, and the tough vines of wild blackberries, God's own barbed wire. I took a deep breath and searched for a route through the undergrowth. There was an earthy smell of wet moss, slow-decaying leaves, and the decomposing bodies of microscopic animals.

But I hit it lucky. To my right, I found the remains of an old path, maybe the trace of a lumber road, maybe the vestige of a long-dead friendship between neighbors whose houses had sunk into cellar holes. With the filtered beam of the flashlight aimed at my feet, I took firm steps on the packed-down earth. Then the barking of a couple of dogs gave way to a voice entirely different from theirs. I have no ear for human music, but I am a connoisseur of howls. This one lacked the volume, range, and melody of Rowdy's—he is a canine Pavarotti—but it was unmistakably the song of one of his kin, the howl of an Alaskan malamute. Missy? Or maybe not. But a malamute, one of my own.

As if the sound waves carried scent, at the exact second the howl reached my ears, the stench invaded my nostrils and pressed like a determined finger on the back of my throat. I'd eaten breakfast. Maybe I should have started out on an empty stomach. The fresh coffee I'd drunk had turned as stale and bitter as if I'd swallowed the filter and grounds. My breath stank of indigestion, and the damp air reeked of dogs and filth.

I reached the clearing around the Simmses' place. The road was somewhere to my left, hidden in the night. The sagging roof of the shabby little house dipped in a U-shape against a patch of sky visible through the cloud cover. The ruins of the sheet-metal broiler farm were straight ahead. Scattered between the remains of the big, ugly building and my spot at the edge of the woods were three little sheds that looked something like outmoded and abandoned overnight cabins and even more like miniature outhouses, which, in case I've lost you, is the only word for privies ever spoken by loyal natives of the State of Maine.

In the shelter of the woods, I turned off the flashlight, slipped off the backpack, and transferred the camera, a collar, and a lead to the pockets of my parka. I removed my gloves, stowed them in the pack, and hefted it on again. Then I made for the nearest little shack. The closer I got to it, the more it smelled like an outhouse, but the less it looked like one. It was roughly the shape of a prefab tool shed intended for the suburban yard of a diminutive gardener. To avoid stumbling on the pieces of unidentifiable junk that seemed to be strewn everywhere, I circled carefully around and located the door on the side that faced the back of the property. With the little shed and the high walls of the ruined broiler farm between me and the house, I removed the penlight from my pocket, held it against my hand, flicked it on, and used its beam to find a big, sturdy hook and eye, the door's only latch. I had to push up hard on the cold, wet metal to raise the hook, and it cleared the eye with a sudden snap that sounded loud enough to awaken Diane Sweet. I held perfectly still. Inside the building, something stirred. I switched to the big flashlight, and holding it poised to turn on, I inched open the door.

I'm not afraid of dogs, of course, but I'm not naive, either. Ever been bitten? And I mean *bitten,* not just pinched or nipped. Like being slammed with a nail-spiked baseball bat, right? Intense pain and sorely wounded feelings, too. But I lost my pride a long time ago. Sure, dogs understand that I love them, but they'll bite me nonetheless.

Consequently, before entering the windowless little shack, I braced the door with one hand, and with the other, I raised the flashlight and inserted it in the crack of the door. I flicked on the beam and peered in. The first thing I saw was a slowly moving mass of white that momentarily baffled me. A motherless litter of Westie puppies? For a second, I scanned for tiny heads or eyes or tails, details that would let my brain read this pale, teeming blob as squirming newborn pups. For God's sake, the stench should have told me; I didn't really need my eyes at all. And even the ugliest, wettest newborn pup looks nothing like a thick swarm of maggots feeding on a disgusting pile of feces.

I tugged the door closed behind me and turned on the big flashlight. There were puppies, too, an unborn litter that swelled the belly of the emaciated golden retriever bitch who barely dragged herself to her feet when I entered. I was raised by golden retrievers; compared with goldens, my hu-

man parents were the incidental figures of my early child-
hood. Vinnie and Danny were goldens. I have handled goldens in breed and obedience. I have trained dozens of them,
groomed hundreds, and admired thousands. This bitch's coat
was so caked with filth that it took me a second to identify
her breed. Or maybe I just couldn't let myself see her as a
golden. Lack of food and exercise had left her with bone in
place of muscle and flesh. Although she managed to rise to
her feet, she didn't approach me. In fact, she seemed neither
friendly nor wary, but merely stood there aimlessly, her tail
immobile, her eyes vacant. The golden retriever is a superb
obedience breed, of course. Acting as her own trainer and
handler, this golden seemed to have taught herself the trick
of feeling nothing at all. In her circumstances, she couldn't
have chosen more wisely.

My hands dripping with sweat, I pulled out the camera
and photographed the living things I saw: the golden retriever bitch and the maggots that lived on the feces she'd
pitifully tried to confine to one end of the shed. Then I got a
couple of tiny dog biscuits from my pack, placed them on my
open palm, and slowly extended it toward her. At the sight of
a moving hand, though, she cringed. I'd been wrong. She
hadn't lost all feeling after all. I dropped the treats onto the
dirt floor and left.

28

THE DAMP AIR OUTSIDE THE shed should have seemed almost fresh after the toxic-smelling fumes the poor golden breathed, but it didn't, and my mouth tasted as though I'd caught a gum disease that was spreading to my tongue and throat. I wanted to find Missy and get out. But was she here? I leaned against the shed and gave my eyes a chance to recover from the camera flash and readapt to the darkness. I was facing the back of the property. Ahead of me were two more little outbuildings. A black mass of trees rose in the distance. In the cleared area to my left, between the trees and the nearby ruins of the massive chicken coop, I could make out a scatter of low, dark lumps. Oil drums? Then one of them moved. A chain rattled. I glanced around the corner of the shed to check out the house. No lights were on. Stepping much more slowly and carefully than I'd have liked, I started toward that moving lump chained in the field. The darkness made the Simmses' whole spread look vast, but, by daylight, it had seemed small, and my feet covered the ground quickly. In what seemed like seconds, the lump came into focus as a big, wolflike dog.

As I stepped forward, the clouds opened, and I saw the white of the dog's bared teeth, the flattened ears, the stiff legs, the low angle of his head and tail, the whole posture of fearful aggression. Carelessly and stupidly, I stared directly at him, and with an almost inaudible growl, he took two quick paces, the warm-up for a powerful lunge. By the time he hit the end of his chain, I'd backed up out of reach. I shouldn't have stared at him, but I couldn't help it. Even in the darkness, an Alaskan malamute is unmistakable. Besides, Rowdy and Kimi had dulled my reflexes. If you stare at either of them, what you'll get is a highly polished see-how-cute-I-am routine designed to convince you that you're the greatest thing to come along since Eukanuba. Their ridiculous and universal friendliness to human beings is as typical of the Alaskan malamute as the bulky muzzle, the brown eyes, or the plumy tail waving over the back; and, to my mind, bad temperament is a far worse fault in the breed than the snipiest muzzle, the palest eyes, or the shortest, baldest little whip of a snap tail. Where does it come from? Careless breeding. Human cruelty.

I gave this guy the benefit of a doubt. "My God," I whispered to him as I backed away, "what have they done to you?"

Underfed him? Even in the darkness, his body was skeletal. And his thick chain was moored to bare ground. In a fierce blizzard, he could have nestled snugly in the snow, but he had no natural shelter from the rain and, worse yet, the summer sun, not so much as an empty barrel, not the poorest excuse for a doghouse. Inflict this misery on Rowdy, and how long would his lovely temperament endure? How long would Kimi's?

But they were safe at home. Where the hell was Missy? I turned away from the malamute. Showing him my back may have been a mistake, or maybe I suddenly gave off a scent of terror. In any case, since my arrival, there'd been a few low barks and growls, but nothing even approaching the deafening canine warning I'd feared, the sudden outbreak of cacophony: Intruder! Intruder! But now? And from a *malamute*? The breed that can bark, but almost never does? The world's worst guard dog? His sudden roar must have doubled my heart rate. Within seconds, the pack was off my back, and my right hand was gripping a rawhide bone, knotted at both ends, shaped more or less like a wooden dumbbell. I'm no good with balls of paper, but even under pressure, I can hurl a dumbbell-shaped object through the air and place it in the exact spot I choose. Hardest part of teaching a dog to retrieve, right? Teaching yourself to throw the dumbbell. *Dog* training? People training. If the rawhide bone landed just beyond the dog's reach, where he could see it and smell it? He'd stretch, bellow, and tear the ground to get it, and he might snap his chain.

But I have dead aim. The malamute fell silent. How long had his alarm lasted? Ten seconds? A few more? I hoped that the dog barked like that every time a raccoon turned its back on him. I almost wished for the sound of a window opening in one of the bedrooms and the sound of Walter Simms's voice hollering, "Christ, can't you ever shut the fuck up!"

But I heard nothing. Almost immediately, I headed toward the outline of the big ruined broiler farm, which turned out to house—if you can call it that—four more golden retrievers—three bitches and a dog—and five Norwegian elk-

hounds—four bitches and a dog. Males don't actually produce puppies, right? Anyway, the nine dogs lived—if you call
it that—on what my hand-filtered flashlight revealed as a
small patch of mud and feces in a chicken-wire enclosure
attached to the building. A ragged lean-to along one side of
the wire offered more shelter than the malamute had. I
caught a glimpse of an open sore on the head of one of the
elkhounds, one of the goldens limped badly, and all the dogs
were hideously thin, but this group was nonetheless in better
shape than the first golden I'd seen.

But maybe Walter Simms had something against moth-
erhood. Jammed into a wire-floored rabbit hutch—honest to
God, a rabbit hutch—at the corner of the building, I found a
Norwegian elkhound bitch with a litter of three puppies. You
know what an elkhound is? Well, if not, this isn't the time to
tell you in detail. Gorgeous breed, wonderful dogs, but for
now, let's just say that an elkhound would remind you of a
half-size gray malamute, at least if you didn't actually know
anything about dogs. This elkhound bitch was jailed in a
space that would have cramped a chihuahua. She had no
room to stand up, and if she'd been able to rise, the wire floor
would have cut into her pads. The pups actually seemed to be
nursing, though, and both the bitch and her litter looked
better fed than the other dogs I'd seen, which is to say that
they weren't skin draped on bare bone. If Simms liked her
enough to feed her, I wondered, why confine her to this cage,
with its pile of droppings underneath where they had fallen
through the wire? Why feed this one? Then the explanation
came to me, cruel and sick: She was fed while she nursed the
puppies, then and only then, while she was preparing the
merchandise for the clean fiberglass cages of Puppy Luv and
the spotless concrete runs of Your Local Breeder. After all,
customers *see* the puppies. But who sees a puppy mill brood
bitch? Who even imagines her?

The elkhound bitch watched me suspiciously, and when she began to growl, I moved on. Where the hell was Missy? The male malamute was chained in the open. The bitches, too? I'd first seen him as one of a series of dark lumps, the one that moved. Should I check out the others? Or try the two little sheds I hadn't yet entered? The sheds had one advantage over the open ground: I could use my camera inside without the risk that Walter or Cheryl would make an early morning bathroom trip and catch sight of the flash. I wanted Missy, but I also wanted more evidence than I'd been able to get so far.

I headed in the direction of the sheds, back toward the woods from which I'd emerged. The shack I'd already entered, the one that held the golden, was to my right. The other two were clustered together to my left. My progress toward them was maddeningly slow, mainly because the direct route led across what seemed to be Walter and Cheryl's private dump. The handgun at my hip was loaded; I couldn't afford to fall. The ground was littered with beer cans that no one had bothered to turn in and the spilled contents of what seemed like a few thousand torn plastic trash bags. To detour around the heap without tumbling into it, I simply had to use a flashlight. With my hand blocking most of the beam and my heart hammering, I picked my way along. Want a survey of the Simmses' product preferences? Oreo cookies, Kraft macaroni and cheese, generic potato chips, and—I swear— Lysol air freshener. The family beer was Miller Lite. Cheryl used tampons with pink plastic applicators. The headline of a soggy but legible tabloid newspaper caught my eye: "The Curse of Elvis Strikes Lisa Marie!" Poetry, right? At every supermarket checkout aisle. No wonder nobody reads Robert Frost anymore.

In spite of my maddening circuit around the garbage, I again had the sense of reaching my goal more quickly than

I'd expected. These sheds were smaller than the first. For no particular reason, I'd intended to begin by checking out the one on the left. I'd even begun to search for the door, but the sudden eruption of frantic thumping in the other shed changed my plan. A dog was in there, a dog trying to batter down the door, which turned out to open outward and to be barred shut by a piece of two-by-four suspended on heavy metal hooks. I had the bar off in no time.

Missy? But I was as careful as I'd been at the first shed. I held the door, braced it, and began to inch it open. I had nothing to fear, though. A big, familiar-feeling creature knocked the flashlight from my hand, scoured my face, bounced at my feet, leapt up, popped down, and nearly made it out the door before my groping hands sank into a thick double coat and finally grabbed a leather collar. I gripped it tightly, retrieved the flashlight, and trained the beam directly on that full mask so much like Kimi's, the black cap, the bar down the nose, the goggles around the eyes.

My relief was so great that a wave of exhaustion suddenly swept over me, but Missy—thank God, Missy—was all energy. Her powerful body swept back and forth, and her tail sailed joyfully above her back like a plume waving, exactly as the breed standard says. I pulled the leash and collar from my pocket, snapped the leash to one ring of the nylon choke, and slipped it over her head. One goal accomplished. I swept the light over the interior of the shed. The floor was dirt, and Missy had, of course, been forced to soil her quarters. She'd tried to free herself, but had succeeded only in digging a series of holes before she'd repeatedly hit chicken wire. Was there evidence to photograph? The absence of food and water? Weak evidence, at best.

But the third shack, only a few steps away? Because I hadn't wanted to use the flash outdoors, I'd taken photos of only one dog, a starving dog cruelly confined, of course, but only one dog. Were those photos enough? I was taking Missy with me, but I couldn't free all of these dogs, not by myself. The elkhound bitch and her three puppies? I couldn't carry the puppies while leading Missy and the bitch, could I? And the two bitches, oblivious to my purpose, might decide to go for each other's throats. The golden? Pregnant, emaciated, maybe dying? She was the legal property of Walter or Cheryl Simms, and if my evidence proved inadequate or insufficient, so she would remain.

I hated to leave Missy in that shack, even for a few minutes, but, with a malamute on lead, it would be impossible to check out the other shed. To enter, I'd need one hand for the door and one for the flashlight. If the place, in fact, held a dog? I'd never manage to handle Missy and the stranger while using the flashlight, never mind the camera. So I barred the door on an eager, puzzled Missy, crossed to the neighboring shed, and located the door, directly opposite the one to Missy's. Like the first shed, where I'd found the starving golden, this one had a door fastened with an oversize hook and eye. I repeated the cautious procedure I'd used to enter the other two sheds. With Missy almost free and the two of us almost safe, I didn't want to get careless and end up mauled, maybe even too badly injured to get Missy away. As I eased open the door, I listened hard for the soft pad of feet or for the sound of a dog panting or simply breathing. I heard nothing. I inserted the flashlight and peered in. The other sheds had been barren. This one was piled with junk: a rusted wood stove, a pile of split logs, a chain saw, a pickax, a shovel, a couple of galvanized metal buckets. Still moving cautiously, I opened the door. By now, it seemed to me, my nose should have adapted to the pervasive stench, but when I stepped in, my rib cage contracted in deep, rhythmic waves of nausea. I pulled out the camera and tried to prepare for the sickening task ahead of me. There was a dog in here, after all, a dog beyond the suffering of the others. The dark, dirty shed reeked of death.

With the camera in one hand and the flashlight in the other, I searched for the body. I found it at the far end of the place, shoved behind the wood stove. The body lay on the dirt floor, but the head and shoulders, weirdly encased in clear plastic, rested on a pile of logs, as if he'd stretched out to rest with his head propped up on a hard, rough pillow. His black shoes were muddy, and flecks of wood and bits of debris dirtied his dark suit. The plastic had slipped from the top of the head. The beam of my flashlight shone on crimped white-blond hair.

I shot ten pictures one right after the other. Then I staggered outside and vomited. When I wiped my hand across my mouth, my own skin reeked.

As always, a dog brought me to myself. Missy was thumping and scratching at her door. I closed and latched the door to the shed that held the corpse. Then I opened Missy's door, grabbed her leash, shut the door, and barred it. Less than a minute later, she was dashing along the rough track that led through the woods and to my car. I stumbled after her.

29

OPPONENTS OF CRATE TRAINING point out that the ancestors of our domestic dogs were not denning animals, and it's true that wolves are nomads who use the den exclusively as a nursery for their pups. When the pups are old enough to rove with the adults, the pack abandons the den until the arrival of a new litter. In many respects, both anatomical and behavioral, though, the domestic dog is like a juvenile wolf. *Neoteny,* it's called, the retention of immature characteristics in adulthood, like the little wolf-pup teeth of grown-up dogs. Face licking? Food begging. And denning? Maybe. But neoteny is no excuse for cruelty; a den is a nursery, not a jail. A crate can be a portable den, welcome protection from car crashes and dog-show chaos, but the dog who's crated half his life is a dog with atrophied muscles and an atrophied mind.

Normally, then, I'm a crate training mugwump. When Missy and I reached the Bronco, though, I felt grateful to

Enid Sievers for what I suspected was an overuse of the Vari-
Kennel she'd tried to sell me. Although the crates in my car
were wire mesh, not polypropylene, when I opened the tailgate, Missy hopped up and in like a show-circuit veteran and
happily settled herself on a threadbare pink blanket. I gave
her a drink of water and a handful of dog biscuits, replen-
ished the supply in my pockets, and latched the cage. The
rain had stopped. I pulled off the poncho, stowed it in the
back of the car, and closed the tailgate.

Then I headed back.

Why? Neoteny, maybe. I'm an honorary malamute now,
but I was raised by goldens as a golden. If I abandoned that
bitch? She could go into labor any time, and I wasn't sure
that she'd survive it on her own. The presence of a dead
human body would immediately rouse the police, but would
they also raid the puppy mill and save the dogs? A raid could
involve the MSPCA, the Colley Society, local animal control
officials, and the local health department, as well as the state
police or a deputy sheriff. Also, a raid would inevitably mean
the arrival of a veterinarian, and I was as worried about the
vet as I was about delay. Euthanasia is a sad and sometimes
necessary fact of raids on puppy mills; the attending vet
euthanizes the dogs deemed beyond salvation. The golden?
She was filthy, wasted, and miserable, but she'd shown no
sign of acute illness or pain. I thought she stood a chance of
recovery. But would the attending vet agree? The extra crate
was sitting empty in the Bronco; the golden's miserable,
filthy shed was only a short distance from the edge of the
woods; and I'd discovered a quick, smooth route that would
get me there and back in under ten minutes. A faint prelude
to dawn was just beginning to color the sky: I wouldn't even
need a flashlight. If she couldn't walk? A mature golden retriever bitch weighs about sixty pounds. This one, although

heavily pregnant, couldn't be more than forty-five pounds; if she couldn't cover the distance on her own, I'd carry her.

It took me less than five minutes to reach the far end of the rough trail through the woods. The predawn light was already reducing the dimensions of the cleared land around the Simmses' house. I glanced around, stepped into the open, and crossed rapidly to the shelter of the golden's shed. Then I hesitated. If she'd started to whelp? I hadn't promised to save her; I was here only to give her a chance. I pulled out my big flashlight, but, this time, instead of inching open the door, I walked boldly in. The golden hadn't gone into labor, and she'd eaten the dog biscuits I'd left. Once again, she struggled to her feet.

I slipped the training collar over her head, attached the lead, and whispered, "Good girl." Then I patted my left thigh and added, "Let's go!"

And you know what? With a feeble wag of her tail, she followed me out the door. To delay the Simmses' discovery of my visit, I stopped briefly, closed the door, and forced the hook into the eye. Then, leading the golden, I took a couple of steps and tried to assess her strength. Could she make it to the woods on her own? Or should I carry her? But if I stooped and lifted her, would she panic? Although she was pitifully weak, she seemed in no danger of losing her balance, and she was obviously willing to accompany me.

"Let's go, girl!" I murmured. "You can do it! Let's go!" I moved ahead of her, and she gamely followed. Then I slowed down to match her pace; if she stumbled on the rough ground, I wanted to be at her side to support her.

We'd covered about half the short distance back to the shelter of the woods when, for the first time, she began to totter a little. Just as I was leaning over to rest a supporting hand on her shoulder, a door clattered. I looked up. The back of the house was now in view and, beyond it, the top of the ragged wire fence that ran along the road. The only thing in motion was a speeding dog.

How fast can a healthy, young Rottweiler run? Thirty miles an hour? Forty? It looked like a hundred. Within seconds, Walter Simms's big, sleek Rottie, Champ, was zooming toward us. If Champ was out, he'd been let out; the household was beginning to awaken. Walter and Cheryl Simms, though, were a distant threat. At the moment we had an immediate peril. About two yards from me, Champ slammed to a halt, his legs stiff, his jaws open to display a set of clean white teeth.

Ever hear a Rottie growl? Very deep, very serious. And ever so slowly, he moved. Terror seemed to wire my pounding heart directly to my gut. Great dog expert, right? I had no idea what to do. I tried to avoid Champ's glaring eyes, but he had no desire to avoid mine, and his growl grew louder and louder. When he began to circle, I went rigid. Then my hands started to shake. Time was up. In a second, he'd strike.

In desperation, I used the only resource I had. Moving as slowly as Champ did, I eased a hand into a pocket, grabbed a fistful of tiny dog biscuits, and said softly and cheerfully, "Here, boy! Treat!" Then I tossed the biscuits behind the snarling Rottie. A trained guard dog would have ignored the food, of course, but Champ was startled. He took his eyes off me, veered around, sniffed, found a biscuit, and wolfed it down. I threw a few more biscuits, and, while he was distracted, I slipped off the backpack and fished desperately for one of the rawhide bones. The ploy had worked with the malamute, hadn't it? What other option did I have? As if in answer to the question, the twenty ounces of Ladysmith suddenly felt like twenty pounds.

Shoot a dog? I almost yelled the words aloud. *Me? Shoot a dog?*

And yet my right hand went to the holster, groped, and closed firmly around the revolver. To protect this helpless golden, this emaciated, pregnant bitch, could I do it? Even if I wanted to, could I aim and pull the trigger? *Kill a dog?* I glanced at Champ, dropped the golden's leash, and anchored it with my foot. Then I reached back into the pack and finally located a rawhide bone. Would Champ go for it? My right hand was so drenched in sweat that the rawhide felt slimy. I slowly raised my arm and was just aiming the rawhide at a spot halfway to the Simmses' house when I heard the sound of approaching engines. My arm froze. Cars? Maybe not. Loud and powerful engines. An oil delivery truck? But at daybreak? Oil companies don't—

Before I could complete the thought, the first cruiser appeared on the road. Behind it were a second cruiser, two vans, a station wagon, and probably several other vehicles as well. I didn't stop to count them. Oblivious to the signs of a raid on his master's puppy mill, Champ was circling and snarling again. He'd spotted the rawhide bone in my right hand. If I didn't throw it fast, he'd go for it—and probably take my fingers with it. My aim was rough this time. The rawhide sailed high in the air and toward the house. My eyes followed its arc. I hoped Champ's did, too. If he lost sight of the bone? He'd assume I'd been teasing, and he'd look for the rawhide in the last place he'd seen it: my right hand. And he wouldn't search gently, either.

But Champ started toward the rawhide, or so it seemed. As soon as he found it, I intended to bolt for the woods and the Bronco.

But the back door of the house banged open. Walter Simms had seen or heard the cruisers and vans. Only a few minutes earlier, he must have awakened briefly, let Champ out, and gone back to bed. At the approach of the vehicles, he'd evidently thrown on his jeans and a pair of shoes, snatched up his shotgun, and decided to get out as fast as he could. He hadn't even pulled on a T-shirt. He was facing away from me, scanning the area on the opposite side of the house and softly calling, "Champ! Here, boy!" Simms hadn't yet seen me, but the second he turned, I'd be in plain view. Police cruisers at the front door and someone—anyone—at the rear? And with a dead body on the property? I'd seen the body, and I'd seen how Simms treated his dogs, all but Champ, that is. Unless I acted fast, Simms would turn, aim, and shoot me.

Only four or five yards ahead of me, Champ was ignoring his master's voice and still searching for the rawhide. I had a few dog biscuits left in my pockets. Could I lure the Rottie toward me? The dog was a well-fed, obviously untrained pet. "Champ's not like them others. Champ's *my* dog," Simms had said. I could almost hear him. With the police at the door, Simms was delaying his escape by searching for Champ. A man who'd do that, it seemed to me, could be trusted not to risk shooting that dog. Could I use Champ as a safety shield? Or should I make for cover? The woods? Or back into the golden's filthy shed?

But the Ladysmith tempted me. Walter Simms had caused immeasurable suffering. He'd starved the dogs I'd seen tonight. He'd undoubtedly caused the death of many others. He'd probably murdered a man. He was on the verge of escape, and I could stop him. If he caught sight of me? But I could take him out first. I knew I could. I could pick him off like a scurrying rat. I am, in fact, a very good shot.

The golden, who'd been standing patiently by my side, gave a brief, soft whimper of pain. Slowly and calmly, I drew out the Ladysmith, raised it, cocked it, and took final aim at the dead center of Simms's naked back. My hands and mouth had gone dry, but I was eerily calm. I felt complete confidence in my aim. Otherwise, though, for that half second, I felt nothing at all. The Smith & Wesson manual advises never to touch the trigger until you're ready to fire. My target was sharp, bare, and oversized, as if an anatomist had stepped in to replace Simms's lean, live body with a twice-life-size drawing—muscular system, trunk portion, dorsal view, outer layers stripped back to reveal the man beneath the skin. My finger had moved inside the trigger guard when an authoritative male voice shouted, "*Halt!* Drop it and put your arms *up!*"

And Walter Simms obeyed. So did Champ, who abandoned his search for the rawhide bone and tore toward his master, across the mounds of trash and the tussocks of dry grass washed yellow in the morning light. A uniformed man appeared around the far corner of the house. Then another. And another. I decocked the Ladysmith very carefully—dangerous procedure, that—stowed it in the holster, picked up my backpack and the golden's leash, and led her to the trail in the woods. I wasn't going to stick around to have some veterinarian tell me that this golden couldn't be saved. In rescuing her, I'd almost ended up shooting Walter Simms. I have no doubt that if I'd fired, I would have killed him.

30

ALTHOUGH I HAD A KEY to the door of Steve Delaney's apartment above the clinic, I was standing in the parking lot, hurling gravel at his bedroom window, and calling his name. Steve has two dogs, India, his U.D. shepherd, and an incredibly sweet, timid pointer bitch named Lady. Kenneled downstairs were Steve's hospitalized canine patients and a few boarders. Once the clinic opened for the day, there'd be dozens of dogs coming in. I was so terrified of infecting them with whatever organisms my clothes and hands might carry from my predawn raid that I'd removed my boots and left them in the car before I'd stepped out. I wasn't even willing to touch the doorbell.

"Steve, wake up!" I pelted the window with another spray of gravel. "Wake up!" My voice sounded high and hoarse.

India, who must have been maintaining her usual vigil

over Steve's deep sleep, finally pressed her nose to the window, assessed the situation, and vanished. A few seconds later, Steve repeated her performance and then appeared at the door. Except for his scalp, which remained almost hairless from Rhonda's clippers, he hadn't shaved, and his eyes were heavy. He was barefoot, but he'd put on a pair of tan cords, and he leaned placidly against the door frame slowly buttoning his white shirt.

All of a sudden, tears were running down my face. I'd rescued Missy—I'd brought the golden to Steve—I'd done my part; it was his turn now. I'll bet that when the patient's anesthetic wears off, the surgeon's does, too. "Steve, I have two dogs here." I sobbed and caught my breath. "One is very sick, but I can't bring her in—Steve, I've been to a puppy mill —It was worse than—"

He started toward me.

"Don't touch me!" I ordered him frantically. "I'm covered in filth. You'll make the other dogs sick. Stay away from me!" By then, though, his arms were wrapped around me. I shoved against his chest and tried to push him away, but, malamutes or no malamutes, his arms are stronger than mine. "Don't touch me!" I yelled.

"Hey, let me worry about that," he said calmly. Then he asked to see the dogs. Have I ever told you how much I love Steve? He is honestly the greatest veterinarian in the world. Even so, I was scared to have him examine the golden, terrified of what he'd conclude. Steve and I met the day I brought Vinnie to this clinic for the last time. I held her in my arms while he gave her the peaceful release she wanted. Vinnie was eager to leave; she could hardly wait. Steve was her celestial travel agent. The pain at the end was mine, intense and physical.

"The golden is in bad shape," I warned him. "She's pregnant, and she's starving, and God knows what else. The malamute is okay, I think, except for whatever she picked up there. She wasn't there very long. Steve—"

"Keys?" Steve was peering into the back of the Bronco. "What?"

"Your keys. Unless you want me to examine the dogs through—"

"No, I guess not."

"And put some shoes on," he said. "You're shaking."

The temperature must have been close to freezing, but my socks were wool—warm when it's wet. I looked down. Steve was barefoot in a puddle of water.

I handed him the keys. "Steve, there was a dead man there," I blurted out. "At the puppy mill, in one of the sheds, there was a body. A tall man with weird white hair. Steve, I think I know who he was."

But Steve wasn't listening. He'd opened the tailgate and half-crawled into the Bronco. His voice rumbled softly; he was talking to the dogs. He cares more about live dogs than he does about dead men. So do I, of course. So do I.

An hour later, I was sitting at Steve's kitchen table drinking sweet, milky tea and patting Lady, the pointer. I didn't even have to move my hand. I held it still, and Lady kept running her smooth, soft head under it. Pointers make wonderful companions, beautiful, intelligent, affectionate, and, if need be, self-patting, too. I must have looked like hell. My hair was wet from a long, hot, decontaminating shower, and I was dressed in a vet tech's baggy blue-green pants and top, the only clothes available in anything close to my size. Everything I'd worn at the puppy mill was sealed in a trash bag for me to take home and empty into a strong solution of chlorine bleach. I'd reached Rita, who reported that when she'd been filling the dogs' bowls from the big bag of food in the closet, Kimi had somehow managed to weasel her way in, stick her muzzle in the bag, grab a gigantic mouthful, dash away, and then toss the food all over the floor. Rowdy had then decided to claim his share of the scattered kibble. Rita had wisely let them fight it out. The food had vanished in seconds, neither dog had been hurt, and Rita was never, never feeding those monsters again. As I've mentioned, people are the real challenge. I'd instructed Rita, but she'd ignored me. First you tie up the dogs, or you put them on a down-stay. Only then do you open the closet. But I apologized to Rita, thanked her, made sure that Rowdy and Kimi had water, and thanked her again.

The door to the inside stairs opened, and Steve appeared. He'd rescheduled his morning surgery to give himself time to check out the golden and Missy. "The malamute's overweight," he told me. "Otherwise, she's fine. Something could turn up later, and we should check a stool sample sometime, but that's it."

"The golden?"

Steve leaned against the door. His expression turned professional. He folded his arms and avoided my gaze.

"Steve, I know you have to make these decisions sometimes, and I know she is just . . . she is *so* weak. I couldn't tell if . . . Steve, if you have to . . ."

"It's not a question of euthanasia," Steve said, taking a seat at the table. When he grins, his eyes narrow and, honest to God, they twinkle. A wave of exhaustion nearly knocked me over. Steve got serious. "We're going to have to watch for eclampsia. And bitches like this are prone to mastitis. They're getting her cleaned up now. I'll take another look at her later. She's emaciated, probably anemic, loaded with parasites. Holly, uh, who owns this dog?"

"I do. For now, I own both of those dogs." I hate lying to Steve. "They don't exactly belong *to* me, but they belong *with* me. Is that good enough?"

"For now," he said.

"Honest to God, Steve, I am too tired to tell you about it. Look, I *cannot* stay awake. I was just waiting to . . . it'll be . . . it'll probably be on the news tonight. Maybe it's on the radio now. Steve, I'm going home. I'll call you when I wake up. Can I . . . will you keep the malamute here? Just for a while?"

He reached for my hair, squeezed, and dripped water on my face. "Not a chance," he said. "The minute you're gone, I'll turn her loose on the street. It's the kind of responsible veterinary practice I always run."

I can remember rejecting Steve's offer of a pair of his size twelve shoes. I have a blurry memory of driving home in my stocking feet, or rather, with my feet in a pair of Steve's socks. He'd assured me that if I didn't wear my boots into the house, it was okay to expose myself to the dogs. I believed him, and, of course, I'd showered and changed my clothes, but I still felt contaminated. And desperately tired. When I entered my kitchen, Kimi and Rowdy went wild, but the scent of India and Lady on the blue-green baggies distracted them, and I managed to stay on my feet. While the dogs were in the yard, I remembered that when I'd been driving home, I'd forgotten to listen to the radio. Then the dogs came tearing in. I remember feeding them.

At four-thirty in the afternoon, I awoke to the sound of heavy breathing and the sense that four happy brown eyes were trained on me. Rowdy was stretched out on the bed with his head on my pillow, and Kimi was sitting on the floor with her face about two inches from mine. When I stirred and opened my eyes, Kimi leaped over me and landed on Rowdy, who threw her a warning stare, growled, lunged, and ended up with his snarling jaws encircling her muzzle. She squirmed, kicked, flew through the air, landed on the floor, sprang back onto the bed, nipped at Rowdy's ears, dashed to the far edge of the bed, and crouched. I wrapped my arms around my head and braced myself. Just as the iron bulk of Kimi's body hit my back, Rowdy twisted around and kicked me hard with his hind legs, and then the two dogs became a single roaring mass of teeth and fur that abruptly disappeared from the bedroom, sped back, crashed into a wall, veered around, and vanished. Play, of course. This *is* how malamutes play. I sat up in bed. Every bone in my body ached. A pile of white dust lay on the floor beneath the new dent the dogs had made in the wall. Now and then it occurs to me that instead of taking all these handling and obedience classes, most of us should study something really useful to the dog owner, for example, plastering, auto reupholstery, or invisible weaving.

Despite the shower at Steve's, I still felt filthy, as if I'd breathed and drunk the evil stench of the puppy mill. The taste lingered in my mouth. My body smelled like rancid fat. I started to fill the bathtub with hot water and impulsively squirted in some foaming skin conditioner left by my cousin Leah on her last visit, but the rising bubbles reminded me of Diane Sweet and Walter Simms, so I drained the tub, stood under the shower, washed my hair twice, and scoured my body with soap. I rinsed off, wrapped myself in towels, brushed my teeth three times, and burned my lips and gums with full strength mint mouthwash.

After I'd dressed and fed the dogs, I carried the portable TV from the guest room to the kitchen, made coffee, and drank it while I watched the five o'clock news. At least one of the vehicles in the caravan on Old County Lane had obviously carried a camera crew and equipment. The bad color of my little TV turned the Simmses' house—and everything else—a pale, sickly green. According to the voice-over, today's early-morning raid on a suspected puppy mill in Afton had resulted in the seizure of sixty-eight dogs from the home of Walter Simms and his sister, Cheryl. The coffee cup almost fell from my hand. *Sixty-eight dogs?*

The camera now panned the back of the property, and the voice went on: The raid had taken an unexpected and sinister twist when authorities searching for dogs had come upon the body of a recently deceased man, identified as Joseph Willard Rinehart, 55, of Burlington. Miniaturized and washed in green, the shed appeared.

Then the little TV showed tiny lime-tinted figures, human and canine, heading toward a row of vans and station wagons. The announcer said that the tip on what officials were calling a puppy mill had come from Jane M. Appleyard of the Eleanor J. Colley Humane Society, who credited an unidentified friend of the Simms family with serving as informant.

A friend of the family? I wished the unrelenting flow of the story would stop and give me time to work things out. A friend? Someone who dropped by to watch the Celtics? Who sat around drinking Miller Lite? I couldn't imagine anyone liking Walter and Cheryl enough to ignore the nauseating odor for the sake of their company. I couldn't even think of Walter and Cheryl as a family, never mind as a family with friends.

Mrs. Appleyard's face filled the screen. Her hair stood up in rough clumps. In the powerful, dulcet tones of old Bryn Mawr, she said, "We've known about this situation for a long time, but, in the absence of probable cause, when one's suggestions are ignored, there isn't a great deal one can do." The name, address, and phone number of the Colley Society flashed on the screen, and one of the TV anchors, a woman, said that the Colley Society was appealing for donations of money, supplies, and grooming services to care for the rescued dogs. She ended on a firmly conclusive note, as if she'd done her part, and the male anchor took over. I watched as a still shirtless Walter Simms ducked into a cruiser and was driven away. The polished male voice said that Simms had been taken into custody and that Rinehart's death was being treated as a homicide.

The female anchor began to report on delays in the construction of the new harbor tunnel. I channel-hopped in search of more news about the raid, but found none. Then I checked my answering machine, which blinked red with messages. The first was from Betty Burley, who apologized for not helping with Missy, wondered if I'd made any progress, and suggested that if Missy hadn't turned up, we might want to consider advertising for her and offering a reward. The second was from a guy who'd seen the Malamute Rescue notice posted at a pet supply and grooming shop in Newton and who wanted me to call him. Most of the people who call about adopting a rescue malamute want an obedience-trained watchdog under a year old who'll get along great with six cats and stay in the yard if he's turned loose, but I wrote down the name and number, anyway. Next, Gloria Loss reported that she'd quit her job. Kevin Dennehy had called to ask where I was. Sally Brand wanted me to return the photos I'd borrowed from her.

The machine lacks a date and time stamp. I had no idea when anyone had called. The last message, though, was from Steve, who said that it was three o'clock and that the golden was loaded with whipworm and coccidia, among other things, but that he didn't want to hit her hard with worm medication because she was within a few weeks of whelping. He'd wait until the puppies were born and then treat the whole family. What the bitch needed now was improved nutrition, and that's what she was getting.

I erased the messages, went back to the TV, tuned in midway through another story about the raid, and learned that I'd missed most of the dogs because forty-eight of them were discovered inside Walter and Cheryl Simms's little house. I gathered from the TV footage that the indoor dogs were small—I spotted some cockers, Shih Tzus, bichons, and dachshunds—and that only the big dogs lived outdoors. According to the announcer, the golden retrievers and what he crassly referred to as "huskies," meaning malamutes and elkhounds, I guess, were in better condition than the little indoor dogs, whose small, filthy cages and boxes were stacked throughout the house. Bitches of big breeds are usually free whelpers. But tiny breeds? Forced to bear litter after litter? Their agony was unimaginable. I wondered how they'd survived at all. Many hadn't, of course.

At the end of the story, the camera zoomed in on Cheryl, who stood on the sagging porch in her pink raincoat, her thin, blotchy face a mindless mask of rage. She opened her mouth and wailed directly at the camera. "Me and Walter didn't do nothing wrong. You'd've thought we was in Communist Russia the way they just come and took all our dogs away." She fell silent for a second, then added fiercely, evidently as an afterthought, "And Walter, too."

31

KEVIN DENNEHY APPEARED AT my back door that evening wearing a rumpled blue suit and, as befit both his profession and the damp weather, a tan trench coat. Clutched between the thick fingers of his enormous hands was a heart-shaped box only slightly redder than the blush on his face.

He stammered his routine greeting: "Hey, Holly how ya doing?" Before I had a chance to answer, he added, "Where you been?"

"At a tracking test," I said more or less truthfully. "Kevin, I had totally forgotten it was Valentine's Day. This is—"

Let me say that Kevin was really embarrassed. He looked like an overage kid forced to serve as the ring bearer at the formal wedding of some despised relative. He thrust the candy at me, two pounds of dark chocolates with all soft centers. As Kevin had obviously remembered, I don't like milk chocolate, and my fragile dental work won't stand up to anything more solid than cream fillings and squishy cherries.

I thanked Kevin for the chocolates and offered to share, but he refused. I ate one, made happy noises, and then, to relieve Kevin's discomfort, changed the subject. "So Simms murdered Rinehart, huh? How come nobody noticed he was missing?"

While I was stashing the box of chocolates in the refrigerator, one hidey-hole that Kimi hasn't yet learned to penetrate, Kevin said, "Joe was the kind of a guy who didn't like people sticking their noses in his private business. The salesmen out there and the mechanics and the secretaries and whatever kind of wondered what happened to him, but what with Enzio and all and what with the economy and all, they weren't going to come running to us and then have Joe turn up."

"I guess it wouldn't exactly have earned them any bonuses," I said. "You want to help me walk the dogs?"

Kevin agreed to take Rowdy. Unlike Rita, Kevin considers the malamute a walkable breed. The policeman is your friend, right? Strong and brave. In fact, Kevin is always glad to take Rowdy, but he hates being in charge of Kimi. Although Kevin never admits it, I'm convinced that he doesn't like being seen with a girl who lifts her leg.

The rain had started up again, but the air was warm, at least by the standards of coastal Maine, where *warm* is any temperature above forty degrees. I wore my yellow slicker and Wellies. Kimi and Rowdy wore matching red training collars and leads. The light over my back door showed a few crocuses breaking through the frozen ground in a patch of earth between the fence and driveway. Kimi cocked a hind leg over them. Ever the gentleman, Kevin looked away. Rowdy, though, watched, sniffed, and covered her scent. In his own way, he's a gentleman, too.

"But, Kevin," I said, "didn't *you* notice that Rinehart was gone? I mean, Diane Sweet did business with Rinehart, Simms worked for him, Simms was at Puppy Luv. . . . So didn't you try to . . . ? I mean, I would've thought that a guy like that would've—"

"Yeah, yeah, they want to look like the upright citizen, got nothing to hide," Kevin said, "but they're kind of like a housewife with company coming. They want a couple of days to get the accountant in there and get a little housework done. But even if his body hadn't turned up, sooner or later, we'd've put it together. And if the scene hadn't been such a godawful mess, they could've got it sorted out easier. They can tell dog hair from human hair, no problem, but it would've taken them a while, what with that much of it to look at. But once the body turned up . . ."

"Rinehart was *at* Puppy Luv?"

"Oh, yeah, Rinehart was there. No question. Everything matches up. The dog hair on him comes from there, traces of the dog shampoo they use. He's got Puppy Luv written all over him. The head . . . when they found the body, the head was wrapped in a piece of this clear plastic, and it matches up. Covered with traces, Diane's saliva, lipstick, an eyelash. And a piece torn out of the plastic fits with the little piece that got caught on her earring. No question."

The dogs brought us to a halt at a lamppost on Concord Avenue that looks like every other lamppost in Cambridge, but obviously smells utterly distinct and fascinating. Kimi sniffed the base while Rowdy was checking out the area above her head.

"We'll have to wait for them," I said. "So it was Rinehart who strangled Diane Sweet? Kevin, that doesn't make sense. Why would Rinehart kill her? She was a good customer, I think, and she was no threat to him. I mean, what kind of trouble could she have caused? Being a puppy broker is evil, but . . . Well, except that according to USDA regulations, Rinehart was supposed to hold the puppies for twenty-four hours, or something, and he probably didn't. But, you know, when the USDA even bothers to inspect, they don't do much. If they find a violation, all they usually do is tell the people to correct it. I can't understand why Rinehart . . . Kimi, enough! Let's go!"

Kimi lifted her leg on the interesting lamppost. Kevin hauled Rowdy away and looked back at Kimi. "You ever, uh, ask Delaney about that?"

"It's perfectly normal," I said. "A lot of bitches do it, but, of course, some of them just do it once in a while, and a lot of them don't actually . . . And sometimes she squats. Anyway, it's perfectly normal. So Rinehart—"

"Probably didn't even touch her," Kevin said. "Diane could've been dead when Rinehart got there. This plastic from the dog bed went from her to him. If Rinehart had been standing ten feet from her and sneezed, the lab could tell you, but Rinehart had on a dark suit, and Diane was wearing a fuzzy white sweater, so if he'd got close enough to strangle her, you could've seen it with your naked eye."

"But, Kevin, I don't see . . . The thing is, Rinehart . . . Kevin, on Wednesday morning, someone placed an order with Rinehart. Someone ordered puppies from him."

"From his people," Kevin said. "The business is still there. It's an office, is what it is. Rinehart Pet Mart. Deals in cats, too. Kittens."

"Jesus. So Rinehart got to Puppy Luv after—or probably after—Diane Sweet was dead? So Rinehart wasn't—"

"Couldn't've been," Kevin said. "Rinehart tries to use this plastic on her, and that doesn't work, so he strangles her, and someone comes along and grabs him and cracks his head on a bathtub, and wraps him up in the same piece of plastic he just used . . . ?"

"A bathtub?"

"The one in the back. Raised up high so's the top is about level with your waist."

"Right. So . . . ?"

"Hair all over the place," Kevin said, "including the drain of the bath tub, and, like you'd expect, most of it's dog hair."

"But?"

"But in the drain of the bathtub, we find a couple of strands of human hair. And just a little trace of human blood."

"Thorough," I said. "You guys are very thorough. From Rinehart?"

"From Rinehart," Kevin agreed, "who happened to have had his head bashed against a solid object."

"By Walter Simms," I said. "Eliminating the middleman, right? So that was it? Brokers are the middlemen, and they're the ones who get rich, and that's what Simms was doing after all, right? Eliminating the middleman. Or wrong. I mean, I told you that Simms wasn't trying to do that, because he couldn't supply what Rinehart could, you know, that many puppies, all the breeds. But, Kevin, does Simms say . . . Look. Simms got there first, right? He got to Puppy Luv, and he killed Diane, and then—"

"You're getting there," Kevin said. "But you need to back up."

"Janice Coakley? Simms goes to Your Local Breeder. He delivers the puppies Janice ordered from Rinehart, plus a few he's selling her himself that Rinehart doesn't know about." Kevin said nothing. Then I got it. "But Rinehart *does* know! Rinehart knows. He's caught on to Simms." I paused. "And to Janice Coakley. And to Diane Sweet."

For reasons perceptible only to dogs, Rowdy and Kimi had lost interest in the lampposts, fire hydrants, and trees, and were now setting a fast pace down Concord Avenue toward the Armory and Fresh Pond. Kevin and I were trotting after the dogs.

The words started to tumble out of my mouth. "And, Kevin, Janice Coakley knew! Or I think she did. On Wednesday, yesterday, Janice Coakley knew that Rinehart was dead, because yesterday morning, she placed two orders for puppies, some from Rinehart—or from Rinehart Pet Mart—and some from Walter Simms, and if she knew Rinehart had caught on, and if she thought Rinehart was still alive . . . So Walter Simms *told* her, right? Either he told her he'd killed Rinehart, or else he just told her that Rinehart was dead. Anyway, she knew it was safe to keep ordering from Simms."

"You're ten steps ahead," Kevin said.

"So Rinehart had caught on to Simms and the whole deal. Rinehart knew they were cheating him."

"How, I haven't got that worked out yet, but, yeah, Rinehart caught on. More likely, he got told."

"Okay. So Simms goes to Your Local Breeder, and . . . I'm lost. Anyway, he leaves there, and he drives to Puppy Luv. And then, he, uh, either he delivers the puppies first and makes love to Diane, if you can call it that, or he delivers the puppies after. And then, for some reason, Simms murders her. He gets this dog bed, and he starts to smother her, only he ends up strangling her? Anyway, for some reason, Rinehart is there, and Simms murders him, too, because . . . Well, for some reason, he does. And then, obviously, Simms isn't just going to leave Rinehart's body at Puppy Luv, because he wants it to look like a robbery, right? So he puts Rinehart's body in whatever he's driving. And then when he gets home, he dumps it in the shed. That part makes sense. The ground is frozen. Simms was waiting till the ground thawed to bury him."

We turned onto Fayerweather Street, the Concord Avenue end, of course, which is like my block of Appleton Street, two-family houses, cops, writers, students, professors who live on their salaries. The neighborhood on our side of Huron Avenue is Fresh Pond, but once you cross Huron Avenue and head toward Brattle Street, twenty-room mansions replace the two-family houses, and . . . Well, congratulations! You've moved up in the world. Now you're Off Brattle. Kevin voted for Governor Weld, who lives at the Brattle end of Fayerweather, but he avoids crossing Huron Ave. except in the line of duty.

With justifiable pride, Kevin said, "You don't get it, do you?"

"Of course I do." My voice was huffy.

"No, you don't. And, geez, you're the dog expert, and here am I—"

"What does my, uh, expertise—?"

"You pull out this pedigree, and you tell me all about—"

"What does that have to do with . . . ?" It seemed to me that Kevin hadn't been all that interested in Missy's pedigree. Mostly, as I recalled it, he'd been morally outraged.

"You remember what you said?"

"I guess so," I said.

"Well, what you said was that dogs don't know. Like, uh, one stud and two sisters."

"Walter Simms. Diane Sweet. Janice Coakley. But, Kevin, if Janice Coakley . . . *Janice* found out? And after Walter Simms left her, she followed him, and—Okay, Kevin, this has gone far enough." I was actually angry, more at Walter Simms than at Kevin and his guessing game. Running a puppy mill is no crime. Even with blatant evidence of neglect and cruelty? That son of a bitch Walter Simms would pay a small fine and spend maybe a few months in jail. I'd wanted him convicted of one crime that everyone, even the AKC, would take seriously, namely, murder.

"Mrs. Coakley didn't find out until today when yours truly opened his big mouth and told her, and, once he did, you should've heard what came out."

"So . . . But Diane found out. Who told her? Walter Simms? He told her and then . . . Just *tell* me, would you?"

"Joe Rinehart gets a tip about the ripoffs, or else he tumbles to it, but whichever way, he gets to Mrs. Coakley's. This is Sunday night, quarter of ten, somewhere around then, and Simms has just left to go to Puppy Luv, but Rinehart reads her the riot act, scares the shit out of her, only he only knows *half* of it. Rinehart knows about the puppies, he knows Janice and Simms are pulling one over on him, but he doesn't know about her affair with Simms. So Rinehart scares the pants off her, and then he takes off after Simms."

"So Janice calls to warn Simms! Only, of course, Diane answers the phone, right? I mean, she owns the place, and her voice is on the tape. So did Janice talk to Simms?"

"That wouldn't've done it," Kevin said. "Remember, like I told you about the dogs. If they know, they care. Janice calls Diane, and she wants to talk to Simms, and when Diane asks why, Janice makes a big mistake, not for her, for Diane. She tells Diane that Rinehart's on his way and she has to talk to Simms, and she lets it slip that they've got this special relationship. Or maybe she says Walter is special to her. Something like that. She can't remember exactly."

"So basically Janice told Diane. Diane thought Simms sort of belonged to her, and then she found out he was sleeping with her sister, too. Oh, okay! So Diane never passed on the message, right? She heard *special*, and she probably heard something in Janice's tone of voice, and so she never told Simms that Rinehart was on his way."

"Cool customer," Kevin said. "Businesswoman type."

"And then?"

"Conjecture. Diane doesn't pass on the word about Rinehart. She just tells Simms that she knows all about him and Janice, and while she's yelling at him and maybe he's yelling back, Rinehart shows up, and I think he comes to the back door. That's where Simms's van is, and Rinehart's on a kind of back-door errand, anyway. So Rinehart's at the door, and when Diane hears him, she knows who it is. She's expecting him."

"And Simms could've . . . He could've thought it was her husband, I guess."

"Not if he heard Rinehart's voice. Simms worked for Rinehart. He would've recognized his. So when Simms heard Rinehart holler to open the door, that's when he decided to shut her up, and while he was at it, he decided to make it permanent."

"He knew Diane hadn't warned him. He realized why Janice had called, and he knew Diane hadn't warned him. Oh, and Simms hadn't talked to Janice, so he didn't know for sure that Rinehart had caught on, did he? And maybe Diane could've told Rinehart, I don't know, more than he knew already, like how long it had been going on, whatever."

"Or maybe Simms just does what little Walter does when he's really pissed off."

"I don't—"

"You will," Kevin said.

As predicted, at the intersection with Huron, the great sociogeographical divide, Kevin turned right instead of crossing over into Off Brattle. Rowdy darted toward a tree, raised a hind leg, practically wrapped himself around the trunk, lowered his leg, sniffed the tree, and then lifted his leg so high that he almost toppled over.

"Macho," Kevin said with approval.

"So how did Rinehart get in? Did Simms open—"

"Tire iron. We got that one wrong to start with. We figured that was part of the business of faking a robbery, like emptying the cash drawer and all, but the tire iron's covered with Rinehart's prints. Rinehart did that. Dumb guy, when you think about it. You know, I've been thinking about that, about him and Enzio, and I was thinking maybe what Enzio always had against him wasn't that he wasn't Italian. Maybe Enzio just always figured Rinehart was stupid. Anyways, he should've pulled his gun."

"Rinehart was carrying a gun?"

"*Ça va sans dire*," Kevin said and added, rather unnecessarily, "like the Frogs say."

"So then Simms—?"

"Socked him one in the gut, gave him a swift kick where it hurts, and dragged him around the corner to this bathtub and banged his head." Kevin paused. "Contusions. Not a lot of blood."

"So the plastic was to keep the blood off the van or truck or whatever. Hey, wait a minute. What happened to Rinehart's car? If he drove from Janice Coakley's to Puppy Luv . . ."

The streetlight near Henry Bear's toy shop showed Kevin's grin. "Just like Mabelline."

"What?"

"Coupe de Ville. Like the song. Mabelline. Cadillac Coupe de Ville."

"So where is it?"

"Parked on the street, couple of blocks away, covered with tickets, tire iron in the trunk, right where little Walter put it. Like I said, we would've worked it out sooner or later."

"Okay, so what's the 'You will'? There's something else, right? I can tell from your face."

"Little Cheryl," Kevin said. "You catch her on TV?"

"Yes," I said.

"I don't know what Rita'd call it, but, in my opinion, she hasn't got all her marbles. Christ, poor kid, no wonder."

"*Poor kid?* Kevin, they seized sixty-eight dogs from that disgusting place. Walter wasn't the only one responsible for that. Just because she's simpleminded or whatever she is, it doesn't excuse that. You don't have to be exactly brilliant to understand that animals are suffering. So don't tell me—"

But Kevin interrupted. He'd interviewed Cheryl Simms after the TV segment had been taped. He had some news that hadn't made the five o'clock report I'd watched. Kevin is a good cop. Smart. He asked Cheryl about Joe Rinehart, and she said, predictably enough, "Me and Walter don't know nothing." Then Kevin asked her about Diane Sweet, and, of course, she said the same thing. Finally, Kevin thought about the background information he'd been given on the Simms family, and he asked Cheryl what had happened to her father. Her reply? "Me and Walter don't know nothing." The excavation of the dirt floor of the same shed that had held Rinehart's body revealed the largely decomposed remains of Cheryl and Walter's father, who had died of gunshot wounds about two years earlier. When Walter Simms was informed that Cheryl could be charged in the death of their father, he confessed to the shooting and claimed that he'd been protecting his sister. Kevin believes him. The pedigree? I told you to look, didn't I? Yeah, the father-daughter breeding. Kevin was right, of course. When people know, they mind a lot.

32

DOG'S LIFE PUBLISHED MY article on Sally Brand, who was so pleased and flattered that she offered me a free tattooed portrait of the dog of my choice anywhere on my body. I had to decline, though. I finally realized that every dog I've ever loved is already written all over me, plainly visible to the canine eye. Who knows what smiling face or wagging tail Sally might inadvertently cover up?

I'm the tattooed lady, and I'm not unique. In fact, if you've ever loved a dog, check out your arms, your legs, your torso, even the palms of your hands and the soles of your feet. Look into a mirror and stare into the depths of your eyes. The retina's a tender place for a tattoo, of course, but you know that already, don't you? When you lost that dog, you nearly died of pain.

We are the *irezumi*, the tattooed ones, engraved, emblazoned, permanently decorated with elaborate patterns of rich design, and together we form a kind of benevolent, joyful *Yakuza,* too, the legal, happy Mafia of dog fancy, neither secret nor exclusive, but open to absolutely anyone who's ever bragged about a dog. *Mafia?* The literal meaning? Boldness, bluster, swagger. Dog lovers, and proud of it. And we're everywhere, of course. We're the guy pumping gas at your local garage, the pharmacist who filled your last prescription, the UPS driver who delivers your orders from Cherrybrook, and the homeless woman in Harvard Square who feeds herself on garbage, but begs change to buy food for her dog. We're Barbara Bush and Cleveland Amory, and I sure hope we're Robin Williams. We're Doris Day, Brigitte Bardot, and Dan Quayle. We're the queen of England.

And damned if we aren't Enzio Guarini, too, who despite his involuntary residence in Rhode Island, has never visited Sally Brand's studio, but who bears on his heart the portraits of two beloved Norwegian elkhounds. When the news broke, Guarini made a large donation to the Eleanor J. Colley Society in memory of his late daughter, Maria, and also arranged to have a quick-setting concrete boot hand-fitted to the foot of Rinehart Pet Mart. Rinehart Motor Mart is still in business, but the associated animal brokerage firm sank so fast that no one even saw the bubbles. So you see? We're everywhere.

Jane M. Appleyard confided to me that the tipster who provided probable cause for the warrant and was thus responsible for the raid on Cheryl and Walter Simms's puppy mill was, in fact, Bill Coakley. I should have guessed. A friend of the family? I mean, who else could have ignored or endured the stench? According to Mrs. Appleyard, Bill Coakley was trying to buy her off; he informed on Walter Simms, and, in return, she was supposed to leave Coakley alone. She hasn't, of course. She hasn't got him yet, but I have faith in her, and I have faith in you, too. If the AKC-registered mini dachshund you bought from Bill Coakley looks suspiciously like a pug, or if Coakley sold you a kennelful of cute little pet tapeworms, whipworms, and roundworms as well as the Pomeranian you wanted, complain! For a start, call Mrs. Appleyard, the Westbrook Health Department, the SPCA, the Humane Society of the United States, the American Kennel Club, and the United States Department of Agriculture.

But I'm pretty sure that Mrs. Appleyard is wrong about why Bill Coakley informed on Walter Simms. I can't prove it, but I have a hunch that my bribe worked. I'd bet that Bill Coakley wanted my five hundred dollars, tried to buy Missy back from Simms, and decided to get revenge when Simms refused to part with her.

With regard to the Coakleys, I regret to report that, in spite of the recent scandal that hit all the papers ("Scabies Cases Traced to Local Kennel"), Your Local Breeder is still in business. Although *Sarcoptes scabiei,* the itch mite, is not yet registrable with the AKC, Janice Coakley apparently received a large shipment on a litter of Italian greyhounds flown in from Missouri. As I hope you've never had to learn, scabies itches like crazy. It's caused by female mites that burrow in and lay their eggs under your skin.

Oh, while we're on that topic—under your skin—I have happy news about Gloria Loss, who kept the braids, lost the acne, and, at my suggestion, responded to an ad that read TATTOO FOR LOVE AND PROFIT. Gloria still doesn't believe that we have a right to own companion animals, but she realizes that our dogs and cats are better off with us than they are in a research laboratory and that, at least until they're all returned to the wild, a tattoo is the best protection we can offer them. And speaking of research laboratories, I'll confess that I introduced Gloria to someone from my past who knows a lot about them and doesn't like what he knows. Let's just say that he's committed to change, okay? And so is Gloria, of course.

Steve offered to spay Missy free of charge, but refused to perform the surgery until I'd obtained written permission from her owner, Enid Sievers, or a signed document stating that Missy belonged to Malamute Rescue. I'd intended to call Enid Sievers, anyway. I wanted to have another go at persuading her to hand over Missy's papers; I didn't like the sound of the gentleman friend who'd recommended Bill Coakley's boarding facilities.

On the early March day when I stood on her doorstep, Enid Sievers's house looked even more intensely raspberry than it had in February, almost as if the fruit had ripened. When Mrs. Sievers answered the bell and welcomed me in, she wore a chartreuse dress with dyed-to-match pumps. Prancing and yapping at her high heels was an incredibly cute little short-haired brown-and-white mixed-breed dog, half smooth fox terrier, I guessed, half something much smaller, anyway, a lively, yipping character with alert eyes and a bold expression. Within thirty seconds, he'd produced more noise than I'd heard from Rowdy and Kimi in the entire time I'd lived with them.

Bending from the waist, Enid Sievers leaned down to the little dog and coyly shook an admonishing finger. "*Friend,* Pedro! *Friend!* Pedro, *hush!* Pedro, Mommy has company!"

Pedro leaped in the air, danced in circles, and kept up the high-pitched barking. Eventually, though, Enid scooped him up in her arms and cooed at him until he quit.

"Pedro is adorable," I said. "Some terrier there, huh?"

Enid Sievers's expression was one I recognized immediately. I don't usually see it, though; I just feel it spread across my own face whenever someone admires my huskies, my shepherd mixes, or, believe it or not, my beautiful Akitas.

"Pedro," she informed me, caressing the dog's little head, "is a Chihuahua." I sealed my lips. She read my face and asked in a tone of arch condescension, "You've never seen a Chihuahua like Pedro before, have you?"

"No," I admitted. "Actually, he seems a little, uh, bigger than usual."

"Well, that's what *I* said when I first saw him," Enid Sievers said. "So I said to the salesgirl, 'Isn't he big for a Chihuahua?' But she explained that Pedro is supposed to be big like this because he's a *standard* Chihuahua, not just an ordinary one. That's why he was a little bit extra, of course. They're *very* rare."

Rare? The standard Chihuahua is a member of the rarest group of dogs on earth, the AKC's famous Nonexistent Group, which also contains the mini Saint Bernard, the hairless puli, and the legendary unicorn hound. Pedro came from Puppy Luv. But he must be a Chihuahua, I guess. After all, he has AKC papers to prove it. Enid Sievers showed them to me. She also parted with Missy's, and, while she was at it, signed a form turning Missy over to Malamute Rescue.

But you don't care about Enid Sievers, Bill and Janice Coakley, Enzio Guarini, or Cheryl and Walter Simms, do you? You care about what happened to the dogs. Walter Simms's arrest and the raid on the Simmses' puppy mill resulted in the removal of all dogs from Cheryl Simms's custody, but she managed to get back Champ, who obviously hadn't been abused, and six of the small dogs, none of them spayed or neutered. The court felt sorry for Cheryl because of her diminished capacity and her sad history. I'm sorry for her, too, but I don't believe that the dogs should have been returned to her. The court paid too much attention to Cheryl's mental limitations and too little attention to her real disability: She has a diminished capacity for kindness.

And the other dogs? The Eleanor J. Colley Society and

local purebred rescue organizations took most of them, but Lorraine, Rhonda, Pete, and the rest of Steve's staff fell in love with the golden retriever bitch. They named her Val—Valentine, of course. High-quality protein was a wonder drug. Val's litter was very small, only three puppies, but they all survived. Because of superb veterinary care, Val is doing very well, and the puppies, now cured of the intestinal parasites to which they were exposed before birth, are little golden teddy bears come to life. After a really terrible fight, Rhonda gave in and said that Pete could take Val if she could have pick of the litter. Lorraine is taking one of the remaining two pups, and the third, a darling little male, has been promised to a carefully selected client, a guy named Ron Coughlin, who's my plumber as well as the treasurer of the Cambridge Dog Training Club.

Missy's sire, Yukon Duke, the male malamute who growled at me, went to Malamute Rescue, of course. When I visited him in his isolation kennel at Betty Burley's and got my first good look at him, I felt heartsick. It's hard to find good homes for beautiful, friendly, young dogs. What in God's name would we do with this rangy, badly proportioned, cranky ten-year-old? And the damn thing was that despite the horrible life he'd led, Duke was perfectly healthy. Also, although he didn't have the ideal malamute temperament, he wasn't vicious, just reserved, crotchety, and, of all things, protective. Even so, absolutely no one would want to adopt him. These decisions are terribly hard to make, but Duke was taking up space at Betty's that we might need for a friendly, young, readily adoptable rescue dog. His situation seemed hopeless.

Fortunately, though, reality is not my father's strong point. Buck is convinced that one of these days, the right adoptive owner will come along, and, until then, the now-neutered Duke will live in Owls Head.

The raiding party discovered Icekist Sissy inside the tumbledown broiler farm. She'd given birth to a litter about three months earlier. Her coat was a thin, ragged mess, and she was suffering from malnutrition. Also, she was frightened of almost everything. But, to my surprise, Lois Metzler made good on her promise to take responsibility for Sissy. Lois paid her vet bills, including the cost of spaying, and she's even paying Betty to board Sissy until we can place her. It may take a while. Sissy needs a very special home. She's not a typical malamute, of course. You can already see that once she puts on a little more weight and gets her coat back, she'll be gorgeous, but she's hand shy and rear shy. Loud noises startle her. She's terrified of strangers. Even the most gentle word of correction makes her cringe. Amazingly enough, though, she loves other animals, especially cats.

Missy, too, is still looking for a good home. It's only fair to warn you that she'll shed copiously about twice a year. Also, she's tremendously strong, she isn't great with cats, and she turns out to be a food thief, too. But she's healthy, outgoing, spayed, fully housebroken, very pretty, and, at least for an Alaskan malamute, she's almost docile. Interested?

And the malamute puppy at Puppy Luv? When John Sweet reopened the pet shop two weeks after his wife's murder, I tried to talk him into letting me leave some breed and obedience-training information with the puppy's papers, but he refused. One day in Harvard Square, though, I happened to spot the puppy, and I talked to the couple who bought her. The wife is an assistant professor of economics at Harvard, and the husband has a Ph.D. in biology. Educated people, right? And decent people, too. But when they came to my house to meet Rowdy and Kimi and to pick up some information about malamutes, I tried to suggest that they might consider buying their puppy chow someplace other than Puppy Luv. I explained that pet shops that sell dogs support

the puppy mill industry. A Harvard professor and a Ph.D.,
right? Economics and biology. They asked me what a puppy
mill was. Believe me, I told them. They listened, too.

And you? We can close the puppy mills, you know, we
really can. The AKC won't do it, and the USDA won't do it.
We will. Remember, we're everyone, and we're everywhere,
and, before long, none of us will buy so much as a single
morsel of premium kibble from a pet shop that sells dogs.
Peace will come. Let it begin with us.